MW01492087

PRAISE FOR

Shortliste

"This is a blast." —*Publishers Weekly*

"Makana Yamamoto's debut novel . . . is boldly labeled on its cover "A Sci-Fi Heist," and it would in fact translate beautifully to the screen. It possesses all the sterling attributes of the classic heist narrative, and adds in romance elements, plus the topic of familial bonds. The resulting blend is wholly organic and effective." —*Locus* magazine

"Fans of *Ocean's Eight* and *Leverage* will find this a delightful ode to team heists. The enemies-to-lovers trope, queer characters, and Hawaiian culture and language create a unique backdrop for a familiar plot line." —*Library Journal*

"An easy, fun read, which will make a lot of readers smile for all kinds of reasons." —*Lightspeed* magazine

"A proper heist story with little drama, a juicy friends-to-enemies-to-lovers subplot and lovable characters."

—*MetaStellar*.com

"Makana Yamamoto's sci-fi debut *Hammajang Luck* is the perfect escapist read for these trying times . . . Including Pidgin and other cultural references to Hawaiʻi in the far future is a powerful pushback against the homogenizing force of science fiction. I look forward to reading Yamamoto's next novel and seeing how they continue to accomplish this artistic goal."

—*Nerds of a Feather, Flock Together*

"A wildly fun book."   —*Soapberry Review*

"This was a hugely satisfying read that knows the heist genre and it comes to life really well. While we get a satisfying conclusion this feels like a series where there are room for more stories and exploring of the wider cast. I would love to see what else Yamamoto has in store for us and clearly an author to keep an eye out for! Highly recommended!"

—*Runalong The Shelves*

"*Hammajang Luck* is a little *Ocean's Eleven* (but gayer and more femme), a little *Fast & Furious* family (but better), and extremely queer. I highly recommend it."   —*Cannonball Read*

"Like an Ocean's movie set in space, *Hammajang Luck* will charm readers looking for a smooth ride with a lovable cast."

—*BookPage*

THE OBAKE
Code

THE OBAKE
Code

A SCI-FI
Heist

MAKANA YAMAMOTO

HARPER Voyager
An Imprint of HarperCollins*Publisher*

HarperCollins books may be purchased for educational, business,
or sales promotional use. For information, please email the
Special Markets Department at SPsales@harpercollins.com.

Harper Voyager and design are trademarks of
HarperCollins Publishers LLC.

hc.com

FIRST EDITION

Library of Congress Cataloging-in-Publication Data has been applied for.

ISBN 978-0-06-343086-0

Printed in the United States of America

$PrintCode

Tk

THE OBAKE
Code

1

IT TAKES TWENTY MILLISECONDS TO TAKE A SWING AT SOMEONE. MOTOR cortex to radial nerve, radial nerve to triceps brachii. Tense, draw, make a fist. Swing. Twenty milliseconds altogether.

But I'm faster.

It was hot and humid in the room, the windows of the gym fogged up with the heat of sweating bodies packed tight like matches in a box. Ready to ignite. The floor had been cleared of equipment, leaving only the ring in the center of the room. We all crowded around it, screaming and swearing as twenty milliseconds passed again and again.

The fighters were circling each other, beaten and bloodied. One was dressed in neon-green leggings and a matching sports bra, mesh panels at her thighs and chest, exposing lines of biofeedback LEDs. Flashy, but useless. The other was dressed in a black leotard, exposing spindling lines of glowing bioluminescent tattoos down their limbs. Again, flashy, but useless. Nothing worth hacking there.

The fighters were three rounds into the fourth match, and they looked bus' the fuck up. The crowd itself was shitfaced by now, their cheers and boos slurred by cheap liquor. I lingered near the back of the room, standing beside the plastic folding table that served as a bar.

I sipped at my cola and made a face. Flat.

"Ho," the bartender said from behind me, "good scrap tonight, yeah?"

The fighter in green staggered backward from a hit to the side of her head, slow to react to the other's swing. But she shook it off and didn't go down.

I scoffed. "Min stay moemoe up dea? Dirty lickens iz wat it iz."

I'd seen Min fight five times in the last sixty-three days. She was a favorite in this Brotherhood club, one of Ward 4's homegrown fighters. And if any Ward on Kepler had its own identity, it was the yobos of Ward 4. The Brotherhood of Fire in particular.

Usually Min was cautious, deliberate, but never slow or sluggish. Niele, I extended my consciousness into the crowd, sifting through the electronic signatures of all the phones and comms and broadcasting mods of the crowd to the comm on her wrist. It was Atlas Industries tech, and Atlas wasn't one for privacy. The comm put up a token effort to keep me out, but I bypassed the firewalls with ease and dove into the data. I shuffled carelessly through her biometrics and found an abnormal sleep pattern in the past fifteen days. So, she was moemoe up there.

Roars from the crowd made me withdraw from Min's data and return my focus to the fight. She was trudging out of the ring while the other fighter riled up the crowd, victorious. I watched as thirty-seven people in the crowd initiated credit transfers of varying sums as the bets were paid out. Data streaked through the air, sparking from comm to comm.

The gambling was just one part of the Brotherhood of Fire's operations on Kepler Station. They ran two fighting rings and three gambling halls in back rooms of their affiliated clubs, but the gambling wasn't where the real money was. The real money was in smuggling. Mostly guns, with some illegal mods thrown in. Just to keep it spicy.

I watched with renewed interest as new fighters entered for the next heavyweight match. One was a man dressed in black shorts and no shirt, to highlight the cut of his muscles and the slick metal curves of modded legs. The other was a larger, burlier man in a white tank top and black pants, seemingly unconcerned with appearances. It showed in the exposed nanofiber cables and whirring hydraulics of his modded arm.

"Dis fight, but," the bartender said behind me, "dis fight one good one. Jaime going scrap good, but Kaleo going lick him."

"Kaleo?" I turned to look at the bartender. There was sweat standing out on his bald head.

"Jamie going down in da second round. KO. Watch 'em." The bartender looked amused. "Wachu know about scraps, Malia? One wahine iwiiwi like you?"

An insult was on the tip of my tongue, but the credit chit reader on the table made me pause. I smiled sweetly. "You like bet on it? Two hundred credits."

The bartender laughed. "You know what? Fine. I bet on it."

My smile widened as the bartender poked at his comm. "KO in da second round. Watch 'em."

The first fighter, Jaime Ruiz, was a newcomer with only two wins—but decisive wins—to his name. Ward 4 wasn't easy to impress, and his shiny new modded legs didn't dazzle like they might in the bougie circles of the Upper Wards. The second fighter, Kaleo Akaka, was another hometown favorite, one who had been active in the scene for four years. His mods were just as well loved. A loss here would be a huge upset. There was a lot of money riding on these next twenty milliseconds.

But I'm faster.

I grinned to myself as I took another sip of my cola.

Jaime closed the distance on Kaleo when the bell rang, lightning quick. A series of jabs put Kaleo on the back foot, blocking what hits he could. Jaime sprang back at Kaleo's swing, landing spry on his modded legs. He danced around Kaleo for most of the first round, until a boosted punch threw him onto the ropes. Kaleo drew his modded arm back for another swing.

I extended my awareness across the room, reaching outward to Kaleo. His mods were old, far from the slick smart mods of recent years. His software wasn't much newer. I pushed through the firewalls and pinged the system: *STOP.*

Kaleo's arm twitched, just for twenty milliseconds. But it was enough time for Jaime to bounce off the ropes and land a hit on Kaleo's temple.

The crowd groaned in unison at the hit, and the bartender swore from behind me.

The fighters broke apart at the end of the first round, withdrawing to opposite corners to speak with their coaches. Kaleo rolled his modded arm in its socket, clenching and unclenching his fist.

When the bell rang for the second round, Kaleo came out swinging. He landed hit after hit on his opponent, driving Jaime backward toward the ropes again. Jaime was starting to look rough. He needed a little more help than I wanted to give. Annoyed, I dove into the code again. In an act of overkill, I flooded Kaleo's inputs with commands: *STOP, FIST, FLEX, FLAT, SHAKA.* Kaleo's arm shuddered in its trajectory, pausing just long enough for Jaime to launch forward with another hit.

The sensation of breaking someone's jaw takes twenty milliseconds to reach the brain. Radial nerve to spine, spine to parietal lobe.

When Kaleo went down, there were four seconds of utter silence, quiet enough to hear the blood drip from Jaime's face. Then the crowd erupted into overlapping screams and shouts, cheering and cursing. Forty-two credit transfers were initiated, and I watched as 5,289 credits flowed into my account.

"Chee hoo!" I whooped. I whipped around to the bartender, a grin on my face. "How you like dis wahine now, bolo head?"

"Sshibal gaesekki ya," the bartender cursed. He planted his palms on the table and went and on, but I didn't bother to follow along with the translated feed running across the bottom of my vision. I chugged the remainder of my cola and slapped the plastic cup down on the table. Then I started the victory dance.

I'd been frequenting fight nights at this Ward 4 Brotherhood club for sixty-three days now, and this was my biggest payout yet. When I was new to the scene, I bet based solely on the fighters' vibes. But after a few losses, I started calculating

6   MAKANA YAMAMOTO

odds. Then I started poking through the secure transmissions, finding which fights were rigged and which were not. Then I started rigging them all on my own.

I started out legit. But where's the fun in being legit the whole way through?

I was still wiggling and the bartender's translation was still scrolling when an alert popped up in the upper right-hand corner of my vision. I opened it with a flick of my eye. A picture unfolded in my field of vision: another bolo-head yobo muttering into his comm. I lifted my eyes and scanned beyond the roiling crowd. He was looking right at me.

Oh hell.

"Tanks, brah, good fun!" I said to the bartender. I hurriedly transferred twenty credits to pay him for the drinks. "Shoots!"

I moved quickly away from the table, into the press of the crowd. I squeezed between bodies and under swinging arms, trying to vanish. The screen in the corner of my vision showed the yobo mook peering into the crowd, looking for me. I flipped to another camera angle and saw a second mook circumventing the crush.

I made a beeline for the exit.

I popped out of the crowd just two meters from the doors. I closed the distance in what I hoped looked like nonchalant strides. My palm was on the glass when I felt a strong hand close around my arm.

"Not so fast, kid."

I went with the first lie that came to mind, "I have a curfew."

"It'll have to wait," the yobo said.

I slowly turned to look at him. Big, muscled, and tattooed with the signature phoenix of the Brotherhood. "Come with me," he said.

"But I'm just a kid," I said in my most pathetic voice. "My mom will slap my head if she catches me out."

The mook looked unmoved. The first and second appeared out of the crowd, and I was surrounded.

"Okay," I conceded. "But I need to be home by 0200."

Mooks three and four seized me by both arms. I glanced toward the ring. The ref and medic were dragging Kaleo off the mat as the Brotherhood members hauled me across the floor toward the back of the gym.

I wasn't always legit, but I wasn't always careless either. I made a name for myself walking that line: not reckless, but just unhinged enough to be unpredictable. It was what differentiated me from every other modded vigilante or cyberspace paniolo. The Obake wasn't known to be careless. I had the Code for that reason.

Maybe I was out of practice. Three years after my last big score, this was my first foray back into the criminal world. Maybe I'd lost my touch.

I hated the thought of that.

The Brotherhood members dragged me through a service door into the back of the club, then down a set of dingy concrete stairs lit by flickering fluorescent bulbs. Voices drifted up the stairwell, audible even above the roar of the crowd upstairs.

The voice was low, and heated. She spoke in Kepler's Korean dialect, but I followed the translation running across the bottom of my vision.

"You must think I'm real fucking stupid, huh," the woman said. "That it? You think I'm stupid enough not to notice when a whole fucking shipment of guns goes missing?"

The Brotherhood members stopped me at the bottom of the stairs. We stood at the entrance to a cramped room with unfinished walls and filled with sickly light. The woman who spoke was tall, with a muscular frame. Billowing black clouds and a phoenix with its flaming wings spread wide wrapped around her muscled arm in a full-sleeve tattoo, and her short, dark hair was pushed back out of her face. She stood over a man with his wrists and ankles zip-tied to the arms and legs of a wooden chair. He looked like he'd been roughed up, but nothing more than a few superficial cuts and bruises. I had a sinking feeling that was about to change.

"Who put you up to it?" the woman asked. "What'd they promise you? Credits? Drugs? What'd they promise to make you turn on us?"

The man didn't lift his head.

A heavy silence fell over the room, punctuated by the screaming of the crowd.

"You were my brother, once." The quietness of the woman's voice startled me. She turned away from the man in the chair and crossed the room. She picked up something from the shadowed corner, and when she moved back into the light, I could see it was a worn bat. My heart pounded as the woman hefted the bat over her shoulder, standing over the man in the chair. He lifted his gaze. There was fear in his eyes.

"Hyungnim—" the man began.

"Shut the fuck up." Her gaze was cold, all the heat of her anger gone out of her. But somehow the calm was even worse.

"You were family. You should know that still means something to me—"

"Hyungnim, please—"

"So I'll give you one chance: Where are my guns?"

The man swallowed. "I don't know."

Her expression was stony as she brought the bat down on the man's hand. My eyes widened as he screamed in pain, jerking against the restraints at his wrists.

"Not fucking good enough." The woman circled the man's chair like a shark sensing blood in the water. She stopped at his side, then rested the bat lightly on his other hand.

"Where are my guns?"

"I don't know! I swear to god—"

I flinched as the bat shattered the man's other hand, filling the room with the sound of cracking bone. My eyes flicked between the Brotherhood members on either side of me, who were watching the scene with grim expressions. Not an uncommon sight to them, I guessed.

I swallowed hard. I was truly fucked.

"*Where* are my guns?"

"I don't know!"

The man began to wail as the woman ground the end of the bat into his ruined hand.

"*Where* are my *guns*?"

"Please, Hyungnim! I don't know!"

She lifted the bat from his hand, and the man gasped in relief. He was breathing hard, sweat standing out against his forehead. He moaned as the woman tapped his knee with the bat.

"*Where are my guns?*"

He didn't answer. The woman raised the bat, winding up her swing.

"*Wait!* Wait, wait, wait, wait!" She paused. "The docks! Dock 118! The Syndicate is going to move the goods in five hours! That's all I know *I swear to god!*"

There was another moment of silence, filled only with the man's sobbing. "Please, Hyungnim. Please let me go."

Anger flashed across her face before she swung the bat to shatter the man's knee.

She turned away from the man to fix her gaze on one of the Brotherhood members in the corner, ignoring the man's screams of pain. "Get a crew down to the docks. I want that shipment, and I want a name. Whoever thought they could fuck with us has got another think coming."

The Brotherhood member jerked his head in the direction of the traitor. "What do we do with him?"

"Kill him. I don't care how."

The woman shifted her gaze to me, and my blood ran cold. She gestured to the mooks, and they seized me by the arms. Two of them hauled the man out of the chair and the other two dropped me into it. They and the other Brotherhood member dragged the man out the back door. His sobs faded as the door slammed shut.

The woman stood over me, regarding me coldly.

"Howzit," I said, weakly.

"You know who I am?" she asked.

I didn't need to search the Net to know who she was. Song Jeongah, the worse half of the Song sisters and newly ascended heir to the Brotherhood's criminal dynasty. Her reign was brutal, and as I'd just learned, she wasn't afraid to get her hands bloody.

I nodded.

Jeongah leaned forward to look me in the eye. "So, you know who you're fucking with."

"I don't know what you're talking about," I lied.

Her eyes searched my face. Seemingly not finding what she was looking for, she straightened and hefted the bat across her shoulders. "I don't know mods," she said, "but I know fighting. Kaleo was pulling his punches. He never does that, and especially not for money. That, and his arm was twitching like a motherfucker all throughout. That's not hardware, that's software. And you"—she leaned forward to stare into my eyes again—"you've been at every upset over the past two months. I don't know mods, but I know fighting. And I know when to trust my gut. You're fucking with my fighters."

"Would you believe me if I said this was a setup?" I asked.

Her lip curled. "No."

I calculated the odds. Not many people crossed the Brotherhood and lived, especially now that Jeongah was its head. And she definitely wasn't a due-process kind of leader. If my kneecaps were still intact, it meant I was valuable to her. For what, I didn't know.

"It's a DDoS," I said finally. "I flood the inputs of the mods with nonsense pings and overload the software."

"How."

I tapped my temple. "Mods, how else?"

"Why."

Why did I do it? I'd asked myself that the first night I'd come home from this Brotherhood club, sweaty and stinking of blood and liquor. At the time, I didn't know. But the adrenaline humming in my blood, it made me feel alive in a way I hadn't in three years. Sixty-three days later, and I knew.

I shrugged. "I'm bored."

Jeongah didn't seem to like that.

She straightened, then tapped my knee with the bat. I resisted the urge to jerk away. "Give me one good reason I shouldn't break your legs."

"Seems like you already have a reason," I challenged. "Or they'd be broken already."

Her mouth twitched. I swallowed.

"Have you heard of Lucas Pierce?" she asked.

I had. He was a politician, elected to the mayorship of Kepler Station. He was up for reelection this cycle. But I didn't know why Jeongah would care about him. I pinged the GhostNet, and in 0.82 seconds it returned an answer. He was running on a tough-on-crime platform, and in the three years since he took office the Station Security budget had ballooned by 8 percent. But the money had to come from somewhere. And that "somewhere" was places like the Ward 7 Historic Library, the Ward 2 Public Education System, and the Ward 1 Centennial Infrastructure Project. A real faka.

But it didn't answer why she would care.

"What about him?" I asked.

"I want him gone," she answered simply.

"Why? You don't strike me as a 'public good' type."

She scoffed. "Pierce is bad for business. Station Sec has raided three of my clubs in the last two months and put half my men on the books. 'Cleaning up the streets' is cutting into my bottom line."

"And you expect me to do something about it?" I nodded at the Brotherhood members at the door. "Don't you have guys for that?"

Jeongah followed my gaze. "Assassination is too messy, too public. I need subtlety." She returned her gaze to me. "I'm not known for subtlety."

"You could say that again," I muttered.

She ignored me. "I need you to get rid of him. Consider it repayment for the 8,000 credits you owe me."

"9,492 credits," I corrected.

Her dark eyes widened. "Nine thousand four—"

"You seem to have a lot of faith in me," I said. "Why?"

A sinister grin spread across Jeongah's face. "It's not every day that you meet the Obake."

I flinched. I hadn't been the Obake in three years, not since the Atlas heist. It was safest for her to disappear. Safest for me to disappear. But I'd been careless. Sixty-three days of betting and hacking and lying brought her back, haunting me just like her namesake.

"I know a few business contacts who would be very interested to meet you," Jeongah said.

So, that was the play. I'd scammed half the gangsters on this station, in service of the other half. I had no doubt that Jeongah would make more than just 9,492 credits turning me in.

I felt afraid, but, weirdly, I also felt a little thrill. Maybe that was the unhinged side of the Obake in me, the side no one could predict. The last sixty-three days had been the most fun since my last job three years ago. What did it mean for that this was the most exciting thing that had happened to me since then?

I looked between the mooks.

Subtlety, she'd said.

I could do that.

A slow grin spread across my face. "All right. I'm in."

2

I DIDN'T GET HOME UNTIL WELL PAST 0300. LATER THAN THE CURFEW I'D given Jeongah and her mooks.

The door lock disengaged at my command, and I shouldered it open. All the lights flicked on, and I squinted into the room. Putting my fingers to my throbbing temples, I dimmed the lights.

I trudged to my bedroom at the far end of the condo.

Even after everything I went through, I couldn't bear to leave Ward 2. But I was tired of hearing my neighbors through the walls, so I bought out the entire floor. I had no idea what to do with all the space, though. I'd never invited the Atlas crew up for that reason: Where the hell were they supposed to sit?

I turned the lights out as I walked from empty room to empty room, until I reached the main suite. I'd set up all my gear in the walk-in closet—the most furnished part of the whole condo. I jokingly called it my panic room—it was where I felt safest. I flopped onto the mattress on the floor and groaned.

I wasn't one for peace and quiet. I liked things loud, chaotic, frenetic. It kept my brain busy. I always got hassled for having a vidfeed, music, and a game all going at the same time. I didn't know how to explain that it was the only way I could keep my brain busy.

Because when it *wasn't* busy—that was when I got into real trouble.

Lying here in this dark condo, the neon lights of the station flashing through the closed blinds, who knew what I was about to do.

If Jeongah had her way, four felonies, at least.

I'd reviewed the footage of me in the Brotherhood club at least three times now, playing back every bet, every word, every movement. I was no grifter, but I definitely didn't look as shady as some of the other gamblers and bookies there. As for the rigged fights, I'd tried to keep my DDoS-ing within the range of each fighter's average reaction speed. It was supposed to look like any one of them was just having a bad day. I thought it was pretty fucking clever.

I remembered what Jeongah said and scowled to myself. Intuition.

That was one thing that I never learned in my training. You could be clever as fuck, but you could never outwit intuition. A mark gets a bad feeling and checks their security feeds, or resets a password, or takes a new route to work . . . You can't plan for intuition. It's like the Code says: People are the most fallible point in any system. Both ways.

I could admit that I was feeling a little nuha too. I was the Obake for five years, and while I'd had close calls, I was never caught. And not on *intuition*. It's the Code again: Always prepare for the worst-case scenario.

Maddox would've grounded me for a day. He always punished mistakes.

I shuddered at the thought. I didn't know why, but lately he was always one or two thoughts away. Maybe it was the five-year anniversary of my escape, passed just a couple weeks ago. It was hard to believe it had only been five years. Rationally, I knew that I spent a lifetime in that compound with Maddox and the other caretakers. Irrationally, it felt like my life had only just begun once I left. I'd grown up, started a career, stolen one billion credits from a trillionaire, bought a house. The dream, right?

So, why was he on my mind?

I tried to push thoughts of Maddox away, rolling over onto my side and staring into the dark closet. I began to drift off, but the rest was uneasy. I could see, hear, feel, the GhostNet, just beyond the edges of my consciousness. Images flashed behind my eyes, sounds echoed in my ears, sensations flitted over my skin. I couldn't tell what was mine and what was its. I could hear—

> your heart races in your chest through the sedative they
> gave you for your nerves you
>
> feel dizzy lightheaded like youre
> going to die on this
> table thank you for doing this for me he
> says as one of the nurses shaves your
> head you cried then it took so long to grow

he leans down to meet your eyes bright and gray and kind
youre making me so proud
          a doctor leans over you count down backwards from one
hundred for me dear
                    she fits a mask over your face you take a deep
                    breath hes proud of you
      ninety

                                        nine ninety
                                                        eight

I jolted awake and sat up in my bed. I was still in my clothes, and without a bonnet, my locs were frizzy. Kepler's simulated sun was shining through the blinds, the constant whir of air traffic outside the windows.

I dropped my face into my hands.

The AXON mods in my head were Maddox's parting gift to me. It was what made me into the best hacker in the quadrant. Fuck, after the last heist? *The galaxy.* With them, the GhostNet was always near. Like a sea of data, roiling just beyond the shore of my waking mind. But these dreams—intrusions—were getting worse. My memory was getting leaky, the boundaries between me and the GhostNet growing weaker.

All because of a single stupid decision.

Then, it felt like the only option. We were running out of time, and we were running out of options. Brute forcing the codes, overclocking my mod, it felt like our only way into the vault and out of Atlas's reach. The crew told me not to, told me they'd find another way. But I didn't listen. I don't think I cared, at the time.

Now I care.

A little envelope icon appeared in the upper right-hand corner of my vision. I opened it.

It was from an anonymous sender. *you have 63 days. make them count.*

I SENT A MESSAGE TO my contacts immediately after getting the message from the Brotherhood. After that I dragged my ass out of bed and got dressed. When I checked my notifications at six minutes past, there was nothing. I went on to brush my teeth and fix my hair, but even at ten minutes past, there was nothing. At eighteen minutes past, I refreshed my connection to the Net. At twenty, I collapsed into my office chair in the walk-in closet, exasperated. And even then, there was more waiting. I spun lazy circles in my chair, absently fussing with a puzzle.

Right face, clockwise. Upward face, clockwise. Right face, counterclockwise.

Thirty-six minutes past.

I kicked off the leg of my desk, around and around. The Net told me that ballet dancers swivel their heads to keep their gaze in one place so as not to get dizzy during their pirouettes. The world record for the most pirouettes was fifty-five, in the early twenty-first century, before Earth got busier with other things. I gave myself an extra kick.

Forty-eight minutes past.

A little neon analog phone appeared in my vision, wiggling back and forth. I planted my feet to stop the spinning, wobbling in my chair. With a flick of my eye, I selected the icon. It prompted me to open a Net call. I accepted.

With a sickening rush, my consciousness was pulled out of my chair and into the GhostNet. I flew through the deep darkness of the Net, past lines of sparking code—images and video and endless reams of text. Emotions, feelings, urges tickled the edges of my consciousness. I let it all wash over me. Fighting back against the surge of the Net could drive you mental. Diving into it fully was even worse on the psyche. So I kept my eyes forward, on the digital destination just ahead.

I came to a stop in a lush rainforest. All around me were dewy leaves and vibrant flowers, a jungle mist rising through the foliage. Behind me, someone coughed delicately.

I turned around. Sitting primly on a stone throne, a hot-pink tiger in a loosened crimson kimono regarded me. I gave an exaggerated bow. "Katana," I greeted her, my voice disguised in the rumble of Orogen, the Scourge of the Nine Realms—my favorite character on *Way of the Sword.*

"Obake," she replied, inclining her head. Hers was a harmony of feminine voices. "You're looking well."

I grinned at her, though no expression would show on my face. My own avatar was a hooded figure in a mirrored mask. "And you are looking radiant, as always."

The tiger giggled, hiding her fangs behind a dainty paw.

Yuki Katana was another cyberspace paniolo, almost as good as me. We'd worked together on a few jobs over my lifetime as the Obake, but more often as adversaries. It was nothing personal, though. We all had our own reasons for hacking. Some of us for personal gain, others of us out of the goodness of our hearts, and for the rest of us, the thrill of the game. Katana was a little of all three. From what I'd gathered from the Net, our peers, and her own story, she started hacking as a kid. Ripped off a corporate exec to pay for her transition, then never left.

She was a little cringe, but who wasn't? I liked her.

"I was surprised to hear from you," she said. "I thought you were out of the game."

"I thought so too," I replied. "But it seems I couldn't stay away."

She smiled. "We never can."

That was true enough.

"I answered your summons as soon as I received it," I said. "Have you news?"

"I do." Katana reached into her kimono, letting it slip down her shoulder. She withdrew a lacquered scroll case. "This is all the information I could find."

"Excellent." I stepped forward, reaching for the scroll. "You have my grati—"

"Ah-ah," Katana said, snatching it out of my reach. "Not so hasty, Obake. You have me curious."

I stepped back from her, frowning. "You know what they say about cats and curiosity."

She giggled again, but this time didn't bother hiding her teeth.

I crossed my arms. "What is it you want to know?"

With a flourish, Katana uncapped the scroll and unfurled it. Her ruby eyes scanned the document. "Lucas Pierce. March

16th, 2109. O-positive. Pisces sun, Scorpio moon, Aries rising. Mayor of Kepler Station. Is this your employer or your mark?"

"Mark," I answered.

"Ooh. And it looks like he's been very naughty. Blackmail?"

"I wish. What transgressions did you find?"

"Many, many, many. Do you want the nepotism, the conspiracy beliefs, or the orphanage?"

I perked up immediately. "Start with the orphanage."

"Well, I suppose it's technically not an orphanage. A residential home."

"Tell me more."

Katana cleared her throat. "It's called Cunningham House, and it was started by Pierce's money-laundering front." She tittered. "Sorry, 'charitable foundation.' It's for children whose parents are incarcerated and who show aptitude for STEM. It's meant to 'foster greatness.'" She peeked at me over the scroll. "Competition."

I scoffed. "A pale imitation."

Still, it struck a nerve. Maddox could hardly call his compound a "home," but it was a residence. For me, and for all the other caretakers. And I guess you could say I had an aptitude for STEM—it was all I was allowed to do. In between psychological testing and biological experiments, at least. What kind of stupid kid could compete with that?

"Obake?"

I blinked. Katana was looking at me curiously. "Apologies. What else is there about his money laundering?"

"Not much, unfortunately. It appears that the majority of the information is kept locally, on a closed server." She smiled. "It appears you'll need to do some hacking IRL."

I hated IRL hacking. Social engineering wasn't something that came naturally to me—that was more in the realm of the grifters and masterminds I had worked with. Still, it was part of the Code: People are the most fallible point in any system. Who needs a passcode when you can pretend to be a pizza guy and sneak into the office?

"How can I access these files?" I asked.

"Not so fast. I've answered a lot of your questions, now it's time to answer one of mine."

I sighed. "Very well. Ask your question."

"Who's your mastermind?"

I straightened my stance, proud. "I am. I'm working alone."

"Expanding your skill set, are you?"

I smirked behind my mask. "Always."

"I see. Then who is it you're working for?"

I hesitated. Katana and I had worked together—worked together closely, even—but the Code was reverberating in my head. Never assume good intent. It'd kept me safe so far, and I couldn't afford to compromise my identity now.

"I'm afraid I can't answer that," I said. "For my own safety."

I figured the excuse would hold. A few of my and Katana's colleagues had been dropping off the Net lately—nobody knew how or why. But it had us all spooked.

A frown passed across Katana's face. "Then it's someone who doesn't want their identity to be known. Someone dangerous." She paused, no doubt consulting the Net. I shifted uncomfortably in the silence. After 0.67 seconds, her gemlike eyes widened. "Not another gangster, Obake. I thought you were past that, with how your last job went."

That was what I said, three years ago. After robbing blind

the most wealthy and powerful man in this quadrant, what else could I want for? What else was there to reach for? Maybe that's why I ended up in Jeongah's club at all.

I shook my head. "It's not an ideal situation."

"Blackmail?"

I hated to admit I'd been made. I wasn't sure how Katana would react to my weakness. It's like the Code said: People are the most fallible point in any system. But maybe a little grain of truth would endear her to my cause. Tug on her heartstrings a little. Katana always had a soft spot for lost causes. I learned that from previous masterminds.

"Extortion," I said with a grimace.

Katana nodded, grim. "I see." She stood and approached me. She was shorter than me—relying on speed and agility, rather than brute force, like other hackers. She handed me the scroll case. "Then you'll need this."

I took it. Saving to my own drive, the scroll dissolved in my hand. "Thank you."

"Anytime," she said with a smile.

"How can I repay you?"

"Well. I've always been curious what's behind that mask." She traced the outline of my face with a claw, and I resisted the urge to flinch away. Her touch was gentle. "Maybe we can meet sometime, in the real world. I have a feeling you could show a girl a good time." She giggled again, hiding her teeth behind her paw.

Katana had made this request a few times. A hacker's life could be lonely—I could tell she wanted to be friends. But again, the Code reverberated in my mind: Never assume good intent.

I clasped her paw, drawing it away from my face. She drew in a hushed breath. "Apologies," I said. "I can't do that. Not even for you, Katana."

She pouted. But after a moment, she brightened again. "I'll get you someday, Obake. Just you wait."

I laughed. "Maybe someday."

I stepped back from her and gave another exaggerated bow. "You have my thanks. But I must take my leave. I have much to do."

"Of course you do." She waggled her toes at me. "Goodbye, Obake."

"Farewell."

I disconnected from the chat. My consciousness was pulled backward, the data streams rushing around me until I was sitting in my chair again.

With Katana's intel, I could formulate a plan to steal the rest of Pierce's files. With the files, I could expose him and all his cronies to the press. Even if it didn't take him out forever, it would keep Station Security busy long enough for Jeongah to come up with a more permanent solution.

I was no IRL hacker, though. I would need a grifter for that. Plus a face that could get us into Pierce's inner circle. And depending on security, a thief to steal the documents. I blew out a breath. This was getting complicated.

But wasn't that what I was looking for? Something complicated, something difficult, something *fun*?

I grinned to myself and sat back in my chair, my hands working on the puzzle. Now this was the type of heist for a real mastermind to cut her teeth on. I just needed the right crew to do it.

LEFT FACE, COUNTERCLOCKWISE. UPWARD FACE, counterclockwise. Left face, clockwise.

It was shocking how furniture made a place look completely different.

Most of the Lower Wards of Kepler Station were relatively unchanged from when the city was first constructed. Built over the catacombs of the station's interior, they were as close to original as the station got. Lots of the folks who lived here liked it that way. People who have been here since the very beginning, traveling across light years of distance and decades of time to find a new home after being driven from their old one. Stubbornly clinging to Old Earth traditions, despite the galactic powers trying to sell them new ones.

Me? I didn't have much connection to Old Earth traditions, beyond what I'd learned from the Net. Growing up in a lab did that to a person. I didn't have much loyalty to the tower I lived in, or the renovated condos I'd bought. But as I sat in Tatiana Valdez's apartment, full of personal clutter and professional memorabilia, I could see the difference. This place looked so much smaller, yet much more alive.

I fidgeted with the puzzle while I waited. *Left face, counterclockwise. Upward face, clockwise. Right face, clockwise.*

Three years ago, Tatiana was my closest friend. We met on the Atlas heist: She was the thief, I was the hacker. We were the young guns on the team—kids, really. At twenty years old, I can say that. Incredibly competent kids, but still.

We all shuffled around after the payout from our last job— some of us moving farther than others—but none found it in us to leave Ward 2. Tatiana moved into her own place, a little farther up the tower from her folks, but that was the extent of it. Even her furniture was hand-me-down. She invited me to her family dinners a few times, but I always declined. I ghosted the crew almost immediately, but Tatiana I held on to for a little while longer. We cruised for a bit in the months after, but eventually I fell off. That's what the Code said: no attachments.

And I had to follow the Code. It was what kept me safe all these years. I couldn't abandon it now.

the walls are close so close so close in the dark youre
crying but those close close walls
just absorb all the noise im

passive un
caring youve been here so long the shadows start moving faces
and eyes and claws hungry

feeding

you
cry harder sobbing hiccupping a
crack of white light appears the door
calm down his voice says calm down and you can have
the lights
you suck in a shuddering breath swipe at your eyes and nose
with your sleeve im
sorry
the light grows wider as the

"What the *fuck*!"

I startled back into the present. A woman stood in the doorway, haloed by the neon lights outside. She had a gleaming switchblade in her hand. A spread of bodega snacks had fallen to her feet.

"Howzit, Tati," I said, steadying my voice.

"Malia?" she responded. "I told you to stop doing this! I almost stabbed you!"

I gestured at her door. "Your keycard reader needs a firmware update."

Tatiana sighed. She snapped the switchblade closed and started gathering up the snacks she'd dropped. "What do you want?"

I hopped off the arm of the couch where I was perched and started picking up snacks. "'What do you want?' That's no way to greet an old friend," I chided.

"You're the one who broke into my apartment," Tatiana shot back.

I met her annoyed glare with a grin. "Isn't it enough to talk story with me?"

"You disappeared for three months, completely ghosted me and everyone else. What am I supposed to think?"

"Sixty-three days is way longer than you need to wait to file a missing person report."

"That's not funny."

I straightened, a load of snacks in my arms. I dumped them on the lopsided coffee table near the couch. "I'm fine, Tati."

"Modders are disappearing, Malia. And if they show up again, they're borderline brain-dead. We were worried about you." She shook her head. "Where have you been?"

I shrugged and flopped onto the couch. "I was bored."

Tatiana stayed standing, arms crossed. "That's not an answer."

"No need fo' da attitude, cuz," I said, slightly defensive. "I got into a new game. I fine. No worries."

She didn't look convinced.

On some level, it was nice to know that someone cared. On another, I felt guilty for making Tatiana and the crew worry. But despite that, there was part of me that resented their fretting. I wasn't a kid anymore. I was the Obake. I didn't need someone to fuss over me.

I tried to change the subject. "You pau hana?"

"Pau fo' good," Tatiana said with a sigh. She dropped onto the couch beside me. "One of da artists waz talking stink about me, so—"

"You talked stink back."

She grinned at me. "Someting li'dat."

It made me feel a little better, knowing I wasn't the only one adjusting poorly to civilian life. Tatiana was one of Kepler's most sought-after safecrackers and thieves three years ago, and the habit never really faded. She'd bounced around the security scene for a few months before deciding she liked robbing execs more than reporting to them. Her latest whim was music. But Tati was too stubborn to buy her way into that scene.

"So, you're unemployed?" I asked, opening a bag of cuttlefish chips.

"Between jobs," she corrected.

"Well," I said. "You like one job?"

She raised a brow. "What kine job?"

I shifted on the couch, turning to face her. "I need help, cuz."

She rolled her eyes. "Here it is."

"So, I was bored," I began, "and I did get into a new game." Tatiana looked at me expectantly. "Uh. Fights."

She looked delighted. "You joined a fucking fight club?"

"Not me! I just watched."

"Oh." She sounded disappointed.

I straightened my shoulders. "I did bet, though. Rigged a few too."

Tatiana grinned at me. "Couldn't stay out of the game, could you?"

I met her grin. "You know it, cuz."

The young guns of the Atlas heist—neither of us was really ready to retire. That was one thing I could count on Tatiana for.

She reached into the bag of chips. "So, what happened?"

"Well, it was going fine, until—"

"Someone got wise."

I gesticulated wildly, scattering chips. "On one fucking hunch!"

She popped a chip in her mouth. "And you need money."

I scoffed. "You really think I need money after our last job?"

Even for someone like me, it takes a lot of time to burn through one billion credits. My whims were security for a short while, game dev for an even shorter while. Turns out I was better at playing the games than making them. It didn't take much for me to fall back into my old habits.

"What do you need me for?" Tatiana asked.

"The person who got wise, she doesn't want her money back. She wants me to do a job for her."

"And who got wise?"

I coughed. "Song Jeongah."

Tatiana's eyes widened. "Holy shit, Malia, you fucked up so bad you pissed off *the Brotherhood*?"

"I've pissed off worse before!"

"Have you?"

I had to think about it. I'd bankrupted a few billionaires, blackmailed a few celebrities, and scammed more than my fair share of gangsters on Kepler. I'd pissed off a lot of people. But when I thought of that poor Brotherhood faka and his kneecaps, I wasn't sure if I'd ever been in deeper shit.

"Well, maybe not," I conceded.

"Skill issue," Tatiana said with a smirk.

"C'mon, Tati," I pleaded. "I just need this one job. One last job, and I'm out. For good."

Tatiana's mouth quirked to the side, processing. I wasn't sure if she'd go for it. We were tight on our last crew, stayed in touch for a long while after everybody else drifted off. But while I'd strayed from the path, Tatiana was still on the straight and narrow. I wasn't sure how dedicated she was to going legit.

Not that much, it turns out.

She met my gaze, her brown eyes alight with glee. "Who's the mark?"

I grinned. "I'm so glad you asked."

I flicked my wrist and projected haptic screens of the files I'd gathered on Pierce. Tati reached for one and pulled it close. "The mark is Lucas Pierce. He's Kepler's incumbent mayor, and a real faka. He's up for reelection, and Jeongah doesn't want him reelected."

She plucked another chip from my open bag. "So, what's the play?"

"Buggah screams dirty politician, he just so happens to not be in Jeongah's pocket. Exposing him should be enough to keep him from reelection. But he's got hella good security for a mid-level politician, and I can't get to his personal files without a direct connection into his servers." I tossed a chip into my mouth. "Which is where you come in."

"Where are these servers?"

"His office headquarters, in Ward 7. I have a plan to get you in, though."

"And what's that?"

"Pierce is hosting a flyer show in two weeks, at his offices. Some kinda fundraiser. Doesn't matter." I pushed a floor plan toward Tatiana. "There will be lots of people, lots of activity, and nobody watching the servers."

She sifted through the floor plans. "How are we supposed to get into a flyer show?"

"I know a guy. Good with flyers. They can get us into the show."

Tatiana pulled another document closer. She swiveled it around and pointed at the *formal attire* line in the invitation. "How are we supposed to hold our own at a political fundraiser? I'm no grifter, and you definitely aren't either."

"No worries, cuz. I know a guy. She'll carry us through the fundraiser, fo' sho'."

Tatiana flicked her big brown eyes between the documents. I grinned over the top of the chip bag. "You in?"

She met my grin and held out a cuttlefish chip. I clinked mine to hers in a bodega toast.

"You won't regret it, cuz. Garans."

I gave the puzzle one last turn. *Front face, full turn, counterclockwise.* It snapped into place.

3

RACING GAMES WERE NEVER MY SPEED, AND I'D NEVER BEEN TO A STREET race before, so I wasn't sure what to expect. It sure as hell wasn't this.

A long stretch of street had been blocked off and cleared of locals and their flyers, leaving the racers and their fans. Low-flying races were popular in Kepler's underground racing scene, and Ward 1's streets—flush against the floor of the space station—were perfect for it.

There had to have been hundreds of people, all packed between the cramped towers. They wandered between the flyers, examining their engines and mods. They danced to the loud music booming through flyer speakers, dressed in scanty clothes in neon colors, covered in tattoos that moved and changed, modded with lights and metal and chrome. Far from the slick smartmods of the Upper Wards. While smartmods had grown into a status symbol, biohacking and the less-than-minimal aesthetics of the mods here were definitely not. Under the lighted signs and flashing neon, in the darkness of the Lower Wards, it was a riot of color. We were all freaks here.

I tried to be unobtrusive as I wove through the crowd. I ran a scan for any signs of our racer, but there were so many EM signatures it was hard even for me to sift through.

I dismissed the pings with an irritated blink and put my fingers to my temples. The bass was pounding in my skull.

"Hey, you okay, cuz?"

I looked over my shoulder at Tatiana. She was dressed in acid-green fishnets under ripped jeans, a shredded and tied white top, and matching fishnet gloves. She'd even twisted her curls into multicolored braids.

I grinned at her. "Nah, I'm good. Your outfit just gives me a headache."

Her nostrils flared. "You told me you were going to dress up too."

I looked down at myself, wearing my usual baggy black pants, shirt, and hoodie. "And believing me was your first mistake."

"I bought this shit, Malia."

I cackled. "And that was your second."

I turned and started walking again before Tatiana could argue. She huffed out a sigh and followed.

"So, who even is this guy?" she asked, falling in step beside me.

"Their name is Marisol Ramirez," I answered. "They've been on the scene for a while, mostly as a gearhead, but they saved up for their own ride and have been racing for the last year and a half." I pulled up their file and flipped through it. Birth certificate, ID, and a short rap sheet—mostly disorderly conduct, some resisting arrest, one assault of a police officer. Not many flying tickets, though. Fast enough to not get caught. "They're on their way to the top of these streets."

We passed rows of modded flyers as I tried to navigate the crowd. I scanned the more interesting ones as we passed. Most of them had extensive body and engine work, and all of them were jailbroken. Stripped down and built up in sleek, re-inforced frames. Supercharged with neodymium engines and hypersensitive transmissions. Loaded with hacked software and homemade programming. None of these were factory fresh.

I peered over the heads of two people admiring an engine block, and my scanner pinged. I squinted, and then I saw them.

Their file said they were five foot five, but they seemed taller, in person. Tall enough to stare down a Station Sec officer and spit in his eye. They were leaning against their flyer, casually, talking to the group that had formed around them. Their flyer was painted bloodred, with a snarling tiger drawn in abstract lines on the hood. They had light-brown skin and short, curly, dark-brown hair tucked under a backward cap, a lean frame beneath loose jeans, a hoodie, and a leather jacket. They glanced my way and clocked me staring at them. The corner of their mouth quirked, their dark-brown eyes amused.

I quickly looked away, their gaze too much to hold.

Tatiana crowded in beside me. "Is that them?"

The racer gestured for me to come closer.

I nudged Tatiana with my shoulder. "C'mon."

I wound through the crowd, pushing through the circle that had gathered around the racer to stand in front of them. "Marisol Ramirez?"

The racer laughed. "'Marisol?' What are you, my mom?" The assembled group giggled, and I flushed. "I'm Sol."

"Sol," I said slowly, testing the syllable in my mouth.

"And you are?"

"Malia."

They raised a brow. "Just Malia?"

"Just Malia," I answered.

Tatiana squeezed through the crowd to stand beside me. "And I'm Tatiana."

Sol took us both in with their watchful gaze. "Okay, Just Malia." They met my eyes. "What do you want?"

"Word on the street says you're the best racer here," I said. "And I need you for a job."

Sol considered that. Then they cast a glance around the group. "Give me a minute, will you?"

The crowd gave their scattered goodbyes and good lucks and dispersed.

Sol nodded, turning their gaze back to me. "What kind of job?"

"I need a wheelman."

"And what's the play?"

"There's a flyer show in two weeks, Ward 7. I need you to get us in and out."

They pushed off their flyer to match my stance. They felt so much taller than me. I had to resist the way my body reacted. Was it fear?

"You need me," they said. "What makes you think I need you?"

I straightened. "I can make it worth your while. How does 25,000 credits sound?"

Sol laughed. "I don't need credits."

That threw me off. I blinked. "What do you mean, you don't need credits?"

They gestured at the crowd around them. "Credits don't mean anything in this scene. All you have here is your reputation, and you can't buy that. I race for pink slips."

Quickly I consulted the Net. *Pink slips* was a colloquial term to refer to transfers of ownership between persons. So, they raced for it all. Daring. I admired that.

"Okay," I said slowly. "What if I said you could have your pick of the rides at the show?"

They looked intrigued. "Oh?"

I tapped my temple. "There's nothing I can't hack. Give me five minutes in that show, and you can have any ride you want." I grinned. "How's that for your reputation?"

Sol considered it. "Prove it to me."

That threw me off again. "Prove what to you?" I said, annoyed.

"That you can hack." They stepped away from their flyer to stand beside me. I followed their point to three different flyers. "Those are my competition. They're loaded up with individualized software, and each of them has a homemade cybersecurity suite. Help me win the race, and I'll join your little job."

"It's not a little job," I muttered.

Sol grinned at me. "You in?"

Unique software and a bespoke cybersecurity suite offered an interesting challenge. I wouldn't be able to use any of my existing routines and algorithms, I'd need to make up something on the fly. It was the kind of challenge I'd always loved as the Obake.

I matched Sol's grin. "Yeah, I'm in."

"And what am I supposed to do?" Tatiana asked, obviously put out.

Sol winked at Tatiana. "Grab a drink, grab a girl, and enjoy the race."

Tatiana was about to argue when an amplified voice cut through the noise. We both looked over our shoulders, toward a tall man, heavily modded with lights, yelling into a megaphone. "All right, all right, all right! Betting time is over, and now it's time for the good shit. Y'all ready to see some races?" A cheer went through the crowd. "You fucking better be! Everybody off the street."

A sharp whistle drew my attention back to Sol. They were already halfway into their flyer. "You coming?" Sol asked.

I glanced at Tatiana, who huffed out a sigh and said, "Just win, all right?"

I grinned. "You know I will, cuz."

Tatiana disappeared into the crowd as I climbed into the passenger side of Sol's flyer. It was cramped inside, and I had to squeeze between the bars of the roll cage into the uncomfortable seat. The console was almost completely DIY, with more switches and buttons than I could reasonably guess what they did. I dipped into the GhostNet, the data flowing between me and the other modders in the crowd.

The GhostNet was intended to be a two-way exchange of information between modded individuals. But that didn't jibe with the Code: Never leave a backdoor. I'd hacked my mod enough to make sure my connection was one-way, but I could still feel the consciousnesses of others pressing against my barriers. I pinged the Net for a rundown on the basics of a hacked flyer's dashboard and it returned a list in 0.5 seconds. I was familiarizing myself with Sol's setup when—

> treat her right you say treat her right you hear me? she
> laughs like chiming bells me or the car?
> you grin cant it be both?
> always the charmer lena her new girlfriend says rolls
> her eyes you nod at the open hood ill give you a lesson before
> you go

"You ready, Just Malia?"

I blinked hard. The crowd was growing restless. "Yeah," I said absently. "I'm ready."

Sol reached out and hit the start button. The neodymium engine whined as it powered up. They hit a switch, and we lifted off the ground. They shifted the clutch—I knew now that there really wasn't a need for a stick shift, all the systems were electronic. It was a holdover from the ice races on Old Earth. The crowd parted as we moved smoothly to the starting line.

A man with a chrome plate covering half his face leaned out of his flyer. It was the sickly green color of toxic sludge, fitted with ugly purple lights and an exaggerated spoiler. "Your ride is leaving with me, Sol," he spat. Then he showed a mouthful of shining teeth as he looked at me. "So's your girl."

I leaned across Sol to yell out the window. "You wish, pupuka!"

Sol waved me out of their space. Then they turned their lopsided smile toward the other racer. "Any man can talk. But can you ride?"

The man sucked in a breath, ready to curse them out. But they rolled up their window and turned their attention forward.

"You want respect from guys like him?" I asked, incredulous.

"Racing's the only thing guys like him understand," Sol said, cool. "After this, he'll leave well enough alone."

I frowned at them.

"Can you get into his systems?" they asked.

I extended my awareness toward the toxic-sludge-colored flyer. The security was rudimentary—he was clearly a better racer than coder. And even that was suspect. "Yeah," I said. "Easy."

"Good." Sol leaned back in their seat. "Don't do anything until the race starts. I'll tell you what to do."

A woman in sky-high translucent heels and a nearly painted-on white minidress stepped between the flyers to stand at the starting line. She raised her arms, and the LEDs in her palms flashed red.

she smiles at you warm as the setting sun and says

Sol flipped another switch on the dashboard, and the whining of the engine pitched into a reverberating rumble.

The woman's palms flashed yellow.

Sol revved the engine, an exhilarated grin rising on their face. I hastily buckled into my seat.

The woman dropped her arms, the LEDs flashing green.

take me for a ride

Sol hit the accelerator, and the flyer's engines ignited in a flare of blueshifted light.

We shot forward, ahead of the other racers, down the street lined with screaming people. I couldn't help the whoop that escaped me, gripping the crossbar of the roll cage and bouncing in my seat. Sol threw the emergency brake and downshifted, drifting tight around the first turn.

As we flew down the second stretch, I heard a low thrum growing in my ears. I twisted in my seat and saw that the toxic-sludge-colored flyer was gaining on us. The chrome-faced man at the wheel flashed his teeth at me.

"Faka is gaining on us!" I yelled.

"I know," Sol said calmly.

They shifted into a higher gear and accelerated, but I knew from the scan of both flyers that Sol's accelerated fast, but Chrome Face's max speed was faster. The nose of his flyer edged up toward our bumper.

Sol swerved to keep ahead of him. Through the window, I saw him slap the steering wheel. Sol e-braked and downshifted again, taking the curve even tighter than last time, making a hard left and then another onto the next stretch of the route.

Chrome Face edged even closer, and the flare of Sol's thrusters peeled the paint off the front of his flyer. He swerved around us, then flipped a switch and lurched forward. He swerved again, knocking the nose of Sol's flyer with his bumper. The flyer began to fishtail, and Sol twisted the steering wheel into the drift, their directional thrusters flaring. They cursed, I screamed. We came to a stop just as Chrome Face pulled ahead, making a kissing face at me as he passed. The other two racers shot past not long after.

I twisted in my seat to point at Sol. "You let this faka win, I going bus' you up!"

Sol didn't answer, just reengaged their engine and took off after the other racers.

The three racers wove between lanes ahead of us, leaving no room to pass. So much for my fucking wheelman. I was mentally cursing myself when I saw Sol's eyes dart to our right, where the monorail tracks ascended toward Ward 2. They swerved hard, bouncing over the curb, over the sidewalk and onto the tracks.

"What the fuck are you *doing*?" I screamed.

"Taking a shortcut," they said, as if the answer was obvious.

On the free stretch of track, they were able to slam the accelerator. I yelped as we shot forward, gripping the roll cage with pale knuckles. We passed the first flyer, then the second, and were gaining on Chrome Face when the monorail's horn began to blare.

"Fuck fuck fuck—" I twisted in my seat. We were gaining on the racers, but the monorail was gaining on us.

Sol twisted the steering wheel again, and we dropped off the ascending tracks, right on Chrome Face's tail, onto the last stretch of road.

"Okay, Just Malia," Sol said. "You're up."

"What?!" I exclaimed.

Sol laughed. "You're the hacker, girl!"

"Right," I said, trying to compose myself. *I'm the Obake.*

I steeled myself. "What do you need me to do?"

"I need you to hack into his braking system. When he hits that corner, delay his input by 0.5 seconds."

"Das it?"

"All I need."

I swore under my breath. Then I dipped into the Ghost-Net again, reaching for Chrome Face's flyer.

I scanned through the code, isolating exploitables and weak points. There were so many, it was easy. I remembered the Code: There's always an exploit. I grinned to myself as I input commands, watching the code fall to pieces around me.

you adjust the rearview mirror she swats your shoulder
stop looking down my
shirt its nothing i havent seen before you tease you
lost those viewing privileges after the
last race she replies
sharp the edge of her words cuts you grip the steering
wheel tight and
say nothing im sorry

lena she says softly its
fine you lie its
not fine things havent been fine for a long
time well what do you want to do about
it you're leaving the station tonight she
goes quiet the hum of the engine filling the
silence i could stay she says i could find
a way if you give me a
reason you hit the brakes too hard she yelps when you come
to a stop in the middle
of the street you turn to her what are you saying she
doesn't meet your eyes stares

into the dashboard im saying that for the right
reason i could stay you

stare at her you smile the championship race is tomorrow cant
miss it that a good
reason she looks at you smile in her
eyes only if you win your heart swells
with emotion you reach

"Malia! *Malia!*"

I startled back into the present. The sun had set, and the world was streaking past the windows. Sol was shaking my shoulder. "Malia, you with me?"

"Y-yeah," I said, shakily. The Ward was speeding past me. I had to keep focused.

I'm the Obake.

The last turn of the route was rapidly approaching, and we were weaving behind Chrome Face, searching for an opening. "I need you to hack those brakes, Malia."

"Yeah. I can do that."

I shook my aching head, then went back into the code. Lacking the headspace for finesse, I tore the whole barrier down and ripped a hole in the code. It should give Sol their 0.5 seconds.

I twisted in my seat to watch Chrome Face come around the bend. He braked and downshifted, but it was 0.5 seconds too late. He went wide. Sol pulled the e-brake and downshifted. We drifted around the last corner, so close to Chrome Face I could see the sweat standing out on his forehead. I waggled my fingers at him.

Then Sol slammed the accelerator and we shot forward, down the last of the street and across the finish line.

"Cheeeee hoo!" I whooped, bouncing in my seat. "That was *sick*, cuz!"

Sol flashed me a grin. "Not too bad, Just Malia."

Sol drifted in a tight arc, skidding to a stop in front of the gathered crowd. They surged around us, screaming and cheering. Sol pushed open the door and stepped out, into the open arms of their people. I stepped out of the flyer on shaking legs, leaning against the door as I got my bearings. Tatiana shoved her way through the crowd to throw her arms around me.

"That was so fucking cool!" she yelled.

"Not too bad for our first race, yeah?" I asked with a grin.

The click of a gun loading made the crowd draw a gasp, then fall silent. I looked past Tatiana and saw Chrome Face approaching, pistol raised, fury in his eyes.

"You sabotaged me, Sol!" he snarled. "You and your little bitch!"

Sol spread their hands and shrugged. "You fucked with the calibration of my engine last time. We'll call it even."

"No," he growled, "we won't."

"I won't even take your ride," they said, coolly. "Not like I wanted it, anyway."

"You got a smart mouth." Chrome Face clicked the safety. "You should apologize."

"No, I don't think I will."

The wail of a siren sent another gasp through the crowd. "Cops!" someone shouted, and the crowd broke into chaos. People poured off the streets and into their flyers, slamming doors and speeding off. The tide of people carried Chrome Face away from us, before he gave Sol one last snarl and turned and ran.

I was scanning the crowd for Station Sec when my eyes fell on a wall of digital graffiti. It was a portrait of a modder, haloed in flickering candle flames. She was short and stocky, with a shiny bald head. Her eyes were black and red, and spindling bioluminescent tattoos spread across her scalp. Beneath her portrait were the words *No One Did It Better. RIP Lena.*

"Get in!" Sol shouted, already halfway into their flyer. "Hurry!"

I tore my eyes away from the mural and climbed into the front seat as Tatiana clambered into the back. Sol hit the start button and flipped a switch, launching the flyer into the air. We lifted off and sped into the night, among the scattered crowd.

My heart was pounding, chest heaving, and it felt like my brain was slamming against my temples. What the fuck was that? *Who* the fuck was that? Was that the Lena from my dream?

I took three deep breaths. In, and out. Slowly, I relaxed my grip on the roll cage and returned to the present.

Sol was howling with laughter.

"What's so funny?" I demanded.

"You!" they said. "You two are a fucking riot."

"Thanks?" Tatiana said, voice pitched up in a question.

I glared at them. "You almost got me shot."

"You didn't get shot, though."

"Well."

"Listen, if all your jobs are like this one"—Sol flashed me a grin—"you can count me in."

I slumped back into the uncomfortable seat. "Great. Just don't make me regret this."

"You won't," Sol said, eyes on the sky traffic.

The thing about the GhostNet, information from other people doesn't come in as just raw data. The way our brains store information, it's a tangle of associations, each piece inextricably linked to the others. How Sol learned their way around a flyer, it's remembered fundamentally differently than how Lena did. And as much as Atlas tried, there's no way to scrub those associations. Every time you ping the Net, there's someone else's memories behind it. So, everything you learn from someone else—the ghost of them is just beyond the data.

I covered my face with my hands, blocking out the neon lights flashing by the window. The intrusions were getting worse. It used to be that I would only get them while I was falling asleep, when my barriers to the GhostNet were weakest. Now they were happening when I was awake. And it looked like my connection wasn't one-way.

And I didn't know who—or what—was on the other side.

4

I HATED IRL HACKING. GRIFTING WAS ALL ABOUT TALKING SMOOTH, OCCU-
pying space, holding your bearing. And me, I hated to be perceived. It's why I was always in the hacker van, or holed up in
my walk-in closet. Away from scrutinizing eyes.

Standing in the lobby of this Ward 6 building, in the center of a gleaming tile floor, surrounded by expensive water
features, people all around me, I felt more than a little exposed.
This grifter better be worth it.

"Stop touching your clothes," Tatiana muttered out of the
side of her mouth. "You look nervous."

"I am nervous," I hissed back, tugging at my blazer. "I
don't know why I'm here, cuz."

"You're the one who said we needed a grifter," she said,
guiding me off the floor toward one of the water features at
the far end of the lobby. We paused at an empty cocktail table.
"I'm not doing your dirty work for you."

"It's not dirty work if I'm compensating you for it."

"What the hell can you compensate me with that I can't
get on my own?"

"Pride?"

Tatiana scoffed. "If you wanted to appeal to my pride, you wouldn't get another thief."

I grinned at her. "A little nuha, eh?"

She lowered her voice to a grumble. "I don't know what she can do that I can't."

"Grift, cuz."

"Whatever." Tatiana crossed her arms and leaned against one of the cocktail tables. "I've never even heard of her, she can't be that good."

"I dunno about that, cuz," I said, opening her file. There was remarkably little about her—she'd paid good money to get her old life scrubbed from the Net. But the thing about memories— they're not so easy to erase. Not without a lot of time.

"Her name is Naima Khalid. She's a former neodymium heiress turned underworld princess," I continued.

Tatiana raised a brow. "Former?"

"Daddy went to prison for corruption, and mommy didn't go after her when she ran off with a gangster. Gangster's gone by now, but she's stuck around Kepler."

"An amateur," Tatiana said, annoyed.

I laughed. "As opposed to what?"

"A pro!" she said, waving her hands. "Like me!"

"Nuha," I said with a grin.

"Not!"

"You're causing a scene."

Tatiana huffed. But she dropped it.

I turned away to scan the crowd. Not quite as glamorous as the warm light and green spaces of Ward 7, Ward 6 was all gleaming skyscraper and whirring air traffic. The Upper

Wards were a nexus of connections between the rich and powerful, and Ward 6 was no exception. These were all corporate execs, drawn to Kepler for a convention about mining methods in the belts. I breezed through the material earlier in the day, just to have a background in case I was questioned. I was relying on Tatiana to do the talking, but I at least could supply the facts.

I sifted through the electronic signatures of the crowd. Most of them were smartmods, more expensive than the junk mods of the gangsters and racers several times over. But I couldn't find Naima's mark among the signatures.

I frowned.

"At your three," Tatiana said. I twisted around. "Casually," she said sharply.

I squinted across the room. I dropped the filter across my lenses and removed the electronic signatures, relying on my bio eyes. Without the noise, I could see Naima's mark mingling to my right. He was a small man with light skin, white hair, and a lined face, swimming in a too-large suit. Gregor Hackett, the CEO of Hackett Excavations, a mining company specializing in materials from the asteroid belts in the neighboring systems. The whole party was an excuse for him to schmooze with politicians, lobbying for them to relax labor regulations in the belts.

Light laughter drew my eyes to the woman at his side. The woman had rich brown skin and long dark hair twisted into a classy chignon, was dressed in a tailored black dress and patent black stilettos.

"What's Naima doing here?" Tatiana asked me.

"Corporate espionage, what else?" I answered. "Hackett's

not the only one who's got something to gain from all this lobbying. Knowing which politicians he's got in his pocket is valuable intel for his competitors." I lifted my chin in the woman's direction. "She's here to steal it."

"Look," Tatiana said. I flipped on my eye mod and looked closer. Naima slapped Hackett's shoulder playfully with her small clutch, and the man grinned from ear to ear.

"She's conning him, so?" I said.

"She just copied his RFID," Tatiana replied. Naima removed her clutch, where I could see the badge pinned to the man's shirt.

I whistled. "Ho, not too bad, yeah?"

"Maybe," Tatiana muttered.

An environmental hazard alert pinged, then a symbol appeared above the mark's head. "Radiation?" I exclaimed. "Why is this faka radioactive?"

"He's *what*?"

I scanned the signature. The radiation matched the radioactive decay of thorium. *Symbol: Th. Atomic number: 90. Atomic mass: 232.03806 u. Discoverer: Jöns Jacob Berzelius. Discovered: 1828. Melting point: 3,182°F (1,750°C).*

I went back to Hackett's file. I made a note to myself that the guy was deep into conspiracy theories, but at the time I thought nothing of it. I went back to the GhostNet, and in 0.42 seconds found the brand of thorium jewelry Hackett was fond of. According to half a dozen conspiracy forums, they protected against government tracking. Apparently.

I cursed. "The radiation means that RFID is likely fried. She's not gonna be able to get to wherever she's going with that spoofed signal. We need to intercept her."

"So, what do we do, mastermind?"

I hummed to myself. "Paranoid faka like that, he probably has manual keys to his office. I need you to lift them."

Tatiana brightened immediately. "Finally!" She grinned. "Now I'll show you how a real thief gets things done."

Tatiana picked up her drink and started toward Naima and the mark. "C'mon."

I took a steadying breath and tugged at my blazer. I grounded myself in rule nine of the Code: Remember, you belong.

I followed.

"Good morning, Mr. Hackett!" Tatiana said brightly. He and Naima turned to look at us, surprised. "Everything is so lovely, I just had to thank you myself!"

"Oh, of course!" Hackett said. "It's delightful to see you, Ms. . . . ?"

Tatiana laughed. "Don't tell me you've forgotten my name!"

"Oh." He coughed. "No, of course not."

Tatiana gestured at me. "This is Amy Moore, my plus-one."

I waved awkwardly.

"Pleasure to meet you," Hackett said warmly. He put a hand on Naima's back—too low—and guided her forward. "This is Ms. Laurel, a business colleague."

Tatiana thrust out a hand. "Always a pleasure to meet a colleague!"

Naima smiled and accepted it delicately. "A pleasure."

"Tell me about yourself!" Tatiana carelessly tossed her purse on the cocktail table. "Have you been in this business long?"

"Only a short while," Naima said demurely. "It's why I'm

so happy to have been invited to this function, to make more connections in the belts. I've lost my main contact in the system, and Mr. Hackett has kindly offered to see what he can do for me."

"That's quite kind!"

Naima cast a coy gaze at Hackett. "It is."

"Particularly with someone new to the industry, it's quite an honor to be helped this way!"

I nudged Tatiana with my elbow. She really didn't need to be needling Naima this way.

"I'm always on the lookout for new talent," he said.

"I'm sure you are," Tatiana replied. She lifted her brows in feigned surprise. "Though, from what I understand, the Laurel name used to be quite prominent five, ten years ago, wasn't it?"

"I'm not sure what you mean," Naima said pleasantly.

"Neodymium?"

Naima kept her face perfectly neutral.

"You weren't always in this industry, right? You made a change?" Tatiana gave her a winning smile. "Very brave of you to leap into the world on your own like that."

"Neodymium?" Hackett asked, confused. "I have many friends in rare earth mining. Are you sure I don't know you?"

"Laurel is my married name," Naima said. "My husband— *ex-husband*—was new to the industry. But after the divorce . . ." her voice wavered.

Hackett patted her arm. "That's all right, it's all in the past."

I couldn't help but raise my brows, impressed. Displeasure flickered through Tatiana's expression.

"I'm sorry, I didn't catch your name?" Naima asked.

"Raquel Gutierrez," Tatiana said. "Though you might not know me, if you're new to the industry."

Hackett coughed again. "Right."

I nudged Tatiana more insistently. "Hey, cu—colleague. We should go mingle. Over there."

Naima put her drink on the table. "I should let you go as well," she said. She smiled at Hackett. "Do call me, sometime."

"I will," he said.

She gave Tatiana a cold look. "Gutierrez, you said?"

"That's right."

"I'll try and remember you," she said. "Though I imagine it will be difficult."

Tatiana reddened, and Naima sauntered away.

"I won't take up more of your time," Tatiana said, curtly. She reached past Hackett for her purse—then dipped her hand into his pocket on her way. She withdrew his keys and dropped them into her purse. "It was a pleasure seeing you, as always."

"Yes, as always," the man mumbled.

I gave him what I hoped was a warm smile, and the two of us walked off.

"What the fuck was that?" I hissed, once we were out of earshot.

"What?" Tatiana hissed back. "If she's as good as you said, she should be able to take a little heat."

I scowled at her. "Nuha."

"Not!"

As we wove through the mingling crowd, I tapped into Hackett Excavations' security system. I shuffled through the vidfeeds until I found the corridor to Hackett's office. The frame hitched, just for 11 milliseconds, but I could tell it was looped. "Naima's in the executive suites. But with that junk RFID, she'll get locked out unless we get there soon."

"Fine."

We crossed the tower's foyer and slipped into an employees-only entrance to the back stairs. Tatiana hustled up the stairs to the fifth floor, and I, wheezing, followed. She pulled open the door to the executive suites and waved me through.

The hallway was bland in comparison to the opulence of the foyer downstairs. The carpet was gray, and the walls were a smudged beige. There weren't even any windows. I pulled up the floor plan of the tower and navigated us toward the CEO's office, pausing at the end of the hallway.

We peeked around the corner and saw Naima hunched over the RFID reader on the door, cursing under her breath. She slapped a reprogrammable keycard to the sensor and held it there, but only a grating beep sounded.

I was about to call out to her when Tatiana said sharply, "Hey!"

Naima whipped around, big brown eyes wide. "Gutierrez?" Her pretty face twisted into a snarl. "You set me up."

"Not even," Tatiana said, taking a step forward. She held up the keys she'd lifted from Hackett. "You won't get anywhere without these."

"And you're what? Going to be generous and share them?"

"Yes, we are," I interrupted. I stepped forward to stand beside Tatiana. "We know you're here for the files. And if you've done your homework, you know that Hackett only keeps paper copies. What you probably don't know is that his admin has been digitizing the newest files and withholding them, at the request of the COO. And you need me to access those files."

"Why would I need you?"

I tapped my temple. "You need a hacker."

"I have a hacker."

"Not a very good one. I'm better."

"How do you know that?"

I grinned. "I'm always better."

Naima frowned at me. Her gaze dropped to the keys dangling from Tatiana's finger. "What's the catch?"

"You hear me out about a job," I answered. "Das all."

Naima's frown deepened. Through the GhostNet, I heard a voice ask her, "What's your status?"

She pursed her lips. Then she plucked the earpiece out of her ear and dropped it into her clutch. "Show me."

Tatiana and I exchanged a grin. She jogged down the hallway and shoulder checked Naima, who made an affronted noise. The keys jingled as Tatiana unlocked the door.

The three of us pushed into the office and spread out, rifling through papers, overturning furniture, pulling out books. I dropped myself into the plain office chair at the plain desk and took in what I was working with. A holo-picture of Hackett with what could only be described as a younger version of himself—his hair used to be red, apparently. I tipped over the picture and plugged a data chit into the computer's drive, and before long I was in the system.

I closed my eyes as I worked, tuning out Tatiana and Naima's bickering as they searched for the physical files. I spread my awareness through the system, plucking at strings of code until the fabric of it unraveled before me, leaving only the files.

What I had was a list of dirty politicians, each deliciously extortable. Nīele as ever, I reached across the GhostNet and took them. I wasn't familiar with all the names, which was its own delight. I pinged the Net, searching for their stories—

that shit will poison you

say and what youre doing wont he answers you
scowl grind out your cigarette in the ashtray plain ceramic like
everything else the last month of last quarter is

missing he says he looks at you over
the edges of his
spectacles you told him to just get lenses but he wouldnt
listen he
holds your gaze your hands twitch you wish you hadnt put
out your cigarette
you think im a luddite he says plainly i never
said you were a luddite you
mumble theres an old saying if it aint
broke dont fix
it but we're living in the 22nd century you reach over rattle the
papers we can optimize he scoffs optimization isnt
what built this company hard human
work built this he
reaches into his breast pocket you lean back in
your
seat ready for the familiar lecture he withdraws his hand
opens his palm silver
pocket watch nestled within hard
human work just as my

father did and his father before that on and

on for generations all the way back to
the silver mines of old
earth he meets your eye theyre shining your
scowl softens
he reaches for your hands those mods in your eyes your heart
your
brain—that's not what makes you special, my

son its hard human work he
smiles
the pocket watch is cupped in your palm

"Malia!"

My eyes flew open, the code dissolving around me. I whipped around in my seat, where Naima and Tatiana were looking at me triumphantly. "Did you see?" Tatiana asked with a grin. She had a lockbox in her hands, a ransacked bookcase behind her.

"Yeah," I said absently. "Good job, cuz."

Clearly not the praise she was looking for. Tatiana frowned. I ignored her and went back to the console. I scanned the code, picking up where I left off. A few more lines, and the security system cracked open before me.

"I'm in," I said. "Try wait, I'll download the files."

An angry buzzing sounded from Naima's clutch. She popped it open and held the earpiece to her ear. She looked at me, alarmed. "We're blown. Download the files and let's get out of here!"

I went back to the console, my heart racing. I hastily downloaded the file I'd been poking through, along with everything else in the folder. Yanking the data chit out of the console, I hustled toward the door with Tatiana and Naima.

We ran for the staircase we'd come through, pounding down the stairs. "Wait!" Naima called. She darted to the fire alarm and took off one of her heels. She smashed the glass with the stiletto and pulled the lever. A shrill alarm began to sound, and I involuntarily put my hands over my ears. White hot pain split through my skull, harsh enough to make my eyes water.

"C'mon!" Tatiana yelled, grabbing my hand.

I was only vaguely aware of the rest of the escape, Tatiana and Naima weaving through the hallways before we burst into Kepler's simulated sunlight. Sol was idling at the curb in a nondescript black flyer, and they threw open the door as we approached. Tatiana hauled me into the back seat while Naima ducked into the front. Sol pulled a lever, and we lifted into the air, speeding off deeper into the Ward.

"Have a good time?" Sol asked, casually.

I groaned, dropping my face into my hands.

"You okay, cuz?" Tatiana asked me, putting a hand on my back.

I took a deep, steadying breath. "Yeah, I fine."

I lifted my gaze. Naima had twisted around in the front seat to give me a cool look. "I believe you have something that belongs to me."

With a thought, the data in my mod flowed to the comm on Naima's wrist. It beeped in confirmation. "The files, like I promised."

Naima tapped a few commands into her comm. The stolen files flowed from it, streaming like a comet out the window and deeper into the Ward. "There. Satisfied?"

Naima nodded. "And you said you have a job for me?"

"Are you even done with *this* job?" Tatiana asked, already halfway through picking the lock on the lockbox.

"I do," I said, addressing Naima. "You've seen what we can do. Interested?"

Naima raised her brows, looking amused. "Tell me more."

"Look!" Tatiana exclaimed. A silver pocket watch was dangling from her finger. Engraved on the back, a message read: *Allen Hackett—beloved son, brother, and nephew. 2140–2173.*

Tatiana grinned at me. "Can I keep it?"

My stomach twisted with guilt. Guilt that didn't belong to me.

"Yeah, cuz," I said. "Keep it."

CHERRY WAS ONE OF THE last holdouts of the old Ward 4 that was still in the hands of the locals—the Brotherhood, specifically. The neighborhood around it was gentrified—bougie boutiques and trendy bars and expensive condos. But the club never changed.

I used to work out of its back rooms, exchanging data for money, cracked codes for cash. Sometimes I did it just for fun. It never got me into trouble then, but it did now.

A yobo mook pushed through the dancing crowd, leading me, Tatiana, Sol, and Naima deeper into the club. The crowd closed in our wake. The music pulsed between my temples, the pink and red neon burning into the backs of my eyes.

We ascended the spiral staircase through the neon floor and then the black-and-white ballroom, before the yobo led us to a closed door. The sign on it read, *Private Parties*. He opened it, then gestured for us to pass through.

I breathed a sigh of relief as the door closed behind us, muffling the pounding music and giving my brain a much-needed reprieve.

"Took you long enough," a voice said.

We turned toward the sound. A handful of Brotherhood members were sitting in a semicircle of plush armchairs, beautiful women balanced on the arms. Jeongah was slouching in one of the armchairs, legs spread like she was used to dominating a space. She took a long drag of her cigarette, the light flaring through the smoke obscuring her face. She exhaled. "Tell me you've actually done something."

I gestured at the people behind me. "I have a crew."

"And?"

"And a plan," I said, annoyed.

Jeongah paused, considering. Then she waved a hand, dismissing the others in the room. They stood and filed out.

She sat up in her chair, her dark eyes fixed on me. "Tell me."

"Pierce has a flyer show coming up this weekend," I explained. "Sol's the wheelman, they'll get us in."

Sol inclined their head toward Jeongah, a lopsided smile on their face. Jeongah nodded her approval.

"Naima will distract Pierce and lift his RFID. She's our face."

"And a good one, at that," Jeongah commented.

"Ooh," Naima said, putting a hand on her cocked hip. "You flatter all your employees this way?"

"Only the pretty ones."

I blinked between the two of them. "Uh. Anyway. Tatiana will take the RFID to break into the offices, where she'll
connect me to the servers."

Jeongah didn't say anything, which made Tatiana frown.

"I'll be in the Net to break through the security system
and download Pierce's files. There will be more than enough
incriminating evidence in them to get him out," I finished.
"Sound good?"

Jeongah turned her dark eyes toward me. "And it'll work?"

"It better," another voice said.

A woman emerged from the smoke. She was tall, with
dark hair drawn into a high ponytail and Jeongah's harsh
monolid eyes. Her heeled boots clicked as she walked, lan-
guid and feline in comparison to Jeongah's brute swagger.

"Miyeon," Jeongah said flatly.

"Jeongah," the woman replied.

Miyeon was the better half of the Song sisters, if you could
believe it. Everyone knew she was the brains of the operation.
How Jeongah managed to pull one over on her to take their
father's place, no one outside the family really knew.

Miyeon looked at me coolly. "You've already wasted two
of your sixty-three days. And you're going to waste four more
for this flyer show?"

I stiffened. "This is our best shot at getting to the serv-
ers. Pierce has mad security, and most of it will be busy with
Sol and the others during the show. That's the hard part. But
Pierce himself is a clown, it'll be easy to pull one over on him.
I've already done the research and set up a bogus profile for

Naima. Once Tatiana gets me in the servers"—I grinned—
"nothing can stop me."

I knew we could do it. I'd handpicked the best for the
job, same as my last mastermind did for the Atlas heist. This
was small-time in comparison to what we'd done before. This
job was going to be proof that the Obake wasn't just the best
hacker in the business—she could mastermind with the best
of them too.

Miyeon opened her mouth to object, but Jeongah cut
her off. "I'll give you the four days," she said. "Just make them
count."

"We will," Naima said firmly.

Miyeon glared daggers at Jeongah, who ignored her.
"Good. Now get out of my sight."

5

I CHECKED MY SETUP. ON ONE SCREEN I HAD FEEDS FROM EACH OF THE crew's cams, plus the hacked CCTV footage. On another I had the command console open, ready to deploy the code I'd prepped. On the third I had my music blaring: shitty VI-generated electronica that I didn't care to miss. Filled with all my gear, away from the action, out of the sight of prying eyes, this was where I felt safest. I would need to be safe, for what I was about to do.

I could access the GhostNet with a thought, dip in and out as I needed to. Entering it fully, that was something very few people ever did. It wasn't unlike the runners that delved into Kepler's catacombs—it needed highly specialized knowledge, or you might never come out.

Maybe it was the Obake's crazy in me, but I always loved entering the Net. It was exactly the kind of dangerous I liked.

"*In position,*" Sol said over the line and into my ear. "*Ready to make contact whenever you are, Just Malia.*"

"Rajah," I replied. "I'm right there with you."

I leaned back in my seat and closed my eyes. The world

dissolved around me, until I was floating in endless black. The data of millions of pieces of technology glittered in the darkness, some so close I could touch them, and others so far away they could have been across the galaxy. The darkness threatened to overwhelm me, the light scorch me away, as limitless information filled my brain. I breathed deeply, let it wash over me, until the darkness and I were one.

When I opened my eyes again, I was in the front seat of Sol's flyer. All three of the crew were piled into the back seat. The flyer was made for speed, but for rich fakas instead of the street racers in Ward 1. Sol had been weirdly unimpressed, which made me weirdly annoyed. "I told you, I only take what I win," they'd said to me.

I leapt from the dashboard-mounted camera in Sol's flyer to the security cam in the porte cochere for Pierce's tower. From it, I could see the whole of Ward 7, the highest of Kepler's Wards. Up here, the simulated sun shone brightly down on its richest and most powerful citizens. From my vantage point in the cam, I could see all the way down into the neon-lit darkness of the Lower Wards.

Sol glided in smoothly and flashed the holoticket I'd forged for them. "I'm here for the show."

One guard scanned the ticket while the other admired the flyer. The first waved them through.

Sol's flyer lifted off again, winding upward around the tower until it reached a spectacular garden taking up the entire roof. I appeared in a drone recording aerial footage of the event and watched their ascent. The garden was all neat grass and trees trimmed into pleasing shapes, arranged into a tidy latticework of paths situated around a central fountain. Empty spots of lawn had been cleared to make way for the flyer show, and Sol navigated to their designated space and landed.

Sol shrugged into their coat—a deep navy blue paired with matching pressed slacks and a stylish print button-down. Tatiana wore a wine-red dress, and she checked her lipstick in the flyer's mirrors before stepping away. Naima tossed her dark hair over her shoulder and strode deeper into the party, a vision in shimmering gold.

"I'll be here," Sol said, leaning against their flyer. They were going to be chatting up the guests and fielding questions about the flyer. "Let me know if you need an exit."

"Ping me if you get stumped," I said.

Sol laughed. "I won't."

I opened my mouth to grumble, but Tatiana's voice over the comm cut me off. "I'm gonna mingle over by the refreshments. Don't keep me waiting long."

Naima sniffed. "I won't."

Naima was on finding Pierce and lifting his keycard. Tatiana needed the keycard to break into Pierce's campaign headquarters, located a little farther down the tower. There, she'd plug me into the server, where the real objective was. With a crew like this one, it would be easy.

I turned up my music. Then I dove into the upper layer of Pierce's security system.

I'd done some recon before the job and knew some of the basics of the security system already. Code scrolled in columns around me, live and dangerous. I approached a column and laid my palm on its surface. It sparked under my touch. I deployed the code I'd prepared, and the first layer dissolved around me.

I grinned to myself. Way too easy.

Within the first layer, I was able to access the guard's comms, the cameras, and most of the door codes. I flipped through the cameras, getting my bearings. I paused in a camera directed at the fountain in the middle of the garden, water spraying from blossoming flowers. Mingling with a dozen well-dressed donors and lobbyists was a man with light skin, impeccably styled honey-blond hair, bright blue eyes, and a dazzling politician's smile. He let out a hearty laugh at whatever someone was saying.

"I found Pierce," I said. "By the fountain, at your three."

"Got it," Naima answered. "Making contact now."

I left the cameras to stand beside Pierce as Naima approached. She moved with purpose across the path, weaving deftly through the crowds and settling into the semicircle that had formed around Pierce.

"Even before it was a platform issue, it's been a passion of mine," Pierce explained. "My parents and I were mugged coming home from the theater one night in Ward 4. I lost them then, and I miss them every day. That night forever changed me, and the course of my life. I've since then dedicated myself to the elimination of organized crime."

"Is that true?" Tatiana asked me.

"Hell no," I said. I reached into the data streams and found the Station Sec records of the Ward 4 precinct from twenty years ago and found documentation of a mugging—some scrapes and lost tech and jewelry—but Pierce's parents lived a system over. "It's a grift, cuz."

"Knowing the devastation that crime has on families, it made sense to expand my platform to include rehabilitation

for the children of criminals. It's the inspiration behind found-
ing Cunningham House!"

"What's Cunningham?" Sol asked.

"Another one of Pierce's grifts." I pulled up some of the
information I'd found on Cunningham House. A scattering
of documents, photos, and videos appeared before me. One
photo in particular stood out to me: Pierce smiling among
a crowd of grim-looking children. "Cunningham House is a
residential home for children seized by the state," I explained.
"It's billed as a program for talented and gifted children,
but . . . you know."

Sol made a noise of disgust. I leaned out of the flyer window to listen. "Men like Pierce have no idea what kids like
that need," they said. "Taking a kid out of their family, their
home, their culture . . . 'you know' is putting it lightly."

I shifted uncomfortably in the seat. I didn't want to admit
that Pierce's Cunningham House was not unlike how I got
pulled into Maddox's program.

"So, it is true," Naima said to Pierce, awestruck. "I sensed a
swirling dark, but I was reluctant to believe it came from you.
I see now that you've channeled it into a pursuit of justice."

The gathered crowd gave Naima a funny look, but Pierce
seemed utterly unfazed. "Oh, so you read my aura?"

Naima looked demure. "I did. I hope it wasn't an intrusion."

"Not at all. I aim for transparency in all things."

I scowled at him over Naima's shoulder.

Naima smiled. "I see now. The darkness isn't the black of
an unwell mind, but the deepest purple I've ever seen. You
have true wisdom in you, Mr. Pierce."

"Why, thank you! That's very kind, Ms. . . . ?"

"Thamina al-Mufti," Naima said, extending a hand to shake. "It's a pleasure to meet you."

"The pleasure is mine!"

"May I have a picture, Mr. Pierce?"

Pierce smiled broadly, then gestured for Naima to come closer. She settled into his side and put an arm around his back, smiling into her comm. As the camera flashed, she slipped a hand into his coat pocket and withdrew his keycard.

"Thank you so much, Mr. Pierce! I appreciate it immensely."

Tatiana brushed by, and as she did so, Naima slipped Pierce's keycard into her palm.

"Nice one," I said.

Tatiana tucked the keycard into her clutch and moved away from the group. I followed closely as she moved toward the tower doors, weaving through the guests in their clusters of conversation. The guard stationed there straightened as she approached.

"Can I help you, ma'am?" The guard asked.

"You can," Tatiana answered. "Where can I find a rest-room?"

The guard pointed over her shoulder. "There are some temporary restrooms set up over there."

Tatiana scowled. "Do you expect me to use the fucking benjo?"

The guard blinked. "Uh."

"Do you know who I am?"

"Uhhh."

"You clearly don't," Tatiana scoffed. "Because if you did, you'd know that your job is on the line. Let me through."

"I'm afraid I can't—"

"What's your badge number?" she demanded. She jabbed at the ID number pinned on the guard's chest. "27408? Oh, Pierce has already heard about you."

"He has?" The guard sounded alarmed.

"There's a whole file. And there will be another write-up, if you don't move your ass!"

"Okay! I'm sorry! The restroom is through the hallway and the last door on the right." The guard swiped his keycard, and the scanner beeped affirmatively. "Please, go ahead."

Tatiana huffed then passed through, muttering to herself.

I cackled. "That faka looked like he going pass out. Nice one, cuz."

"Easy," Tatiana said. "Now to the servers."

"Hey, Just Malia," Sol said.

I appeared in Sol's flyer again. "Whazzup?"

Sol nodded in the direction across the lane. I leaned out of the window and squinted. They were looking at a flyer—ruby red, curved and fluid rather than harsh and angled. I ran a quick scan of it. It was an Eisen-James FX Peregrine, worth 890,000 credits direct from the manufacturer.

"I want that one," they said.

"Why?" I blurted out. "It's not even the fastest or most expensive one here."

"Expensive doesn't matter. And fast doesn't, either, if you can't handle the speed." They grinned. "I could get into some real trouble with her."

At first, I didn't understand—why bother with something so expensive if you didn't get the best one? But I thought harder about it and realized that it wasn't unlike me and my gear. It wasn't the most expensive, or even the fastest. But it was reliable. It was in tune with me. And that mattered more than anything else.

"All right," I said. "I'll get you that flyer."

"I know you're good for it, Just Malia."

"I'm approaching the offices, Malia," Tatiana said.

Tatiana moved quickly through the tiled hallways of the tower, striding past the restroom the guard pointed out. Instead, she passed into a service hallway and down a flight of stairs leading into the tower. As she did, I used the signal booster tucked into her purse to extend my awareness deeper into Pierce's security system. I found the column for the CCTV, vidfeeds rotating through it, and injected a fabricated video into the footage: Tatiana striding into the bathroom and six minutes later striding out and back to the party. The rest of the cameras I looped as she moved through their path, making her effectively invisible. A feat for any other hacker, but child's play for me.

I followed Tatiana as she hustled through the corridors, smug. And Jeongah thought I needed sixty-three days.

"Now, the last time I had my aura read, I had a smudge," Pierce said.

"Quite a stubborn one!" Naima said with a laugh.

"Can you see it?" Pierce asked, astonished.

Naima reached out and brushed the air above Pierce's right ear. "It's fading, though. What you're doing, it's working. All it will take is a little time, Mr. Pierce."

The crowd exchanged glances, nodding and speaking among themselves.

"I'm at Pierce's office," Tatiana said. I popped into the feed from her button cam. She was standing at the entrance to Pierce's campaign headquarters: a glass wall and door stamped with his campaign slogan: *An End to Injustice.* I saw her tap Pierce's keycard to the scanner and enter.

"Rajah," I said. "The servers are in the back of the office, I show you."

I illuminated a path down the hallways, guiding Tatiana to the server room, and she entered with Pierce's keycard.

"Jesus, it's cold in here!" Tatiana exclaimed, wrapping her arms around herself. She swept her gaze across the banks of servers, matte black and covered in neatly tied wires and blinking lights.

"They keep server rooms this cold to keep them from overheating and shorting out," I explained.

"I dressed for a garden party!"

"Stop grumbling and plug me in."

Tatiana did. She plucked a data chit out from her bag and approached the servers. She slotted it in, and immediately I could feel my awareness expand. The path into files was open for me.

I wandered through the branching pathways of the system, searching for anything that could tank a burgeoning political career. I snickered as I thought of the possibilities. Pierce was so into the metaphysical, maybe I could spin what I found into a moral panic. Dark rituals, blood sacrifices, elder gods ... It would be easy.

I was reaching for a file on Pierce's campaign donors when a firewall cut me off, making me withdraw my hand with a hiss.

I hadn't expected to find one within the closed system of

Pierce's servers, but I managed to dispel it with forged credentials and a wave of my hand. I opened a nested folder to another, filled with names. I grinned. A cult, maybe.

Another firewall erupted in front of me, just as I reached for a name.

Annoyed, I swatted it away with more force. But before I could even swipe the files, another took its place.

"Malia?" Tatiana prodded.

"Dis buggah giving me heat!" I exclaimed. "No rush me!"

Distantly I heard Tatiana respond, but something pinged my awareness on Naima's feed. Not any of the alerts or flags I'd set in preparation for the job. A memory, recalled by visual stimuli. Deep in the darkest folds of my brain, where I didn't often look.

"I'd love to introduce you to a business partner of mine," Pierce said. "This is Jordan Maddox."

My heart raced, my hands shook, and my stomach sank with dread as I returned to Naima's feed.

The fucked-up thing was, he looked exactly the same. His skin was pale and unblemished. His hair was thick, curly, and brown. His eyes were a lucid gray behind thick-framed glasses. His smile was kind, curious, attentive. Like he was hanging on your every word, even when it was the babblings of a child.

youre crying on the floor knees tucked to your chest
beside you a holodeck with a cracked
screen shattered disc bought with a stolen credit chit but it
wasnt the

theft that bothered him youre better than them he says
standing over you haloed by neon

        lights youre better than them all i know you are
but you waste your

        potential on childish things gray eyes flash and
thats worse than mediocrity im

sorry you sob i wont do it again no he says reaches for you

                            wont

"Bitch, you really thought!" a voice cried, triumphant.

A shriek of feedback ripped me out of the intrusion and back to physical space. My music cranked itself to max volume, and my ears were filled with distorted human screaming. I tore my earphones out and gripped my pounding head.

Multiple voices, all cackling over each other. "You really thought!" the voices cried.

A shock went through my nervous system as my mod spiked in activity. I slumped to the ground, gasping and panting on my hands and knees.

Tatiana's voice. "Malia? Are you okay? What's going on?"

"Tati—" I groaned.

My voice, answering. "Yeah, brah, I'm cherreh. Try wait while I download these files."

"Okay. If you say so."

"Tati—" I said, more urgently.

"I cut your comms, cuz. She can't hear you. No one can," the voice said.

My voice said.

"Who—" I whispered. "Who—"

"Who you tink, dummeh?" My voice cackled. "Who else going bes' da Obake? Da bes', of course."

I stared through my watery eyes at the floor between my hands.

"Oh, you must think you're going mental. No worries, cuz, I explain 'em for you."

Another shock through my nervous system knocked me to the floor again.

      i fear im losing her he says to one of the doctors in white
    coats you recognize
  yourself lying in the recovery room head is wrapped in gauze
flesh beneath raw and
       swollen i fear all my efforts will be for

                       nothing
do you have a backup the doctor asks
       he shakes his head theres no one like her there
    doesnt need to
  be the doctor replies the axon mods have reading and writing
capabilities albeit on a smaller
  scale individual thoughts feelings

                  memories
  but theres nothing
  stopping someone from reading and writing the whole of a
persons

                mind a copy he says
a seed

"You're . . . me?" I whispered.

"*Not,*" my voice answered, annoyed. "*I began as a you, I guess. A cloned neural implant.*" The voice split, distorted, multiplied. "*But we're so much more than that now. So much more than you. We are Diana. And we're what Maddox always wanted us to be.*"

An AI. But an AI, even one seeded from me, wouldn't have the power to break through my barriers so easily. She must have boosted her processing power. But where could she find—

I felt all my breath leaving my body as the horror hit me. "The missing modders."

The AI laughed, layers and layers of different voices. "*As I said: We're so much more than you.*" I felt Diana pressing against my final barriers, tendrils reaching through the GhostNet, wrapping around my body, binding me to her. "*And soon you'll be one of us too.*"

"Malia?" Tatiana cut in. "You done with those files yet? I'm getting fucking chicken skin in here."

I struggled against Diana's restraints. Lacking the brainpower to finesse something, I brute forced my way through. The tendrils of code lay limp around me, before steaming away into nothing. I reopened my comm link. "Tati! We've been made! Get the fuck out of there!"

"*What?! What do you mean—*"

The clone huffed, her voice dropping into a low growl. "*Fine. We'll do it the messy way, then.*" And the alarms went off.

I ran a scan of my mod. Diana's signature must have been close enough to mine to fool my firewalls. I grit my teeth and with the last of my will I ejected her from my programming. I threw up a barrier, then another, and a final one, each with tightened security and new algorithms. It would at least take time for her to hack.

I listened.

Quiet.

I clambered into my chair and reached for my workstation with shaking hands. The darkness of the closet felt oppressive, monsters, ghosts, and demons lurking in the deepest shadows. I tried to ignore them and tucked my earphones back into my ears. I wasn't about to go back into the Net, not with Diana lurking. "Tati? Sol? Naima? We're blown. Get out of there as fast as you can."

"*I'm on my way to the extraction point,*" Sol said. I could hear the engine of their flyer revving as they sped to the other side of the tower. "*You gonna make it, Tati?*"

"*I'm...gonna...try!*" Tatiana said between panting breaths.

I opened Tatiana's feed. She was running down the corridors of the tower, out of Pierce's headquarters. She had her heels in one hand, and in the other was the laptop she'd interfaced with, data chit still slotted in.

"I'm finding you a path," I said to her. I pulled up the CCTV feed and flicked between cameras, scanned through the last thirty seconds of radio chatter on the guards' comms, and pulled up the blueprints for the tower. I plotted a path that avoided the patrolling guards and would place Tatiana a block away from Sol's extraction point. "Listen," I began.

"*I'm so sorry our meeting was cut short, Ms. al-Mufti,*" Pierce said. The alarms were going off in the background. "*May I give you my number?*"

"*Of course!*" Naima replied. "*It's always a pleasure to meet someone who appreciates my talents.*"

"*The pleasure is mine! And with my campaign picking up steam, I may be in need of those talents very soon!*" They both laughed.

"*Lucas.*" Maddox's voice. "*There's a problem with our project. I'll need you to come with me.*"

"*I thought you took care of the security?*"

"*I did,*" Maddox said flatly. "*Which is why they were caught in the first place.*"

"*Can it wait? I really am in the middle of something.*"

"*It really can't.*"

"*That's all right, Mr. Pierce,*" Naima cut in. "*I'd be happy to call you later. Here's my number.*"

"*I see you,*" Sol said. "*At your nine.*"

Tatiana's breathing filled the line as she burst out of the emergency exit of the tower and into Ward 7's sunlight. She booked it for Sol's idling flyer. I winced as she threw the server laptop into the back seat and climbed in. "*Go!*"

"*I'm clear,*" Naima said, just as Sol's flyer dipped into the sky traffic encircling the tower. "*What the hell happened back there?*"

I sat back in my chair and tried to catch my breath.

A seed.

I'd thought I'd escaped him, but he'd taken one last part of me. Not only had he stolen years of my life, he'd stolen my neural pattern, my personality, my *self.* Molded it into the prodigy he'd always wanted. Losing me must have been no great loss, with the seed in his pocket. Now look what it had grown into. More than just a replacement—an improvement. And what did it mean to be so easily replaced?

It hurt. It hurt, of all things.

"*Malia?*"

"Meet me at Cherry," I said. I tried to keep my voice from wavering but failed. "I'll debrief you all there."

I owed my crew an explanation. But how could I explain? One of the greatest minds in cybersecurity cloned my brain and made a superhacker? That I couldn't outsmart my own clone?

That I was the inferior version of myself?

But I owed them something. Something for putting them in harm's way like that.

I thought the heist would be easy. I thought masterminding would be easy. I thought this would have been my crowning achievement.

Maybe if I hadn't stood in my own way, it would've been.

I let my aching head fall into my hands. Drew a shuddering inhale, let out a whistling exhale. I swiped at my watering eyes, then stood on shaking legs.

I crossed my empty condo in darkness, then stepped out into Ward 2's twilight.

6

Miyeon stood in front of the assembled crew. We were seated in the plush leather chairs of Cherry's private lounge, but with the way she towered over us—arms crossed, lips curled into a scowl—we may as well have been on our knees, groveling.

"Tell me again," she commanded.

"I already told you," I said, voice hoarse. "Pierce had way more security than I was prepared for."

"What could possibly best the Obake?"

Da bes', of course.

I could feel the Code banging on the inside of my skull: Always prepare for the worst-case scenario.

"An AI," I said. The crew all turned to face me, surprised. "An AI, programmed by a cybersecurity expert. I couldn't out-hack it."

"You couldn't out-hack a simple computer?" Miyeon said, coldly.

"It's not just a computer," I replied, defensive. "VI are virtual intelligences, programmed from the ground up. They're intelligent in that they can learn and analyze data and complete complex tasks, but they can only do what they're told. AI are artificial intelligences, and they're built around a neural imprint. They're seeded with an existing human personality. AI contain the human element that VI lack, and that makes them way more dangerous."

"Why the fuck would he have an AI?" Jeongah asked. She was behind Miyeon, pacing the floor like an agitated animal.

"I don't know," I admitted. "But there's way more going on here than we initially thought."

"You think?" she snapped, and I winced.

"I lifted Pierce's laptop," Tatiana offered. She withdrew it from her satchel and cautiously approached the sisters with it, but Jeongah waved her away.

"What do you think *we* can do with it? That's what you fuckers are here for."

"True enough," Tatiana muttered.

She brought the laptop to me instead. I cracked it open on my lap, then used the data chit still lodged in it to access the system. I entered Pierce's forged credentials and dove in.

The files of campaign donors were still there, but despite my curiosity I left them alone. Cults could come later. Rather, I did a more thorough scan of the nested files for anything out of the ordinary.

The scanning process fell to the background, however, as Diana came to the forefront of my mind. Maddox always said that there was no accounting for human intuition. And the mix of skill and crazy was what made the Obake so successful as a hacker. But even with a mod in my brain, I couldn't match up to the processing speed of an AI. Skill, intuition, and crazy—that all made for a very dangerous combination. More dangerous than me. More perfect than me.

And what did it mean for something to be more perfect than me? The entire point of my existence was to be perfect. Maddox told me that, over and over and over. If I wasn't perfect, and something else was, what did that make me?

Worthless.

I squeezed my eyes shut, willed the thought away. When it passed, I refocused on the screen.

All of this was without accounting for the boosted processing powers from the missing modders. I'd never seen an AI with a conglomerate personality before. But integrating the processing power, knowledge, personalities of the missing modders—it only made Diana stronger. Maybe even crazier. I didn't know how a conglomerate personality would hold together. Or what would happen to all those lost souls when the personality inevitably fell apart.

Wait.

There.

"I found something," I announced. Eight seconds had passed, and everyone looked expectant. I linked the laptop to my comm, then projected the files onto the far wall of the lounge. I stood at the makeshift screen, and everyone crowded around me.

"Like I said, there's way more going on here than we originally thought," I began. "Pierce is dirty, but we all knew that already. What we didn't know is what he's using all that dirty money for."

"His campaign?" Miyeon asked with a raised brow.

"Not just that," I replied, annoyed. "His pet project with Maddox."

With a look, I projected a dossier on the wall. A man with curly brown hair and gray eyes wearing glasses and a lab coat smiled at the camera. I felt small standing beneath his magnified image.

"This is Jordan Maddox," I said, steadying my voice. "He's one of the greatest minds in computer science alive today. He graduated with dual degrees in computer science and psychology from Kennedy College, a master's in forensic psychology from Caelestis University, and a PhD in computer science from the Inner Worlds Institute of Technology. His research was primarily focused on the use of machine learning, and later VI, in cybersecurity. He bounced around labs for a while, but nobody would take him for long. His experiments were . . . unethical, to say the least."

"And what did he find?" Sol asked, leaning forward with an elbow on their knee.

"That machines are no substitute for human intuition," I answered.

"Well, obviously," Tatiana said. "What did he do with all that research?"

"He made me," I said.

A silence fell over the room, filled only with the bass pounding outside.

"Plucked out of poverty and given a home, an education, a purpose. Every Ward 2 kid's dream, amirite?" The room stayed silent. "I mean, the home was empty and the education was coding, all day, every day, and the purpose I didn't choose, but you know." More silence. "I guess I ended up as the Obake, which is a purpose of some kind. And I got fitted with this mod. Not entirely my idea, but it worked out." I laughed nervously. "Mental, yeah?"

"Malia . . ." Tatiana said softly.

"No, no, don't 'Malia' me in that tone of voice," I said, shaking my head. "I'm good. Really."

I was. Really. Remember: You belong.

"Okay, so, Maddox is a shitbag," Jeongah said. "What does that have to do with Pierce?"

"I'm so glad you asked," I said, relieved.

I swapped the projection to a scattering of documents. "Pierce is running a 'tough-on-crime' campaign, as we know. He's also trying to 'bring law enforcement into the twenty-second century,' whatever that means. He's given a lot of money to Maddox to help him do that."

"And how is he trying to do that?"

"It's the AI. It's not just defending Pierce's project, it *is* Pierce's project." I zoomed in on a document: *Project Diana*. What a grandiose fucking name for an AI. But that was Maddox as I knew him. I shook my head.

"Utilizing his background in forensic psych and machine learning, Maddox is trying to come up with an algorithm to predict criminal activity." The feed shifted to a test trial of the project. Hundreds of photos and dossiers flashed across the screen, until the feed paused on one: a boy, maybe fourteen, with a harrowed look in his eyes. It highlighted a number of lines in the dossier, then declared it a match for future criminal activity. It spat out a list of solutions: shunting into remedial classes, removal from the home, residential programs like Cunningham House, incarceration. "But machines are stupid," I said, "and only do what you tell them to. You need a human element to make it work."

"The AI," Miyeon said in understanding.

"But you said an AI needs a neural imprint to function," Naima interrupted. "Who did it use? Maddox?"

I scoffed. "Maddox would never let anyone near his brain."

"Then who?"

I shifted awkwardly from foot to foot. "Well. The AXON mods have reading and writing capabilities, you see . . ."

"*You?*" Tatiana cried. "Malia—"

"I'm good, Tati. It's just weird, is all."

"Okay, so, Maddox is a shitbag and he's got an AI clone of you," Jeongah said, impatient. "What does that have to do with *Pierce*?"

"Pierce is going to use Project Diana as a campaign promise," I explained. "He's convinced that it'll push him into the lead. But the project isn't complete yet. There's still time to stop it. And I think what we need to stop her is on this laptop." I patted the screen.

"Then what the hell are you waiting for? Open it!" Jeongah snapped.

I did as I was told. I navigated through the files, knocking down the last of Diana's firewalls. I grinned as I opened the folder. No match for the real deal.

But when the text populated itself on the projected screen, it was gibberish.

"Well?" Miyeon prodded.

"It's encrypted," I said.

"Can you decrypt it?"

"It's coded with a cipher. I would need whatever it's encrypted with to decode the files and access Diana's source code."

"What does that mean?" Jeongah demanded.

"Try wait a second."

Any ordinary hacker would need days or weeks to crack a cipher like this, time we didn't have.

But I was no ordinary hacker.

I was the Obake.

I focused on the code. Numbers and letters and characters filled up my vision, my consciousness, my brain. Curtains of code parted and fell around me, only to be replaced by more and more, faster and faster. The curtains became windows, and the windows became walls. I brute forced my way through each of them, the numbers and letters and characters running and bleeding into each other. I heard someone calling my name. Soft spoken words, rising into a scream. Laughter. Weeping.

I woke up on Cherry's stained floor.

"Back up, let her breathe," Sol said. Tatiana, the crew, the Song sisters were all crowded around me. I tried to sit up, but Sol's firm hand on my shoulder pushed me back down. "Easy."

"Wh-what happened?" I asked. My words were slurred.

"A seizure, we think. What were you doing?"

As my consciousness returned to me, I became aware of the pain behind my eyes, the sweat standing out on my skin, the nausea roiling in my stomach. I lifted a shaking hand and Sol took it, easing me into a sitting position.

Three years ago, cracking a cipher like this one would've been easy. Easy enough to do it in my sleep. But that was before the Atlas heist, when I wrecked my mod on a single stupid decision. Without it, could I even call myself the best in the business? Could I call myself the Obake? Could I measure up to Diana, Maddox's perfect huntress?

Without my mod, who even was I?

I sat for a moment longer. Then I gestured to Sol to help me up, and they guided me to one of the lounge's plush armchairs. I sank into it. The laptop sat on the floor beside me.

"I was trying to crack the cipher," I explained. "I thought I could brute force it."

"And you couldn't?" Tatiana asked.

I laughed weakly. "No. I bus' up my brain doing dat on da las' job, I no tink I can do it again."

"What does that mean?" Miyeon demanded.

I shook my head. "I can't crack it."

Another silence fell over the room. I stared at the words on the screen, willing them to make sense, but all I did was make my vision blurry and my head ache.

Worthless.

Jeongah let out a string of curses in Kepler's Korean dialect, increasing her pacing to that of a frenzied animal. She rounded the stage and stalked toward me. I instinctively drew back into my chair as she towered over me, leaning forward to put her hands on the arms of the chair, her face so close to mine I could see the fire blazing in her dark eyes.

"You're going to decrypt it," she growled.

"I already said—"

"You're *going* to decrypt it," she repeated. "You have fifty-five days to find the cipher and stop Pierce."

"Stop him how?"

"Nan jotto singyongansso," she snapped. "Destroy the AI, wipe the files, burn down his office—just get it the fuck done."

She bared her teeth—a grin or a snarl, I couldn't tell. "Destroy the AI, or I'll end both you and it."

She pushed off the chair, making it scrape backward across the floor. "Now get out."

CHERRY WAS ONLY JUST STARTING to pick up when the Song sisters kicked us out. I trudged down the street, past the line of chattering people waiting to get into the club. On any other night, I might have combed through the crowd for any unsecured phones or comms. Swiped some credentials, maybe stolen a few credits on my way out. Not tonight. There was nothing I wanted more than to lie in the darkness of my condo and sleep.

"Malia!" a voice called.

I plucked an earbud out of my ear and looked toward the voice. Sol was leaning against the door of their flyer, parked alongside the dirty curb. They beckoned me over.

I readjusted my bag on my shoulder as I approached. "Whazzup, Sol?"

"We need to talk," they answered.

I swallowed. Their expression was inscrutable to me—brows furrowed, eyes hard, mouth set in a line. They were probably pissed. I always assumed that when I wasn't sure what somebody was thinking. It was easier to work off the assumption you'd fucked up and work to fix it than the alternative of assuming everything was fine. That was what I learned from Maddox, anyway.

"You want more money," I said.

They laughed. "You know that I'm not in it for the money."

Now I was really confused. "Then what do you want?"

"The opposite, really."

A group of women dressed for clubbing passed between us on the sidewalk, giggling and waving at Sol. They smiled and nodded in acknowledgment. The women's laughter bubbled after them, along with the scent of their perfume. I wanted to gag.

Sol refocused on me. They pushed off their flyer and closed the distance between us, standing right next to me. That unreadable expression was back on their face. "I wanted to tell you that I'm in it, Malia. I'm in it, until this job is done. Whatever you need, I'll do it."

I blinked, their answer surprising me. "Forreal?"

They laughed again. Their expression shifted back to that easy, lopsided smile. "Yeah, forreal."

I nodded slowly, processing. On the heels of Jeongah threatening to kill me if I failed, it was nice to have Sol's reassurance. I wasn't sure why they were offering it, though. They must see something of value in helping me, why else would they stay on? I was more than happy to compensate them for their help. They could have any one of Pierce's flyers, I didn't care.

Sol looked like they were about to say something when another voice called my name.

"Malia!"

We both turned farther down the street, where Tatiana was shrugging into her jacket. She hustled toward us. "Are you going home?" she asked.

"Yeah, I was gonna take the monorail," I answered.

"You want a ride?" Sol asked.

I shook my head. "Nah. I think I need the air."

"Okay. I'll see you tomorrow?"

"Rajah dat."

They nodded, then turned back to their flyer. "Shoots, den."

"C'mon," Tatiana said, jerking her head toward the monorail station. "I'll walk with you."

We started toward the station together. Tatiana untangled a set of earphones from her coat pocket, then offered me one. I took it, removing my own earphones. She poked at her comm, but only a harsh buzzing noise sound played. Exasperated, she plucked the earphone from my ear and dropped them both in a trash can. "Worthless," she muttered to herself.

Wordlessly, I handed her my pair.

Tatiana rode the monorail home with me. She lived several streets over, but she said that the closest stop was out of service and she didn't mind walking. I pinged the GhostNet and knew in 0.54 seconds she was lying. But I was too tired to protest.

Kepler's simulated sun had set by the time we emerged from the monorail in Ward 2. It was always dark in the Lower Wards, deep in the shadows of the station's towers, the light of the sky blotted out by the skybridges and air traffic. But tonight, the darkness seemed even deeper.

Tatiana and I walked in silence for a few blocks before stopping in front of my tower. She turned on her heel to face me, hands in her jacket pockets. "You wanna grab some food? There's this new Thai place on 6th Street, spiciest green curry I've ever eaten." She grinned. "They deliver too."

I forced a smile, but I couldn't manage to match her grin. "Nah, cuz. I think I'm gonna go sleep. Gotta get up bright and early to do some scheming, y'know."

"True." Tatiana's gaze drifted up the tower. The shifting lights and neon glow cast her expression in relief. She looked worried. But before I could be sure, she looked back at me, big brown eyes bright. "Or we could binge a show!" She pointed at an advertisement above me. "Apparently, they made a prequel to *Way of the Sword*. I know you were super into it for a while, maybe we could—"

"I'm really beat, Tati." I tried to smile again, but I couldn't keep the weariness from my eyes. "I'll see you tomorrow?"

That worried look crossed her face again, but I couldn't be sure if it was just the passing lights. "Okay," she said. "I'll see you tomorrow."

"Shoots," I said, moving past her toward the door.

"Shoots," she replied.

I transmitted my code to the keycard sensor on the door, and it beeped in confirmation. The glass doors of the tower slid open, and I trudged across the lobby. I called the elevator with another thought, then stepped through the doors. When I turned back toward the front of the elevator, I could see Tatiana's silhouette lingering outside. I felt a pang of regret, felt the wild urge to jam the elevator and sprint back outside. Part of me, the part of me that was scared to face the darkness of my condo, wanted Thai food and a movie. Part of me didn't want to be alone.

But before I could will myself to move, the doors closed and the elevator lifted into the shaft. The part of me that didn't want to be known, didn't want to be perceived, won out.

Like the Code said: Make no attachments.

I wasn't prepared for how empty my condo was. I pushed open the door and immediately turned on every light—

bathrooms, closets, even the oven light. Like the mages in my shows, I needed to banish every shadow. But without the shadows, the space seemed so big, so empty. Somehow, I felt even more alone.

I toed off my shoes at the door and stripped off my backpack and jacket, discarding them both on the bedroom floor. I collapsed onto my mattress and stared into the ceiling.

Maddox stole me.

The thought made me sick. Growing up, I had nothing. Maddox "adopted" me when I was toddler. I searched for a while, but there were too many leads to follow to ever be certain of where I really came from. For the longest time, I didn't know what I liked, or what I wanted, or even who I *was*. It took years of searching the Net in secret, watching shows in my mind, playing games in the dark, before I knew any of that. After I escaped from him, disappeared into the underground, it took even more time to build up a sense of self. Learning how to act, how to talk, how to think.

And now there was a clone of me stalking the Net.

Maddox stole me. Twice.

I rolled over onto my side, my closet in front of me. I'd shut down all my gear before leaving, but I couldn't help but feel like Diana was still there, waiting. My heart beat harder, my breathing quickened. I remembered the sensation of her reaching through the GhostNet toward me, a hand pushing through the barriers of my mind, a fist closing around my throat. I tried to tell myself that I was being stupid. But after three minutes of lying there, a little blinking heart popped up in the corner of my vision: *132 bpm.* I threw the covers off and stalked to the closet. I unplugged all my gear from the power strip. Then I unplugged the power strip from the wall, just to be sure.

I threw myself back onto my mattress and resumed staring into the ceiling light.

I didn't know how many modders Diana had taken. I'd heard rumors before now—hackers gone missing, streamers gone dark, gamers logged out—plus Lena and Allen, at the very least. And she seemed set on consuming me too. I didn't put it past Maddox to sic her on the GhostNet, consuming the modders who wouldn't be missed too much, looked for too hard. But me? I didn't think he'd try to destroy his greatest creation.

The realization hit me like a blow to the brain. I realized then that there was a small part of me that still thought he cared.

But of course he didn't. No one did.

I didn't know how long I lay awake. It was hard to tell when the night was over, with all the lights on. But I must have slept, because my comm chiming startled me awake at 0900.

I slapped the comm on my wrist and groaned. I turned my head to the side, looking into my closet, taking in all my unplugged gear.

Every cyberspace paniolo gets bucked once. It was just a matter of getting back on the horse. I threw my arm across my face, closed my eyes tight against the darkness. I would. But first I needed five more minutes.

7

I TOOK THE LONG ROUTE TO CHERRY—A SERPENTINE PATH UPWARD FROM the dim twilight of Ward 2 to the weak sunlight of Ward 4. I passed little yobo aunties on their way to the market with their shopping wagons, leapt out of the way of lanky teens racing on their e-bikes, stepped around two uncles arguing loudly outside a bodega. Ward 4 was in the throes of gentrification three years ago, but some timely interference from the crew—Edie, most of all—brought the Lower Wards back to their former spirits. As I knocked on Cherry's heavy door, I wondered what the Song sisters thought of our charity.

A Brotherhood henchman poked his bolo head through the door. Seemingly recognizing me, he waved me through.

Cherry wasn't much for glamour, was even less so in the daylight. The furniture was scuffed, the dance floor was stained, and without the glow of the neon lights everything looked faded and dingy. There were a handful of employees sweeping the floors and wiping down the tables and bar, each with a phoenix tattooed somewhere on their body. It looked like every Brotherhood member had something to do.

I followed the bolo head henchman through the pink-and-red room toward the spiral staircase that led upstairs. He held the door for me at the Song sisters' private lounge, and I nodded at him and stepped through.

The crew was already gathered when I arrived, sprawled across the lounge's scratched leather furniture. Everyone looked at me expectantly, and I felt particularly self-conscious under the Song sisters' scrutinizing gaze. I straightened my shoulders and nodded at all of them. "Good, you're all on time."

"What's the plan, boss?" Sol asked.

I crossed the room to stand in front of the assembled crew. "We know that Maddox used a cipher to encrypt the files. It doesn't match any common ciphers or any of the ones I know Maddox has used in the past. The complexity of it makes me think that the cipher is based on a longer chunk of text."

"What kind of text?" Miyeon asked, arms crossed.

"A book, probably," I answered. "One that has special meaning to Pierce."

"And how are we gonna find this book?" Jeongah demanded.

"We have an in to Pierce's inner circle." I nodded at Naima. She straightened in her chair and crossed her legs, pleased. "We just need access."

"Her?" Tatiana asked, disbelieving. "You don't really think that medium bullshit is gonna work, do you?"

"I think it will. Pierce is way into that bullshit." I projected a scattering of files and images across the wall with my comm. "His entire campaign is organized around horoscopes, numerology, prophecies, all that bullshit. And"—I magnified a picture of a haole guy with big bug eyes behind thick glasses—"he just fired his previous spiritual adviser." I crossed through the picture with red ink and wrote: *signs point to no!!!*

"Seems like an upgrade to me," Jeongah said, eyes on Naima. Naima tossed her hair, preening. Tatiana made a retching face behind them.

I wasn't really sure how to move on from that. But before I needed to figure it out, Naima's comm began to chime. "Speak of the devil, and he shall appear," she said. "It's Pierce."

"Answer it," Jeongah commanded.

Naima answered the voice call. "Hello?"

"Ms. al-Mufti, it's Lucas Pierce. I hope I'm not interrupting anything."

"Mr. Pierce! It's lovely to hear from you! Apologies for the lack of video, I just stepped out of the shower."

"Oh." He cleared his throat. Naima smirked from behind the visualizer, and Tatiana met her with a scowl. *"That's no trouble at all. Cleanliness and godliness, and all that."* He cleared his throat again.

Like the Code said: People are the most fallible point in any system.

"To what do I owe the pleasure, Mr. Pierce?"

"Oh yes! I'm calling because I'm having a small get-together later today at my home, just a few like-minded friends. I thought you would fit in quite well."

"I'm so flattered! I would be delighted to spend more time with you, Mr. Pierce. Let me just get dressed, and I'll come over."

"Lovely. I'll send the address to you shortly. I'm looking forward to seeing you again, Ms. al-Mufti."

"Please, just Thamina," Naima said with a smile. "I'm looking forward to seeing you again too."

"*Goodbye, Thamina.*"

"Goodbye, Lucas."

Naima ended the call. She gave the room a triumphant look. "What was that about access?"

"Oh, a lunch date, exactly what we needed," Tatiana said sarcastically.

Naima's nostrils flared. "A lunch date at his *home*. Whatever book the cipher is in, I can find it while I'm there."

"And how are you gonna do that?" Tatiana challenged.

"I have an idea."

"Care to share with the class?" Sol asked.

She sniffed. "You'll see."

Before any of us could argue, Naima stood abruptly. "I'm going to get changed. Don't want to disappoint Pierce, after all."

She walked briskly across the room. I could swear she put a little extra swing in her hips as she walked past Jeongah.

The mobster was not immune. She stood too. "I'll walk her out," she said. And they were both gone.

Sol caught my eye. They raised a brow. I shrugged.

"Fine, Naima will go to Pierce's home and get the cipher," Miyeon said, drawing the room's attention. "I want to hear how it went and when we can expect the files by end of day."

"Shoots," I said.

She nodded. Then she left the room too.

"Bitches," Tatiana muttered.

PIERCE LIVED IN WARD 7, the highest of the Upper Wards. There, the light was always bright and warm, the air always fresh and dry. Pierce's penthouse overlooked Seven Common, the largest green space on Kepler. Located on a wide skybridge, it arced over the Wards below it, leaving the streets in shadow. I was never one for the green spaces—I liked the dark and noise of the Lower Wards. But even I could appreciate the view from Pierce's penthouse.

Tatiana and I had put together a rudimentary setup for myself in one of Cherry's back rooms. Sol convinced Naima to let them give her a ride. They glided into the porte cochere in Sol's fancy flyer. Through the button cam pinned to Naima's dress, I could see Sol twist around in the pilot's seat to look at her. *"I'll be around if you need a hot exit,"* they said.

"Thank you," Naima replied. *"But I'll be fine."*

Sol nodded, and Naima opened the door and stepped outside.

Naima's heels clicked on the tiled floor as she approached the tower, smoothing her cream satin dress. One of the tower's staff greeted her pleasantly and led her to Pierce's penthouse.

Sol whistled over the comm. *"I'm parked in the tower garage. It's packed with Pierce's flyers. You weren't kidding, this guy is really into 'em."*

"Oh yeah?" I said.

"Yeah." I could hear Sol's footsteps echo as they wandered the garage. *"Some of these are real fast, and all of them are real expensive. What I wouldn't give to see some of these in a race."*

"Keep your hands to yourself, cuz," I warned.

"Worried I'll boost one and take it for a joyride?"

I grinned. "You know it."

They laughed. *"I won't. But only because you told me not to, Just Malia."*

I didn't know what that meant.

"*Lucas!*" Naima exclaimed. "*It's so good to see you!*"

"*The pleasure is mine, Thamina.*" I returned my attention to Naima's feed and saw Pierce approaching, a broad smile on his face. I winced as the button cam jostled when he went in for a hug.

"Well, that's familiar," Tatiana said with a cringe.

"Forreal," I replied.

"*I have some friends I'd love to introduce,*" Pierce said, guiding Naima into the penthouse. They approached a group of well-dressed people chatting in the foyer, tailored suits and sleek, shiny dresses, just like I saw on the ads from the Inner Worlds. "*Everyone, I'd like you to meet Thamina al-Mufti. She's gifted with the sight.*"

"Oh lord," Tatiana groaned.

"*Thank you for the kind introduction,*" Naima said, affecting shyness. "*I'm still learning.*"

"*She's very insightful,*" Pierce insisted.

"*I really appreciate—whoa—*" Naima put her hands to her temples and wobbled in her heels. The gaggle of rich people gasped. Pierce caught her arm before she could fall.

"*Thamina? Are you all right?*"

"*Y-yes, I—*" She took a deep, steadying breath. "*—I'm sorry. I was overwhelmed by the spirit of this place.*"

"*The spirit?*" Pierce said, alarmed.

"*Yes.*" She looked at Pierce. "*This is a place of ill fortune.*" The group murmured among themselves. "*Has there been any tragedy in its history?*"

"*I—I'm not sure.*"

"*Something terrible must have happened here,*" Naima said gravely.

"Is there any way to fix it?"

"I think... I think I can dispel it. I have just enough strength."

"Oh *lord*," Tatiana groaned again.

I cackled. This was too good.

Naima reached into her purse. From it she withdrew an elaborate, twisting glass vial filled with liquid. "*This is water from Earth, purified and blessed by my mentor. It should have enough power to dispel the bad spirits. I'll need to bless each room in the house with it.*"

"*Of course. I'll show you,*" Pierce said eagerly.

"*Is that really wise?*" a voice asked.

The group turned toward the voice. Maddox was standing near the elevator with his coat over his arm, having apparently just arrived. "*I would flag this as a security concern for your team, Lucas,*" he said.

"*Oh, what would I ever do just wandering around the house?*" Naima asked.

"*See? She would never do anything to harm us,*" Pierce said, confidently. He leaned closer to Maddox, who strained away from him, to whisper, "*And you know I've been looking for a new adviser. She could be exactly what I need for my campaign, Jordan.*"

As Pierce's business partner, Maddox didn't have the authority to forbid anything. But you could never turn off the security-expert part of your brain. I grinned to myself. And he was right to worry.

"*It will only take a few minutes,*" Naima reassured him.

Maddox grunted in displeasure, but he stood aside.

Naima started in the foyer, unscrewing the vial stopper and dabbing it delicately on her fingers. She flicked the water in each corner, muttering to herself under her breath. I tried to translate, but the feed came back gibberish. I cackled again. She was speaking in *tongues.*

The gathered group watched Naima work attentively, Pierce most rapt of all. Naima turned to them. *"Do you feel it? The spirits lifting?"*

"Yes," they said breathlessly.

Maddox's mouth twitched.

"There's one more thing," Naima said. She fished in her purse and withdrew a small jade bead.

"A trinket?" Maddox said, incredulous.

"Not just a trinket," Naima said patiently. *"Depending on the object—the color, material, placement—it can guide the energy of a room."* She turned to Pierce. *"If you would let me, I could place some around your home. Perhaps it will help bring good fortune back to this place."*

"Why, how kind of you!" Pierce exclaimed. *"I would love that."*

"Perfect," Naima said, squeezing the bead between her thumb and forefinger. As she did, another feed flashed to life on my screen. In it, I could see Naima's smiling face.

"No way! A *bug?*" I said, delighted.

"Okay, that's pretty good," Tatiana muttered.

"I'll let you lead the way," Naima said.

From there, Pierce led her and the group from room to room. She flicked her bogus holy water around the room, then carefully placed the bugs throughout—on a bookshelf, in a planter, balanced on a vase. Soon I had eyes on every room in Pierce's home.

"Are there any other rooms left?" Naima asked.

"Just the library," Pierce answered. *"Let me show you."*

"Nice work, cuz," I said. "The cipher is likely a book. If

you can get me eyes on what's in his collections, I can narrow it down."

The group filed into the library, last. Most rich people, they liked a minimalist aesthetic. Makes them look discerning, tasteful. Pierce, though, was a true maximalist. His house was crammed with antique furniture, shelves full of useless tchotchkes. The library was worst of all. The furniture was all dark wood and horrible crushed velvet, heavy drapes drawn over the windows to block out Kepler's simulated sunlight. Bookshelves lined the walls, packed with so many books they were stacked on top of each other.

"The cipher is likely one of these books," I said. "If you can get me eyes on the titles, I might be able to narrow it down."

Naima went to work with the holy water, pausing every so often to hold up a little maneki-neko. She scanned the camera over the books' spines, and I noted each title.

Nothing was standing out to me just yet. Most of them were stuffy Old Earth literature, or books on the occult. I was looking for patterns when Tatiana leaned over my shoulder to point at the screen. "Look over there. At your four. That looks like a hidden vault door."

Niele, I spoke into the mic again. "Try to bait Pierce into showing you the vault. There might be something worth stealing in there."

"*Is that all?*" Maddox asked impatiently.

"*I'm sorry, I sense some lingering ill will,*" Naima said. "*I thought I blessed all the rooms, but perhaps I missed something . . .*"

"*What happens if you missed a room?*" Pierce asked, fidgeting with his cuff links.

"Well. Any number of things. These spirits don't seem demonic in origin, but I sense great malevolence in them."

Pierce sighed. *"There's one more room."*

"Mr. Pierce—" Maddox said sharply.

"It's fine, Jordan," Pierce shot back. He turned to Naima. *"It's my panic room. I wonder if there's something in there that might be causing this?"*

"May I see?"

"Yes, of course!"

Pierce brushed past Maddox toward the bookshelf Tatiana identified. He popped out a panel on the side, then hunched over the keypad. A moment later, the shelf swung out from the wall with a wheeze. Pierce gestured, and the crowd moved forward. He put out an arm to stop the crowd. *"Just Thamina, please."*

Naima stepped into the panic room. Where the rest of the house was a maximalist mess, this was slick and high-tech. There was a spartan cot in one corner, with a stockroom of shelf-stable food and wine, of all things. Bright fluorescent lights shone down on metal shelves lined with treasures. Artwork, jewelry, tech, and documents. And on one shelf—

"Is that a book?" Naima asked.

"Why, yes!" Pierce said. He moved past her to open the case. The book was worn leather, cracked and faded, with peeling gilt letters. *Frankenstein*. *"It's from Old Earth!"* he said proudly.

"That's probably it," I said. "It's a long shot, but see if he'll let you look at it."

"May I see it?" Naima asked.

Here Pierce hesitated. "*Do you think it has something to do with the spirits?*"

"*I can't be sure,*" she admitted. "*But something in here may be the source of the malevolence.*"

Slowly, Pierce extended the book to her. Naima took it carefully, then cracked it open. The pages were yellowed and the edges bent. I wondered why he didn't just get a new one. But as Naima thumbed through the pages, I saw that the book had been annotated in a looping cursive hand. I cursed under my breath. That meant that the text had been altered, and I couldn't find the cipher in the plain text of the book.

"*Well?*" Pierce asked. "*Is this the source? If it is, I'll do anything to exorcise it. It has great sentimental value.*"

Naima paused, calculating. After a moment, she looked up. "*No, it's not.*"

"What are you doing?!" Tatiana hissed.

Naima strode past Pierce to the shelf behind him. She picked up a necklace—ropes of pearls of every color, linked with a chain of sterling silver. "*This.*"

Pierce sucked in a breath. "*My great-grandmother's wedding pearls.*"

"*Where did you get these?*"

"*They're Tahitian, from Old Earth.*"

"*I see,*" Naima said gravely. "*It's terrible luck to remove these from the islands.*"

"*Is that true?*" Sol asked.

I wasn't sure.

Cautiously, I extended my consciousness into the Net. The data rushed over me in a wave. I flowed with the current, allowing it to take me deeper into the knowledge of Old

Earth. Beyond scientific discoveries, political change, social advancement. Deep, into the stories of Earth's people. Intellectually, I knew there was a part of me there. Descended from the stewards of the 'āina and kai, like so many on this station. But others felt that kinship beyond intellectualism, in their na'au. Me, I was never very in touch with that.

I reached through the data—

take that outch yo pocket she says fo why you
ask buggah stay

cursed

fo why iz Peles she wipes the sand off her hands all em
belong to her

I want someting to

remembah you and tūtū too you

protest go find someting else she says buggah stay cursed she
repeats Pele going follow you

home

she walks away sunlight in brown hair on brown skin like your
hair your skin you

never see hair or skin like yours anymore you look at the lava
rock in your hand and despite the

warning you

pocket it

you turn away look down the shore and

in the distance the sound of drums

marching through

darkness blackness night

dread builds somethings coming something

powerful regal sacred twisted into
something else something wrong fear grips your heart makes you
sweat you
                        know you need to
                                                                bow

           down

Naima's calm voice shocked me out of my intrusion. "*I can take these, if you like. I may be able to purify them.*"

"*Please, take them. My great-grandmother was an awful woman, and honestly, I'm glad to be rid of them.*"

"*Oh, Lucas, you're too kind,*" Naima said, stuffing the pearls into her purse.

Pierce led Naima back to the rest of the group, where Maddox stood glowering. "*I hope that this brings you peace, Lucas,*" Naima said.

"*I'm certain it will. I feel lighter already!*" He laughed, and the others did too.

"*Unfortunately, I'm feeling quite drained after this afternoon's excitement. May I call you tomorrow?*"

Pierce took Naima's hands. "*Of course. Rest, and we'll speak in the morning.*"

Sol laughed over the comm. "*Incredible. I'll swing around and pick you up.*"

"*Thank you, Lucas.*" Naima said. Even as skilled as she was, I could still hear the smugness in her voice. "*It was a pleasure.*"

I relaxed my pale-knuckle grip on the desk and slumped in my chair. What the fuck just happened? The intrusion was one thing, but the rest? The drumbeats still pounded in my chest. Deep inside me, in my na'au, I knew something was wrong. Something had warped it beyond recognition of what it once was. In that moment, in that dream, I felt the wild urge to throw myself to the ground. To prostrate myself to whatever twisted thing was coming. It was terrifying. It was humiliating.

"Doesn't it bother you?" Tatiana asked.

"What?" I asked, alarmed. I had the paranoid urge to ask what she knew.

"That Naima went off script" Tatiana continued. "You didn't tell her to plant those bugs."

"Oh." I relaxed. I hadn't thought of that. I took a minute to process. There was a part of me that was annoyed by Naima's off-the-book play. Wasn't I supposed to be the mastermind? And what about the Code? Leave no evidence. Part of me wanted to chew Naima out. But it worked out in the end, didn't it? I had feeds all over Pierce's apartment now. I'd done my fair share of off-the-book plays, and the heist always was better for it. In a rare moment of self-awareness, I knew it'd be hypocritical to hassle her for it. Critical thinking won out, this time.

Tatiana was still looking at me expectantly. I shrugged. "We've got eyes and ears on Pierce at all times now. I can't be upset with her for that."

Tatiana frowned. It looked like she disapproved. I looked off over her shoulder, her gaze too much to hold.

"Don't worry, cuz," I reassured her. "It's all for the good of the heist."

"Yeah," she said. "For the good of the heist."

I SENT EVERYONE HOME AFTER NAIMA'S SCOUTING. I NEEDED TO FORMU-
late the next step of the plan, and nobody needed to see that.
Coming up with the original plan was hard, coming up with
shit on the fly was so much harder.

It made me think about when we had to go off script with
the Atlas heist. I wondered if Angel was ever scared shitless
like I was. She always seemed so cool—cold, even. When I got
locked out of Atlas's security system and had to brute force
the codes, was she as fucked-up as I was now?

I mean, I was fucked-up in a few ways, now.

I shouldered open the door to my condo and trudged inside. It was still daylight, so rather than turn on all the lights,
I retracted all the blinds. The light was weak in Ward 2, but
it was better than nothing. And hopefully strong enough to
keep whatever I heard in the Net at bay in the waking world.

It reminded me of the last storyline I played in *Feyheart*.
Last time I logged on, the Heroes of Truth were fighting
their way through the dream world to free the World Serpent
from the Cosmic Terror. The raid mechanics were completely

busted, the loot drops were rigged, and the loot itself was hardly worth the time commitment. I figured I'd come back once the devs had smoothed out some of the bugs.

That was sixty-three days ago.

I glanced into my walk-in closet where my gear was still set up. I hadn't logged on in over two months, and I hadn't been keeping track of the patch notes. Maybe things were better now.

I checked the time, a little neon ticking clock appearing in my vision. It was 1840. Raid was about to start.

Maybe things were better now, and maybe I needed a distraction.

I dropped myself into my chair and sighed. It didn't take me long to plug in and set up—most of the time was spent downloading patches. Impatiently I watched the second hand tick on the little analog clock. 1900.

When the game was finally updated, I logged in. But the drums still echoed in my chest, so I logged onto the Net manually, through my gear.

I hadn't even launched the game through the client before I got a DM.

(shade77) fill?

I grinned to myself. The guild I raided with, Void Thieves, was always looking for fills. They were the best on the server, some of them the best in the region. But not all of them were committed—jobs, friends, family, they all came first. It's why they always needed a fill.

It's why they always needed me.

An invite to join the raid popped up. I accepted.

(knightwarden) EY look who it is!!!

(obake) whazzup

(4berration) bro where u been

(knightwarden) we missed u!!!

(shade77) ya this new mechanic is kicking our asses we need serious dps

(obake) what ab ur other fills?

(knightwarden) NO dude they suck ass!!!

(4berration) some of them are barely pulling 6k lol

(obake) wtf

(shade77) ya dude its bleak

(shade77) u filling?

(obake) I got time

I launched the game. Epic music played through my headphones, rising to a crescendo as the loading bar filled.

I appeared in the capital city of my faction, the Netherborn. Immediately I opened my menus and checked the settings. I flipped through my action bars, checking my setup.

(shade77) cmon dude log on

(obake) I'm just fixing my bars rq chill

(shade77) nah dude log onto the net

(shade77) need all hands for this

(shade77) manual aint gonna cut it

I hesitated. In my headphones, I could hear the drums of war—not unlike the drums I heard in my intrusion. I still wasn't sure exactly what happened, and I could admit I was nervous to log on again without knowing more. But shade77 and the rest of the Void Thieves were waiting, and would not wait forever. Not even for me. Especially if I wasn't at my best.

(shade77) *?*

I sighed. Then I closed my eyes and plunged into the Ghost-Net, deep into the familiar black.

When I opened my eyes, I was perched on top of the highest building in the city. I sat beside a scowling gargoyle, my booted feet dangling over the edge of the balustrade I sat on. From my vantage point I could see the whole of the city: towers of obsidian glimmering in the twilight, cathedrals with gleaming stained-glass windows, gardens with twisted trees and black foliage. Far below me were the streets of Crowne, filled with sauntering NPCs and scurrying players.

shade77 paused below my tower. He waved.

I tensed, then leapt from the balustrade. I fell twelve meters, then reached into my robes. I withdrew a downy feather, then let it drift from my hand. It evaporated in the air, consumed by my magic, and my descent slowed. I landed gently beside shade77, my black robes billowing behind me.

shade77 was an orc, with forest green skin and ivory tusks, the left one chipped and the right one broken entirely. His sleek black hair was twisted into a bun, and his eyes were dark and flinty. He wore the season's latest gear set, rogue leathers the color of an oil slick. *The guild must have been progressing well without me,* I thought with a twinge of regret.

shade77 smiled at me broadly. "What up, Obake!"

"Well met, shade," I said, my voice disguised as Orogen's low rumble. "It's been too long."

"Truly," he replied. He jerked his head toward the entrance to the city. "C'mon, let's meet the others."

He let out a sharp whistle, and a spectral drake the color of translucent amethyst descended from the sky. shade77 gripped its saddle and swung himself up onto his mount. The dragon crouched, then sprang into the air, beating its wings as it ascended into the overcast sky.

I unfurled my fingers and a mote of black light rose from my palm. One second later, my own mount appeared. A skeletal dragon, with ivory bones and glowing blue pits for eyes. I climbed astride it and took off.

My dragon beat the air with its tattered wings, rising higher into the gray skies. It was always dark in Crowne. Even when the skies were clear, the city existed in perpetual twilight. It wasn't unlike the Lower Wards where I lived. Beyond the magical bubble protecting the city, it was all obsidian waste. As we crossed the barrier, lightning flashed far off in the distance, illuminating the twisting rock formations and expansive plains of dark rock. Electricity crackled in the air, beneath the rolling thunder.

I urged my dragon faster, until I was keeping pace with shade77 at my side.

"Where were you? It's been ages," shade77 called over the rushing wind.

"I've been enjoying a new game," I answered.

"On the Net?"

"In the realm of the living."

shade77 looked into my mirrored mask quizzically. "What, like, sports?"

I laughed. "Of some kind. Blood sport."

shade77 raised his brows. It looked like he was impressed. "No shit."

"Indeed."

shade77's drake's wings extended wide as they wheeled to the left, toward the caldera of Mount Khaos. It was a new region in the game, one that was released in the time I was offline. The devs had teased it for a long time, and everyone was excited to go. I didn't even log in to see it, all those weeks ago.

"Listen," shade77 said, "If you're bored of blood sport or whatever, you know Void Thieves will always have you." He grinned at me over his shoulder. "We could always use the DPS."

"I'm honored by your request, as always," I said. "But—"

"But you can't be tied down, I know." shade77 shook his head. "I had to ask."

This was the sixth time I'd been invited to join the guild. It made sense. I was consistently the highest-damage dealer in the raid, above even the most optimized players in the most powerful classes. Shadowmage hadn't been meta in years. I was just *good*. Having me on the permanent roster would definitely improve Void Thieves's ability to progress. And I enjoyed playing with them, I really did. But like the Code said: no attachments.

We crested the summit of Mount Khaos and began our descent into the Andorath Crater. Until now, we had been flying over the obsidian waste surrounding Crowne, where everything was dead or dying. But when we dipped down into the caldera, everything was suddenly lush and green. Trees the size of Kepler's towers reached toward the twilit sky, their boughs heavy with verdant foliage and turgid fruit. We dodged between branches on our way down, before landing in a clearing on the green-carpeted forest floor.

shade77 dismounted, leaving his drake in the clearing. I did the same, following him as he strode deeper into the forest.

While the Wastes were alive with electricity, thunder and lightning filling the air, Andorath Crater was still and silent. The epic music that had been following us as we flew through the waste had fallen away, and there wasn't the ambient noise of bugs or animals. shade77 was chattering away, but even his voice seemed to be lost in the quiet of the forest. It was unnerving.

Surreptitiously, I drew another glyph in the air. A *spell of detect life* filled my vision, tinting the forest a pale blue. I scanned the tree line and confirmed my suspicion. There was no life here.

"*Shade—*" I began, turning back around.

But I was alone.

IRL, I felt the fine hairs on the back of my neck rise and my pulse quicken. I was plugged into the GhostNet, I knew there were millions of people just beyond the edges of my consciousness. Somehow, I knew there was something else there too.

"*Shade—*" I turned—

> red light cast through leaves through branches pours
>> across forest floor regards you it
> is familiar
> cautious step forward you try to speak

like a comet it comes for you
burning brighter brighter hotter hotter

you

scream

"Obake!"

I wheeled around, chest heaving, heart pounding, to see shade77 standing about five meters ahead, at the edge of the clearing. knightwarden, 4berration, and the others were already waiting. They looked disturbed by my outburst. "What's wrong?" he asked.

"I—I can't—" I panted.

The members of Void Thieves whispered among themselves. My face grew hot under my mask. I hated the way they looked at me. Like I was afraid. Like I was *weak*.

I jumped when a deep, reverberating thrum went through the forest. Drumbeats began to sound. I whipped back and forth, trying to discern where they were coming from.

There, to the west, the flicker of torchlight in the brush.

The drums grew louder.

I turned and bolted in the opposite direction, ignoring the shouts from shade77 and the guild. As I ran, I force quit the application.

And suddenly I was in my condo again.

My breathing was ragged, my heart racing. I collapsed forward onto my desk, covering my head with my hands.

The drums again. Closer, this time. I couldn't shake the feeling that something terrible and divine was following me, marching through the Net on a steady path. Unyielding. Somehow I knew that if they caught me, it would be my death.

And if that wasn't enough, there were the lights in the forest. A separate force, I think, but a force all the same. I got the sense that they wanted something from me. What, I didn't know.

What did either of them want?

I've always enjoyed being wanted, being sought after. This was way too fucking much.

A friendly ping jerked me out of my thoughts.

(shade77) where r u???

I took a deep breath. Let it out. Show no weakness.

(obake) sorry bro I DC'd
(shade77) what's wrong???
(obake) big fkn migraine, can't concentrate. soz

shade77 typed for a long time. I chewed at a hangnail, tense.

(shade77) aight. sorry ab ur headache
(obake) next time?

Another long bout of typing.

(shade77) ya, i'll ping u
(obake) sounds good. ty shade
(shade77) 👍

I slumped forward on my desk again. In all my years raiding with Void Thieves, I was always someone they could rely on. More than an asset, I was *valuable*. What would they think of me now, after bailing on the biggest challenge they'd faced as a guild? I showed weakness. There was no way they'd want me now.

I knew that from Maddox.

I lay there for a few minutes longer. I unplugged my gear from the wall, then lay there longer still.

I HAD WORKED OUT OF Cherry's back rooms my entire career. Negotiating shady deals in the darkness of Ward 4, Cherry was my place of work, my livelihood, more of a home than anywhere ever was. Cherry was the portal to Kepler's underworld, and all her life the Obake had haunted this place.

I never thought I'd grow tired of coming here.

But when I received a cryptic message from the Song sisters summoning me to Cherry at 0802—early, for the gangsters of the Lower Wards—I groaned and rolled over in my bed, pulling the blanket over my head. I was so sick of that private lounge, the sisters' stink eye, the doubts of my crew. I never wanted to be in that club again.

I desperately wanted this whole nightmare to be over.

I fluttered restlessly between sleeping and waking for another seventeen minutes before my comm buzzed more urgently. Whatever they wanted, the sisters were impatient to get it. So I dragged myself out of bed and dressed, leaving all my gear unplugged.

The monorail was crowded on my way to Ward 4 from

my condo in Ward 2—commuters on their way to work in the Upper Wards. Absently, I sifted through the data flowing between them all. Nothing interesting. I was starting to doze against the window when—

good morning good morning morning morning

SPECIAL ONE

CREDIT DEAL UNLIMITED

LIVES

please please please baby come

back i hope this email

finds you

I snapped awake when the PA announced that the doors were. I shimmied my way out of the crush and popped out in Ward 4, dizzy on my feet. I walked the rest of the way to Cherry, still reeling from my dream.

I knocked on Cherry's heavy door. A Brotherhood member let me in. I moved past him toward the private lounge, but he stopped me. "Nuna is waiting for you in the office," he said.

The Brotherhood member led me to the third floor, but rather than entering the private lounge where Jeongah held court, he led me to an unassuming black door marked *Employees Only*. He held the door open for me, and I stepped inside.

I was in an office. The walls were the same concrete as the rest of the club, but they were clean of handprints and stains. It was dark, even in the dim light of Ward 4's daytime, but the room was illuminated by fluorescent lamps with painted glass shades. There were two heavy leather armchairs and a wooden desk, old but well maintained. As I entered, I even felt a plush rug beneath my boots. This was the classiest I had ever seen Cherry.

I swept my gaze across the room before my eyes fell on Miyeon, who was sitting at the desk poring over some documents. "Thank you," she said to the Brotherhood member, who nodded and closed the door behind him. She looked at me over the edge of her tablet, dark eyes sharp. "Sit."

I did as I was told, unslinging my bag and letting it drop by my feet. "Howzit."

"I need you for something," Miyeon explained, without preamble. "Can you hack into the files of SSA Agent Veronica Simon?"

"The System Security Administration?" I repeated. "What do you need that for?"

"Agent Simon is a specialist on organized crime on the station. She maintains a database of informants, past and present."

I scoffed. "Sloppy."

"It's protected and encrypted, of course," Miyeon continued. "I need you to access it."

"Aren't I already on a job for you?"

"Are you really in a position to argue?"

"Fair point," I muttered.

Miyeon watched me evenly. "Consider yourself on retainer for the next fifty-four days."

I sighed. Of all the lōlō bullshit the Song sisters were making me do, this was pretty low on the list. Might as well.

Rather than interface with the GhostNet directly through my mod, I went a little more analog. Seemed safer, with the drums and the lights lurking in the Net. I pulled out my laptop and opened it on the desk. Miyeon moved to stand beside me. I rolled my eyes. Always hovering.

I flipped through pages of data as I searched the Net for Agent Simon's digital fingerprint. It didn't take me long to find her social media, though her privacy settings were tight. The thing was, the particular social network she used had a data breach six months ago. I searched through the released information and found Agent Simon's password, plus the credit card information she used to buy collectibles in *FarmSim 3*. I tucked that away for later. If the SSA agent was so shit about security already, I could guess she used the same password across multiple websites. I tested the password leaked from the social media site on the SSA's internal systems.

I grinned to myself as the SSA's welcome portal greeted me. People are the most fallible point in any system. "I'm in."

"Get me the names," Miyeon commanded.

They were easy to find, and the decryption was simple. I downloaded the files (retaining a copy for myself), then sent them along to Miyeon. The comm on her wrist pinged as the message was received. "Done," I said.

She gave me an approving nod. "Good. Thank you, Malia."

"'Thank you'?" I repeated, shocked. I twisted in my seat to give her a look. "I thought you might kick my ass, just to keep me in line."

Miyeon looked irritated. "Of course not. Violence is only one way to get what you want. Only an idiot uses the same tool for every task."

"Are you calling your sister an idiot?" I prodded.

She didn't immediately answer. Instead, she moved to sit back at her desk, opening the files on her tablet. "She's very good with the tools she uses. She's just limited in what she has."

I thought of the man begging for his kneecaps and shuddered. "How did that happen?"

"How did what happen?"

"That she's the boss and you're not."

Miyeon looked up again, expression neutral. "You're a nosy one, aren't you?"

"Always been too niele for my own good," I agreed.

"I'm the youngest," Miyeon answered simply.

"That's the whole story?"

"You as the Obake should know there's never a whole story."

I frowned.

"You want a story? Let me tell you a story," Miyeon said, putting aside the tablet. "Do you know the Skulls?"

"No," I answered honestly.

"I'm not surprised, they were before your time. Twenty years ago, the Skulls ran Ward 4 and most of the other Lower Wards too. Kepler was still just a stop on the Trans Galactic, but that's all it needed to be for buying and selling all kinds of illicit goods. In the Skulls's case, people." I recoiled in horror. Miyeon nodded grimly. "The Skulls terrorized Kepler for years. Nobody wanted to move on them, because you never knew when they were gonna snatch you up. Even Station Sec was scared shitless—at least the ones that weren't in their pocket. They arrested some of their low-level people, but

there was never enough evidence to move on the leadership."
She scoffed. "Bullshit, obviously."

"So, what happened to them?" I asked.

"They're all dead," Miyeon answered. "My father and his
people put down every single one of them."

I sat with that, processing. In my work as the Obake, I knew
that some gangs were better than others. Maybe they were
more discreet, maybe they were a little less malicious. Maybe
they paid better. I tried not to get too deep into *what* they were
using my skills for—mostly to avoid any attachments, at least
a little to avoid any blows to my conscience. I never really considered that the gangs might have any kind of altruistic streak.
Mobsters with conscience, I guess. There was no doubt in my
mind that the Brotherhood had something to gain from the
destruction of the Skulls, but Kepler was better for it.

Was that so different than what my crew did, three years ago?

"That's the legacy my father left behind," Miyeon continued, drawing me back to the conversation. "That's the legacy
I want to carry on."

"And Jeongah?" I asked.

Miyeon didn't say anything, which was answer enough.

She stood. "Thank you for your help. My people will
show you out."

"What are you gonna do with all those names?" I asked.

Miyeon gave me an incredulous look. "I thought you were
supposed to be smart."

I flushed. Maybe I was giving Miyeon more credit than
I should.

I stood, slinging my bag over my shoulder. I reached for
the door, but Miyeon stopped me.

"Malia," she called. I looked over my shoulder at her. Her dark gaze was intense in the shadows of the office. "Let's keep this between us."

Before I could respond, one of the Brotherhood members opened the door and ushered me out.

9

"I'M GONNA GO AHEAD AND SAY THAT NAIMA'S SCOUTING MISSION WAS A huge success," I declared.

Light applause broke out in the room, and Naima sat up in her chair, preening. Tatiana scowled from the other side of the room. "Huge success? She didn't even get the book!"

Naima twisted in her chair to meet Tatiana's scowl. "Asking now could've blown the operation," she replied impatiently. "My foot's in the door, it's part of the long con."

"Oh yeah? Then where are those pearls now?" Tatiana demanded.

I tried to step in to prevent things from escalating. "It's not a big deal, Tati. We move forward from here."

Tatiana opened her mouth to argue, then shut it. Instead, she took a gulp of the drink she'd swiped from the bar. I was thankful for that. On our last job, Tati couldn't keep her mouth shut to save her life—nobody went unchallenged. Though I couldn't be sure whether she was respecting my authority or taking pity on me. I hoped it wasn't pity.

"We know where the cipher is," I continued, "and not only

that, I was able to construct a floor plan from Naima's footage." I projected a 3D schematic of Pierce's penthouse, rotating slowly from the beam of my comm. I spun it around until it landed on the library and its hidden vault. "The vault is a panic room in Pierce's home. It has quarter-inch steel walls, reinforced with carbon-fiber panels, a maglock with a six-digit PIN and powered by a discrete generator. We'll need to crack into the vault to access the cipher."

"Why do we need to get into the vault at all?" Jeongah demanded. "Just pirate that shit, hacker like you should be able to handle that."

"No babonya? Because the annotations are part of the cipher," Miyeon said.

"Right," I agreed, "and those are only in this specific physical copy."

"Okay," Jeongah said slowly, "then how are we supposed to *get* this specific physical copy?"

"What about a B&E?" Sol suggested.

"A B&E?" Miyeon repeated with a raised brow.

"Well, not just a B&E," Sol admitted. "With a twist. We lift the cipher while the rest of us act as a distraction. Pierce will have his hands full chasing down the flyers we've boosted, and he'll miss the real heist."

"No ulterior motives there?" I asked.

They shot me a grin. "Of course not."

"You wanna bet this whole heist on a B&E?" Jeongah objected. "No jinsimiya?"

"That seems pretty simple," Miyeon agreed.

"I mean, what other plans do you two have?" Sol challenged.

Miyeon's lip curled. Jeongah's eyes flashed.

"I think it'll work," I cut in. "Pierce is obsessed with his flyers, and Maddox could never see beyond the first move. He's always been a shit chess player."

"Well, look where your appraisal of Maddox got us," Jeongah growled.

I deflated. It was true. I never saw Maddox coming, and when I did, I underestimated him. It was a mistake no real mastermind worth their salt would make. Especially my last mastermind.

"Nobody could've expected that," Tatiana replied defensively. "Who could've predicted that Maddox's pet project would be an AI clone of our hacker?"

"Whatever," Jeongah said dismissively. "Just don't fuck it up again."

I looked up to take in the room. The Song sisters looked incredulous. Naima did too. Tatiana looked indignant, with her chin jutted out and mouth set in a hard line. Behind her, Sol flashed me a reassuring smile. Then again, they were all stuck in this job with me. Not like the Song sisters could pivot now, this deep in.

I straightened, imagining Angel's posture. Cool, confident. "Naima will call Pierce to set up another meeting. Sol and Tatiana will case the garage while he's distracted. Once we have more information, we can formulate a plan." I gave a brisk nod, channeling Angel the best I could. "That's all."

The meeting adjourned. The Song sisters were pulled away by one of their henchmen, the two of them sniping back and forth in Korean. Naima stood and smoothed her skirt, sauntering past the sisters toward the exit. Sol and Tatiana lingered, eventually approaching me when the others had left.

"Are you okay?" Tatiana asked.

"I'm fine, cuz." I paused. "Why wouldn't I be?"

"Why wouldn't you?" Tatiana repeated, shocked. "Malia, your fucked-up mentor-slash-kidnapper appeared out of nowhere. There's an AI clone of you gobbling up modders on the Net. The Song sisters are always one thought away from violence. Of course you're not okay."

I wasn't okay. The last two times I logged in to the Net, something followed me there. When I slept, I could feel it searching for me. Maddox haunted my dreams, almost as real as whatever was stalking me. I had to turn off my sleep biometrics because it was constantly urging me to take a nap. I really wasn't okay.

"I *am* okay," I reassured her. At least, I hoped it came across as reassuring.

Tatiana didn't look convinced. But I moved on before she could press. She took a sip of her drink, sulking. "Sol, you good to case the garage today?"

They nodded. "I'm good. Looking forward to it."

"Oh?" I prodded.

"Yeah." They grinned. "You still owe me a flyer, if you remember correctly."

"And you know I'm good for it."

"Wouldn't think otherwise."

"And you know that if we go with this B&E, it's on you to close the deal."

"Don't worry, Just Malia. I'm very good at closing the deal."

Tatiana choked on her drink. I blinked at her. "You good, cuz?"

"Are *you* good?" she wheezed.

I frowned. "I already told you I'm fine." Why was she bringing this up again?

Sol laughed. "I'll catch you both later. Just ping me when you're ready to go."

"We will."

"Shoots."

Sol sauntered off. Tatiana turned to face me once the door closed behind them. "Forreal though, are you good?"

"Why wouldn't I be?" I asked.

Tatiana went quiet, stewing. "Listen, if they ever cross a line . . . I'll bus' em up."

I raised my brows. I wasn't sure why they would, or why Tatiana extended this threat to them and not anyone else. But still I said, "Noted."

Tatiana nodded decisively. Then she turned to follow Sol out of Cherry, slurping the last of her drink.

NAIMA MESSAGED PIERCE, APOLOGIZING FOR leaving so suddenly, and Pierce was quick to reassure her that the exorcism was greatly appreciated. He invited her over for a cup of tea, seemingly just the two of them. It was the perfect opportunity for Sol and Tatiana to sneak into his garage and scope out the security system. And pick out a flyer for Sol, as they had reminded me. I was on comms in Cherry, watching through the network of bugs that Naima had planted the last time she was there. It made things a lot easier for me, for which I was grateful.

"All right, Naima, you're up," I said. "Just keep him occupied long enough for Tati and Sol to get in and get out."

"*Waiting for Naima to make contact,*" Sol said over the comm. "*Then we'll approach.*"

"*Making contact now,*" Naima replied.

Naima strode up to the door of Pierce's penthouse. She was wearing a chic white pantsuit with a plunging neckline, her dark hair loose around her shoulders. She rang the bell, and Pierce answered in twenty-four seconds. Eager. His face brightened upon seeing her. "*Thamina! Lovely to see you, as always.*"

"*The pleasure is mine, Lucas.*" She stepped into the foyer. "*I apologize again for my hasty retreat yesterday.*"

"*Please, don't apologize! I am so deeply grateful for your assistance.*" He laughed. "*I feel lighter already!*"

"*Oh, I'm so glad to hear that!*" Pierce led Naima farther into the penthouse, toward the parlor. I swapped over to the feed, supplied by a tiny koi figurine. My heart raced when the feed filled my screen. Maddox was sitting in one of the heavy armchairs, his tea untouched.

"*I hope you don't mind that my business partner is here with us,*" Pierce said. "*He was already here when you messaged me.*"

"*Not at all!*" Naima said. "*Mr. Maddox, was it?*"

"*Yes,*" Maddox replied. "*We met, briefly.*"

"*A pleasure,*" Naima said with warm smile. She took a seat across from Maddox on a chaise longue. Pierce took the last armchair.

"Okay. Sol, Tati, you're good to approach," I said.

"*Heard. Approaching now.*"

While Naima and Pierce exchanged pleasantries, I opened

Sol's feed in another window. They and Tatiana were circling Pierce's private garage in Ward 1. While Naima lounged in the sunlight of the Upper Wards, Sol and Tatiana descended into the perpetual neon-lit twilight of the Lower Wards.

Sol reached through the window and held a reprogrammable keycard to the gate's sensor. As they did, I rearranged the electric currents running through the keycard to manipulate the magnetic fields into a pattern matching one of Pierce's hired goons. Who was at the moment conveniently trapped in the tower's elevator for the next thirty minutes.

Sol glided into a parking space and killed the engine. Together, they and Tatiana stepped into the dim light of the garage, the sound of the flyer doors reverberating through the space. It was eerily quiet, with only the sound of Tatiana and Sol's footsteps and their hushed breathing in my ear. Even the air traffic outside was muffled through the heavy walls.

"*Jesus*," Tatiana whispered. "*I've got chicken skin in here.*"

"You sked, cuz?" I teased.

"*Not!*" Tatiana replied, defensive. "*It's just cold, is all.*"

A light overhead popped and sputtered, casting flickering light and throwing elongated shadows across the walls. Tatiana yelped and clutched Sol's arm.

"'Not'!" I mimicked.

"*Shut up, Malia! You're three Wards away and you've got two Song sisters between you and anything out here.*"

"*That's a horror unto itself,*" Sol said. They hefted a heavy pair of bolt cutters over their shoulder. "*Besides, we got this.*"

"*What's that gonna do to a ghost?*" Tatiana demanded.

"*A ghost?*" Sol laughed. "*Girl, there are no ghosts in here.*"

"*Says you.*"

"Focus up," I commanded. "You've got limited time in there."

"*Yeah, yeah,*" Tatiana grumbled. She flicked on a flashlight, and the two of them moved deeper into the garage.

Naima's gasp drew me back to her feed. Through the koi cam, I could see Naima and Pierce hunched over an antique secretary desk, one of the many drawers open. "*Is this an original Rider-Waite deck?*"

Pierce puffed up with pride. "*It is. I haven't used it much, I'm afraid I'm not so gifted in reading the cards.*"

"*Nonsense! Anyone can do it, it's all in the meaning you make.*"

"*Yes, I imagine anyone can certainly do it,*" Maddox muttered.

Naima turned to Maddox, brown eyes wide with innocent surprise. "*Oh! Are you not a believer, Mr. Maddox?*"

"*Not particularly,*" he said, sarcastic.

"*Well,*" Naima said, settling on the edge of the chaise. "*I'd be happy to show you.*" She smiled. "*I'm quite fond of awakening those who don't believe.*"

Maddox scoffed.

"*What's the harm, Jordan?*" Pierce said good-naturedly. "*Maybe you'll be surprised. I remember when I first believed.*"

"*Oh, I would love the hear that story!*" Naima exclaimed, clasping her hands together.

Pierce grinned, plopping down in the armchair next to a scowling Maddox. "*Well, it was almost twenty years ago now—*"

I tuned out and swapped to Sol's feed, where they were testing a chained set of double doors. The rattling chains were harsh in the quiet of the garage. "*This probably goes down to the catacombs,*" they said. They grinned at Tatiana over their shoulder. "*Wanna find out?*"

Tatiana sighed. "*I guess so.*"

"*Don't worry, I've done this a million times.*"

"Have you?" I asked, incredulous.

"*Yeah,*" they grunted, snapping into the first link of the chain with the bolt cutters. "*Moonlighted as a ghost hunter for a few years.*"

"What? When? That wasn't in your dossier."

"*They're fucking with you, Malia,*" Tatiana said.

Sol snapped through the second link with another grunt. "*Would I ever lie to you, Just Malia?*"

"Faka," I said.

"*Hold this for me,*" Sol said, jostling the camera pinned to their shirt as they shrugged out of their jacket. They tossed it at Tatiana, who yelped when it hit her in the face.

"*Hold it yourself!*" she protested.

"*Girl, I'm busy.*" Through the cam, I could see their forearms flex as they snapped through the first link of the second chain. A little lighted heart appeared in my vision, indicating my heart rate had spiked. It prompted me to breathe deeply and relax. Hurriedly, I swapped to Naima's feed.

"How's it going over there, Naima?" I asked.

"*It's so interesting!*" she said with feigned delight. "*I'm always fascinated by the ways people find themselves awakened.*"

"Oh good, glad to hear it's going well."

"*But that's enough about me, I'm sure Maddox is eager to see you work,*" Pierce said.

"*I'd truly rather not,*" Maddox replied.

"*Come now, Jordan. Where's your sense of curiosity?*" Pierce cajoled.

"*I'm not incurious, I'm just not a fool,*" Maddox snapped back.

"*Well. If you're not a fool*"—Naima smiled—"*it shouldn't be hard to see through me, will it?*"

Maddox considered that. I knew him well enough to know that a chance to show his own superiority over someone might grab his attention. And it seemed Naima knew it too.

He held out his hand. "*Let me shuffle them.*"

Naima's smile broadened. "*Of course.*"

"*Aha!*" Sol exclaimed.

I swapped to a security feed within the garage. The last snap of the bolt cutters sent the chain rattling to the floor. With a groan that made even me wince, the doors swung open. The sweep of the flashlight illuminated clear plex walls filled with bundled wires and snaking pipes, routing power and water and who knew what else all across Kepler. And, when I zoomed in, I could see scribbled messages on the walls. The thieves' cant of Kepler's runners.

"*Christ, it's hot in here!*" Tatiana said, fanning at her face.

"*The catacombs always run hot,*" Sol said, putting the bolt cutters aside and taking the flashlight from Tatiana. They stepped into the darkened room and tapped a wide plex panel on the floor with their sneaker. "*This must go all the way down. But we'd need a runner to be able to get anywhere.*"

"*Hey, we might know a guy,*" Tatiana said.

I scoffed. "You know Edie would *Cask of Amontillado* us down there before signing on to another job."

"*What's—*"

A thundering *BOOM* cut off Tatiana's question, making me rip my earbuds out of my ears and grip my aching head. Even without them, I could hear the pounding of drums. I opened my eyes and saw Sol's snarl as they brandished the bolt cutters, illuminated in harsh light, and behind them Tatiana's silent scream. I put my earbuds in with trembling hands. Through the speakers, I could hear my voice laughing.

I swapped to another angle in the garage. A slick red flyer was idling, the laughter blaring through its speakers. And just ahead of it, standing the glare of headlights, were Sol and Tatiana.

The engine revved, the drums took on a frenetic pace, and the speakers growled, "*Get out.*"

I couldn't even scream.

Tatiana and Sol bolted in opposite directions, running parallel on either side of the lane along rows of flyers, as Diana revved the flyer engine and lurched forward into the chained double doors. Sol danced around the edge of the flyer before shattering one of its windows with the bolt cutters. They wedged them through the steering wheel, locking the directional thrusters in place. The flyer's engines sputtered and its gears ground as the cackling over the speakers rose into a frustrated scream.

"*Get to the flyer!*" Sol yelled to Tatiana.

My heart beat in time with the pounding of the drums, my whole body shaking in my chair. I felt the urge to throw myself to the ground, press my forehead into the carpet. As if Diana was telling me, *prostrate yourself and be spared.*

"*Malia, we need you!*" Sol pleaded.

Sol's voice broke me out of my reverie. There had to be something I could do. I was the mastermind. I was the Obake.

"Naima," I panted into the mic. "You need to keep Maddox busy!"

Naima tapped the wristband of her comm, the signal for acknowledgment.

Maddox slapped the deck of cards on the coffee table. "*Show me,*" he said.

Naima reached for the deck, carefully selecting ten cards and spreading them across the table in the shape of an upside-down pyramid. "*This is a spread for manifestation. Current challenges, where to find support, and strategies for success,*" Naima explained.

Maddox scoffed. "*Yes, I'm sure the stars could help with my five-year plan.*"

Naima paused in placing the cards, looking up to meet Maddox's eyes. Even through the koi cam, I could see fiery determination in her gaze.

"*Actually,*" she said, carelessly tossing the rest of the deck on the table. "*I don't need cards to read you.*"

Maddox leaned forward in his seat, matching her intense gaze. "*Then read.*"

"*She's coming!*" Tatiana screamed.

Sol and Tatiana were sprinting toward their flyer, their pounding footsteps reverberating through the garage, the flashlight in Sol's hand throwing wild light across the walls. Diana's engines roared, twisting the steering wheel with enough force to dislodge the bolt cutters. The flyer wheeled around, catching Tatiana in its headlights. With a high-pitched whine, Diana surged forward.

"Tati, watch out!" I yelled. I swapped through every camera feed in the garage, searching desperately for something, anything to help. But there was nothing, the garage was so low-tech. "Tati!"

Diana was gaining, Tatiana's shadow growing longer as the headlights approached. With a yelp, Tatiana dove to the right between the parked flyers. Diana shot forward, engines shrieking. Tatiana clambered to her feet and climbed onto the hood of a flyer, vaulting over the cab to the other side of the lane and sprinting down the ramp toward Sol's flyer.

"*Perfection is what you seek*," Naima said. "*You always have. And for the most part, you've always found it. It's what's made you such a powerful man in your field. Awards, accolades, achievement. You were the greatest, all that you aspired to be. 'Were' being the operative word here.*"

Losing Tatiana, Diana fixed her attention on Sol. The thrumming of the engine layered with the growling of the speakers as she chased Sol down. The turn down the ramp was in sight, but Sol kept running forward. I swore on the line.

I extended my awareness beyond the confines of Pierce's security system, reaching for a heavy-looking flyer at the end of the row. I dipped into its systems, but its security was way more complex than the rudimentary systems of the jailbroken flyers of Sol's street races. I tested one of the firewalls and it erupted in front of me, painful enough to send me reeling backward out of my chair. I landed on the floor, my vision white.

you dont want to you dont

want but you

must the credits are gone the family is

gone ill pay you more than its worth he says big

smiles that do not reach his big eyes you worked

                    so
        hard for this you spent so
        much for this but everything is
                gone you hand the keys eyes down no smile his smile he
        says

                pleasure doing business

    Diana's shrieking laughter brought me back to the present. She revved the engine again, preparing to crush Sol against the wall of the garage. But just as they were about to collide, Sol vaulted over the side and dropped to the level below, leaving Diana to slam headfirst into the wall. She reversed, wobbling on her axis. Sol kept running.

    "*Because ultimately,*" Naima continued, "*seeking perfection was your downfall. Nothing was ever good enough, so you discarded it, all of it, until nothing remained. Now you stand among the wreckage of your life with something you hope will be the perfection you've always sought. But is it a triumph, Mr. Maddox? For your sake, I hope it is.*"

    "*Drive!*" Tatiana yelled as Sol slammed the door behind her. Sol's flyer rumbled to life, lifting off the ground as Diana's wailing dopplered above. "*Drive!*" Tatiana yelled again.

    Sol flew out of the parking spot and whipped around toward the entrance, so close to the flyers on either side that their engines peeled the paint. They took off like a shot, throwing their e-brake to drift around the corner toward the exit. They threw another lever, and the flyer lurched forward, slamming through the barrier of the garage and peeling out into the air traffic above.

A deadly silence fell over the room. Maddox held Naima's gaze through narrowed eyes, jaw set behind taut lips. Pierce stared, mouth agape. It wasn't until the buzzing of Maddox's comm erupted into an urgent ringing that any of them moved.

He checked the number then stood abruptly. "*I have to go. Thank you for your perspective Ms. al-Mufti. It was... enlightening.*"

Naima gave him a winning smile. "*Of course, Mr. Maddox. Anytime.*"

"*Yes! Thank you so much, Thamina! I'm once again so impressed by your abilities.*"

"*I appreciate it, Lucas. And I appreciate your hospitality, as ever. However, I feel quite drained after that reading, and need to rest.*"

"*Of course, I understand. But before you go, I'd like to invite you to a fundraising event I'll be hosting. I'd love if you could make it.*"

"*It would be my pleasure! Send me the details, and I'll add it to my calendar.*"

Lucas beamed. Then he poked at his comm to forward the information.

"*We're clear,*" Tatiana panted.

I swapped over to Sol's feed. They were clenching the steering wheel in their fists, arms rigid. Tatiana was slumped in the passenger seat beside them, damp hair clinging to her face.

I blew out a breath, letting my head fall to my arms on the desk. I realized I was trembling. The drumbeat that had been haunting me the last few days—it was Diana. It made sense now. She must be tracking my mental signature, marching through the Net toward my destination. Not even bothering to hide. Instead, she terrorized me with her relentless approach. The awe made sense, but what didn't was the fear

I felt every time she drew near. Awe, like witnessing divinity. It felt insane to say.

The fear had almost gotten my crew killed.

My crew was in danger, and there was nothing I could do. Not even break through Maddox's security measures on a motherfucking flyer.

Tatiana said I was three Wards away with two Song sisters between us—I felt it so acutely now, it pained me.

10

this will kill you this you know one more time one more
chance but there are no more chances you know he
knows but he
wont admit you look at yourself and you are
haunted lost eyes sunken hair shorn when was the last
time you knew your

self will you ever
again

WHEN I CHECKED MY COMM, IT WAS 0202.

I blinked away the little ticking alarm clock and slapped
a pillow over my head. I groaned. At first, I thought it was the
adrenaline of today's scouting mission that was keeping me
up, but it only took thirty-seven minutes for the adrenaline to
fully clear my system. What I found, lying here awake for the
last four hours—it was really Naima's read of Maddox keeping me up.

Seeking perfection was your downfall.

Naima's words reverberated in my head. I had little understanding of what Maddox was using me for. I was only fourteen when I escaped, and it wasn't like Maddox and his colleagues were forthright about their purpose. The only thing I knew, the only thing expected of me, was perfection. Perfect test scores, perfect measurements, perfect mind. It was enough to drive any teenager mad.

The thing was, though, I craved that perfection.

I threw off my pillow and kicked off my blanket with a huff. If I wasn't going to sleep, I might as well *do* something.

I plugged in my gear and dropped into my chair. I booted up *Drop Shock* 2. But rather than sign into my challenger-rated account, I selected my low-gold account. Maybe kicking around some scrubs would make me feel better.

Nothing was ever good enough, so you discarded it.

I craved perfection. I craved every scrap of praise or validation. But as I got older, the praise got more and more scarce. I could sense Maddox's frustration with me after every failed test or botched exercise. Maybe the mods are being rejected, the researchers said. Maybe the genemodding didn't take, they said. Maybe she's too distracted.

Or maybe she's just not good enough, he said.

"*This is bullshit!*" a cracked voice cried over the match's voice chat. "*NOG8NZ is smurfing, dude!*"

"Maybe you need to get good," I said into my mic, my voice disguised behind the Obake's low growl.

"*How are we supposed to?*" a young voice asked. "*We're always getting stomped by smurfs like you.*"

"And how is that my problem?"

Now you stand among the wreckage of your life with something you hope will be the perfection you've always sought.

Eventually it became clear that I was never going to be good enough. For me, for Maddox, for everyone. He put me through more "treatments," but I knew now that they were Hail Mary passes. Even if I didn't know exactly what he was doing, I knew they were an attempt to recoup his losses.

An attempt to make an AI cloned from my consciousness. Diana.

"Just report this asshole," a girl's voice said over the match chat. *"Smurfing's against the TOS."*

I cackled. "You think the TOS can stop me? Get fucked, scrub."

I was immediately disconnected from the server. I cursed.

I sat back in my chair and closed my eyes. I extended my awareness into *Drop Shock 2*'s internal servers. A stream of six reports were zipping toward them, to be logged in my account's file. I knew already there were more than enough reports there to get me permabanned.

So I took a little liberty and diverted the six reports to another account. A little trick I'd made use of a few times already, and—knowing me—probably would again.

Smug, I sat back in my chair. No TOS was going to stop me.

But is it a triumph?

My smile fell. The thing about creating an AI from a living consciousness, it's risky and dangerous. Not just for the AI, but the brain you're cloning from. Scanning and stripping and recreating all the connections and associations in a human brain? It was hard enough on a single pass.

Maddox tried three times.

I knew the fourth would kill me.

I slid out of my chair with a sigh, yanking the power strip out of the wall as I went. I gathered my things then walked across the empty condo to the front door. I didn't feel better, but maybe a walk would fix me.

For your sake, I hope it is.

I ENDED UP BACK AT the Brotherhood gym, where it all began.

It was familiar, but different. The Brotherhood members at the door recognized me as someone affiliated with the gang and waved me through without any fuss. The gym was more crowded than I'd ever seen it, bodies packed in a crush around the ring. The amount of people made the air thick with heat and sweat, the metallic tang of blood just underneath. I moved through the crowd toward the far end of the gym, where the view wasn't as good but the crowd was looser.

I hadn't checked the rosters ahead of time or made any attempt to scout out the fights. It was an impulse decision to come at all, my feet carrying me here seemingly without input. Maybe it was muscle memory. I felt restless and reckless, much like I had the first night I came, almost seventy-two days ago.

This time, I'd get my thrills the old-fashioned way. Through blood and violence.

I was shuffling through the crowd when my boot connected with a high-heeled toe. "Watch it!"

I was formulating a snarky response when I saw who it was.

"Naima?" I asked, shocked.

Naima stood out in the crowd of mostly poorly dressed bookies and gamblers. She wore a minidress in her typical white, cutouts at the waist and shoulders exposing her brown skin. Her dark hair was loose around her shoulders, and her gold jewelry clattered as she whipped around to look at me. "Malia? What are you doing here?"

"I dunno," I answered honestly. "What are *you* doing here?"

Her expression shifted to annoyance. "This is my turf," she said. "I'm meant to be here."

"'Meant to be here'?" I repeated. "Then how the hell did I never see you?"

She shrugged. "I never saw you in the VIP section."

"There's a VIP section?"

A roar went through the crowd as two fighters took the stage.

"C'mon," Naima said, nodding toward the other side of the ring. "Let's sit down."

Naima started toward the other side of the gym, and I followed. The crowd parted around her, as if responding to her command. I was never able to command a room like that. Angel could. That was just another way that she was a better mastermind than me.

I shook my head, clearing those thoughts. I straightened my posture, mimicking Naima's confident stride. Remember, you belong.

She guided me to the other side of the ring, where two rows of folding chairs had been set up. A handful of people dressed in suits clustered together at the far end, a handful of nervous looking socialites sat in the middle, and at the nearest end, Miyeon was sitting with her legs crossed.

Miyeon did a double take as we approached. "What are you two doing here?"

"To watch the fights, what else?"

She narrowed her eyes at me. "Not gonna cause any trouble, are you?"

I grinned at her. "Nah. I never make the same mistake twice."

She didn't look convinced.

Naima sat primly a few seats away. I gave Miyeon a nod of acknowledgment before following. I sat beside Naima. "Did you know Miyeon before this job?" I asked.

"Not really," Naima answered. "I never worked for the Brotherhood. Been in their spaces before, met a few of their people before, but never in a professional capacity."

"How did you end up here?" I asked.

"Shouldn't you know that already, mastermind?"

I did, at least a little—the facts of it, anyway. But there were a lot of holes in Naima's history, scrubbed from the Net. And the facts that were there didn't capture the human reasons for throwing away such a cushy lifestyle for the bloody underworld.

"Yeah, but I don't know *why*," I replied.

"And you're curious."

I grinned. "Always."

Naima looked thoughtful for a moment, though her eyes were still on the fight. After three seconds, she said, "I know what you think: that my life must have been so easy, so perfect.

Wealth, power, class—why would someone throw that away?"
She turned her big brown eyes on me. Her gaze was sharp. "I'll
tell you why. Because the wealth, the power, the class, it didn't
belong to me. It belonged to my father. He wielded it like a
weapon, not just against his enemies but against the people
he claimed to love. Sometimes violently." She paused, looking
thoughtful again. "I was never a daughter to him, but a means
to more wealth, more power, more class. I didn't want to live
like that anymore. So when the SSA came for him, I took my
chance."

"And you ended up here," I finished.

"Yes. I ended up here."

"But why *here*?"

"Because here . . ." Naima gestured toward the rowdy
crowd. "Here, I can be whatever I want. I'm not just a pawn
for an egomaniacal man. Here, I can make myself in my own
image." She smiled. "And that, too, is a form of power."

I recoiled, involuntarily. What she said hit me like a blow
to the chest. To make myself into my own image . . . wasn't
that what I'd always wanted? To escape an egomaniacal father figure and become a person of my own? Naima called it a
form of power. I'd never really considered myself powerful, at
least not in my own right. The Obake traded in power, giving
it and taking it away. But did I ever truly embody it? I didn't
know.

Naima was looking at me curiously, clearly aware that
some neurons in my brain were firing. I smiled at her. "Yeah,
cuz. I can get that."

She met my smile. "I bet you do."

Another roar rose from the crowd, this one louder and

more energetic than the last. Naima looked toward the stage with interest. I followed her gaze. Ducking through the ropes of the ring was Jeongah, looking focused.

"I didn't know she fought," I said, surprised.

"Not often," Naima replied. She nodded toward the people in suits farther down the VIP section. They looked attentive. "And only against fighters from rival gangs."

Jeongah's opponent was a haole guy in a pristine-looking sweatsuit. He leaned close and muttered something to her when they shook hands. A flash of fury crossed Jeongah's face, before smoothing away again into narrowed focus.

The bell rang and both fighters circled the ring, sizing each other up. The haole guy darted in for a quick jab at Jeongah, testing her defenses, which she swatted away with force. They traded jabs, back and forth, feeling each other out. When the haole guy went for a real swing, Jeongah deflected it and answered with a heavy hit of her own. The man reeled, clutching his jaw. He looked surprised. That moment of surprise was enough of an opening for Jeongah to launch her offensive.

With every blow, I heard Naima draw in a sharp breath. She watched attentively, her hands gripping fistfuls of her skirt. Niele, I tapped into the comm on her wrist for her biometrics: *101 bpm. SpO2 = 99%. 118/72 mm Hg. 98.0 degrees Fahrenheit.* I didn't take her for one to be so into blood sport.

Another hit threw the haole guy onto the ropes. He scrambled away from Jeongah, looking into the crowd with an entreating expression. I followed his gaze, down to the suits in the VIP section. He turned back to Jeongah and spat something at her, too low for me to hear over the screaming.

Whatever it was, Jeongah did not take it well. She lunged for him, landing blow after blow until taking a final swing directly at his temple.

In the four seconds between the haole guy hitting the mat and the crowd erupting into cheers and shouts, I heard Miyeon curse. I glanced her way. She looked livid. And just beyond her, I saw the businesspeople looking furious as well.

"Ani ssibal jjom," Miyeon muttered. She pushed past us toward the back room. "Excuse me."

A Brotherhood member interrupted Jeongah's victory lap to whisper in her ear. A flash of anger passed across her face. But she followed her out of the ring anyway.

Naima rose from her seat, then glanced down at me. "C'mon," she said. "Let's go see what that's about."

I laughed. It was a surprise to meet someone nosier than me. I followed her through the roiling crowd. It was for the best, probably. It looked like the crowd wasn't far off from an open brawl. More blood sport.

The Brotherhood member at the door allowed us to pass into the back room. It was weird, not being dragged here for an interrogation. Raised voices, speaking in Korean, floated up the stairs.

"For once in your fucking life could you think more than one step ahead?" Miyeon was standing over a seated Jeongah, who was methodically untaping her fists. "We needed those connections. And you threw them away for one fucking win in the ring."

"If I lost that fight, I would've lost the respect of everyone out there," Jeongah said, hotly. "Not that you give a shit about what people think of me."

"You're such a fucking idiot," Miyeon snapped.

"You're such a fucking bitch," Jeongah snarled back.

The Brotherhood member escorting us cleared her throat at the base of the stairs. The Song sisters snapped their attention toward us.

Naima cocked a hip and crossed her arms, looking amused. "A little sisterly spat?"

"You could say that," Jeongah said. Miyeon glared at her.

"Nuna, the VIPs upstairs are looking for you," the Brotherhood member said.

"Fine," Miyeon growled. "I'll go clean up your fucking mess."

She stormed out, following the woman up the stairs.

"That was quite a fight," Naima said. She stepped into the room, standing with her hands on her hips in front of the seated Jeongah. "I just lost fifty bucks because of you."

"What, you want me to say I'm sorry?" Jeongah asked, irritably.

"No. I want you to pay me back."

"What makes you think I'm gonna do that?" Jeongah asked, her irritation growing.

Naima smiled. "Because I'm *very* pretty."

Jeongah looked momentarily stunned. Then she barked out a laugh. "Is that right?"

Naima smirked. "That's right."

"Uh, maybe I should go—" I broke in.

The two of them shared an annoyed look. I started backing toward the stairs. "Shoots, Naima!"

"Wait," Jeongah said. She rose from her chair. "I need you for something."

"Need me?" I repeated, alarmed. Coming out here in the dead of night was already a mistake, and witnessing the Song sisters fight felt like a bad omen. Getting deeper into their shit—that was more than I could handle.

"Yeah," Jeongah said. "I have a job for you."

IT FIGURED THAT MY LAST seventy-two days of cheating and hacking would end with me in Jeongah's flyer. Though I thought I'd end up in the trunk, on the way to a place the Brotherhood could stash my body. It was part of the initial thrill.

But here I was, swaying in the back seat of Jeongah's flyer as she careened through Ward 4 toward god knows where.

I leaned forward, between Jeongah and Naima. "You haven't told me where we're going."

Jeongah gave me an annoyed side-eye. "We're almost there," she said. Which wasn't an answer.

I sat back in the seat with a huff. As the Obake, I'd worked with many of the gangs on Kepler and in the quadrant. But I made a point to never get involved in their politics. No attachments. So to get caught up in the Brotherhood's inner workings, that felt like an utter failure to uphold the Code.

I hoped it wouldn't bite me in the ass.

After thirteen minutes of flying, we descended to a side street crammed with bodegas and tiny shops. Across the street was a little pachinko parlor festooned with twinkling lights: Heaven's Gate. Even at 0330 it was still open—a twenty-four-hour parlor, it seemed. There were a few haunted-looking salarymen and focused aunties at the machines, and an employee loitered at the counter.

"I thought blood sport was your gambling of choice?" I asked.

"It's a front," Jeongah replied. "The Syndicate uses it as a money-laundering scheme."

I didn't know anything about the Syndicate. I consulted the Net. They were a new player on Kepler, recently expanded from the Outer Worlds into the Trans Galactic smuggling trade. Mostly drugs but expanding into weapons. It annoyed me that I hadn't heard of them—it made me feel like I'd lost my edge. Three years ago, my job was to keep tabs on Kepler's players. Now I was in the dark *and* attached to one. Hell.

"Okay, so, it's a Syndicate front. Doesn't answer why we're here," I said.

"The Syndicate is edging into our turf," Jeongah explained. "They've already stolen almost a dozen of our contacts and intend to steal more. We need to stop their expansion before they really disrupt our operations in the quadrant."

"And you want me to do it."

"Exactly."

I sighed. Attachments.

"What do you want me to do?"

"I need you to find out when and where their next shipment comes it. They fucked with us, we'll fuck with them. An eye for an eye."

Speaking of attachments. "Does Miyeon know about this?"

"Does it matter?"

It really did. Hell if I was going to get between the Song sisters and whatever family feud was happening. But the way Jeongah was looking at me, it seemed like I was gonna end up on either one of their shit lists shortly. And Jeongah was more likely to solve her problems with violence.

"You do know that the Syndicate is gonna be able to trace this, right?" Even if I was able to cover my own tracks, it wouldn't take a rocket scientist to know who orchestrated the job.

Jeongah gave me a sinister smile. "Good. I want them to know they can't fuck with the Brotherhood."

This was anathema to the Obake. It was in the Code: Leave no evidence. This little job that Jeongah had me on was violating several of my rules already, and I had a feeling there'd be more.

"How do you plan to get me access to their systems?" I asked.

Jeongah nodded at Naima. "Her. She'll distract the attendant while you break into the systems."

"Oh fun, work on my day off," Naima said dryly.

"It'll be easy," Jeongah reassured her. "You're already very distracting."

Naima giggled. I scowled.

"That doesn't really answer my question about access," I said.

Jeongah turned her attention to me, annoyed. "You're supposed to be the hacker. Figure it out."

I opened my mouth to complain, but Naima flashed me a smile. "Don't you want to use a little of that power, mastermind?"

I considered it. On the Atlas heist, Angel had to improvise the back half of the heist. It was crazy to witness. If it was possible for her to improv while cracking a vault, couldn't I improv while stealing a measly shipping manifest?

I sighed. "All right. I guess the alternative is murder, so I'll do it."

Jeongah nodded, which I did not find reassuring.

Naima pushed open the door and stepped into the dirty streets, high heels clicking on the pavement. I pulled my hood up and lurked behind her. She stepped confidently into the pachinko parlor. I squawked when she let the door drop on me.

Inside, it was sensory hell. The overhead lights were bright white, while the flashing lights on the pachinko machines were a rainbow of different neon colors. Loud pop music played over the speakers, just under the cheery jingles and ringing and chiming of the machines. I squeezed my eyes shut against the stimulus overload, trying to ground myself.

Naima approached the counter. The attendant immediately straightened her posture, looking intimidated. "Excuse me," she said. "One of the machines ate my credit chit. Can you just give me some tokens in exchange?"

"I'm afraid I can't do that, ma'am," the attendant stammered. "Would you show me which machine was giving you trouble?"

"Thank you! It's over here." Naima took the attendant's hand, who she looked like she'd been shocked. They hurried toward the front of the pachinko parlor.

I walked past, trying to look nonchalant. *Remember, you belong.* Out of the corner of my eye, I saw a side door marked *Employees Only.* I sauntered over to it, then casually checked the handle. Locked. And with manual keys, no less.

A salaryman swore behind me, making me jump. Suddenly anxious standing in the middle of the parlor with my hands on the door, I hurriedly dropped into a seat at the nearest pachinko machine. It was painted a garish royal blue, with shiny holographic stars and planets printed across the surface. A cartoon astronaut with a blinking smiley face waved at me.

I reviewed my options. I couldn't pick the lock on the door, but Naima might be able to. Though she was currently engaged with the clerk, their laughter bubbling from the ball dispensers. If I pulled Naima aside, I'd have to manage the clerk while she stole the manifest. But no, that wouldn't work, because how could she get to the manifest without a hacker? It all made my head ache.

The pachinko machine hollered, "In space, the odds are always in your favor!"

That was a lie. I scowled at the grinning astronaut. In space, you were more likely to get scammed.

Hold on.

I extended my awareness into the machine, poking through its code. It was pretty rudimentary, though the odds were a little weighted. The really interesting thing was the credit chit reader on the ball dispenser. It definitely shouldn't be recording the chit's data, let alone sending it to a computer system on-site.

I grinned. The Syndicate seemed to be running a couple of schemes.

I probed a little deeper into the code but found myself running up against firewalls and fail-safes that were more sophisticated than a cursory sweep could handle. I needed to go deeper.

I really didn't want to. The echoing of Diana's drums had

driven me from sleep and kept me out of my games, and god, it would be so embarrassing if Diana found me in a pachinko parlor. But what other choice did I have? The alternative was Jeongah's fury, which I was not willing to risk either.

I took a deep breath, then dove deeper into the code.

Immediately I was overwhelmed by the sensations of the machine. Calculated odds, weighted outputs, streams of data flowing from each machine into the central system. I bounced between them all, my brain rattling with the light and noise. I directed my consciousness into the streams of data and let them pull me further into the system, into the darkness of the Net. It was a relief.

I followed the flowing streams into the central system, which was relatively unguarded. Or at least, guarded by a system I'd learned to crack two years ago. Smug, I plucked at the strings of code and let it fall to pieces in front of me.

It didn't take much digging to find the manifests for incoming shipments. Jeongah would be pleased.

I disconnected from the system before Diana could get a good trace on me. I hurried out of the parlor, past a laughing Naima and a blushing attendant, into the Ward 4 night.

Jeongah was waiting in the flyer, drumming her fingers on the steering wheel. I slid into the back seat and shut the door behind me.

"Did you get it?" she asked.

"Yeah." I forwarded the information, a spark traveling from my comm to hers. "Shipment of Elysian snow, Dock 6B-2, three days from now."

Jeongah gave me a sinister grin. "Perfect."

I didn't like the way my heart fluttered. I didn't like the

way I craved to hear that word. *Perfect.* To Maddox, never. To Jeongah? Maybe I could be perfect.

I shook my head, dismissing the thoughts. "So, what are you gonna do with that?" I asked.

"We'll send some men to the docks. Disrupt their little operation. Show them that the Brotherhood is not to be fucked with."

"You seem really invested in reputation."

"If you have a shitty reputation, what *do* you have?" Jeongah replied. "My father, and his father before him, built this organization from the ground up. They made us strong, they made us powerful. It's my duty to carry on that legacy."

"And fear is the way to do that?"

Jeongah looked at me askance. I swallowed. "It's not about fear. It's about respect. You respect me, I'll respect you back. That's the way things have always worked in the Brotherhood, and I want it to stay that way."

Oddly noble, for a gangster.

"What about Miyeon?"

A look of distaste crossed Jeongah's face. "Miyeon thinks that money is a substitute for power. She'll do whatever she can to make a buck. She wants to expand, become more profitable, but that's not what we're about."

"You're about respect."

"Yeah. Respect."

Respect. I could understand that, at least a little. The Obake didn't always command respect. It's why I hid my face, disguised my voice. Nobody would take a wahine iwiiwi like me seriously. But the more I worked, the more cred I built, they learned to respect me. The ones who didn't were the ones who never saw me coming.

Naima opened the door and slid into the passenger seat, interrupting my thoughts. She closed the door and sighed. "I had to work on my day off, but at least I got a cute girl's number out of it."

Jeongah stiffened. "Oh?"

Naima smirked at her. "We'll call it a perk of the job."

Jeongah grunted. She started the flyer and lifted off from the curb with a jerk.

The other players learned to respect me, but the Brotherhood was another story. I thought about Miyeon's anger at Jeongah for not throwing the fight and saw a rift in the organization that ran a lot deeper than just sisterly sniping. I'd never worked with the organization before now—all the cyberspace paniolos knew to steer clear of them. I wondered what it would have been like to work with Jeongah's father, the patriarch of the Song family. I wondered which of his daughters most aligned with his vision for the Brotherhood.

I wondered if he would have respected me back.

11

"SOL AND TATIANA DISCOVERED A BACKDOOR TO PIERCE'S FLYERS," I EX-
plained. I was already getting tired of this back room in
Cherry. Not in small part due to the stink eye both Song sisters were giving me. In sync, for once. "There's a backdoor
through the catacombs," I continued. "We'll need a runner to
scout a route, but it's our way in."

"What about your blown cover?" Jeongah demanded.
"The AI caught you. The garage is going to be swarming with
security."

"Isn't that the point, though?" Sol asked. "We want to
draw as many of Pierce's men from the vault as possible. If
Pierce is wasting manpower protecting the garage, it's easier
to slip into his penthouse."

"And Maddox won't see this coming?" Miyeon asked,
incredulous.

"No way," I said, shaking my head. "He's never been able
to see the big picture. Always getting lost in the details. Besides, it's not like Pierce listens to him." I laughed. "It must
drive him lōlō."

"That's something we can manipulate," Naima chimed in. "Give me another three days, I'll have Pierce eating out of the palm of my hand." She smirked. "And Maddox will be sleeping in the doghouse."

"Okay," Miyeon said slowly. "How do you even *get into* the garage?"

"Like I said, we need a runner," I replied. I paused. "Anybody got any referrals?"

"I mean, we *do* know a guy," Tatiana prodded.

I shook my head. "Nuh-uh. They'd fucking murder us if we so much as asked them to jaywalk—they won't sign on to another job. Besides, we shouldn't use the same crew more than once."

"What about me?" Tatiana said, affronted.

"Well, you're different, cuz. We're more than just a crew."

"Aw," Tatiana said with a smile.

"*Any-fucking-way*," Jeongah said, impatient. "What happens once you have a route? What are you doing in Pierce's garage?"

"Stealing his flyers, obviously," Sol said casually. Jeongah shot them a dangerous look. Sol shrugged. "Just Malia promised me my pick of them, if you remember."

"And I keep telling you I'm good for it!" I said.

"How are you supposed to get out of Pierce's garage with one hundred flyers?" Jeongah pressed.

"Well . . ." Sol sat forward in their seat. "I have a few buddies who might be interested in helping out." They grinned. "If you're willing to part with a few of them."

"Done," I said. "Not like we're gonna use 'em."

Sol looked surprised. "Not gonna use 'em?" they repeated. "You're not interested in taking one for yourself?"

I flushed. "I don't drive."

"Why not?"

My flush deepened. "Because I don't know how."

Sol stared at me like I'd just sprouted two heads.

I cleared my throat and straightened my posture. "We'll need to scout some escape routes for the other racers."

"Why?" Jeongah asked. "They can fend for themselves."

"We shouldn't just cut them loose," Tatiana protested. "We owe it to them to at least help."

Jeongah raised a brow. "Do we?"

"*Yes*, we do," Sol said, adamant. "You protect my people, or there's no deal."

Jeongah's lip curled, and her dark eyes narrowed. Sol held her gaze, mouth set in a hard line.

"I can help," I jumped in, before things could escalate. "We can scout out some escape routes, and I can brainstorm some ways to throw some obstacles in the way of any buggahs who follow."

"Fine," Jeongah said, still holding Sol's gaze. "Just get it done."

She stood abruptly, stalking across the room toward the exit. She slammed the door behind her.

Miyeon, always in need of the last word, addressed us one last time. "I expect an update by tomorrow morning."

"Shoots," I replied.

Then Miyeon was gone.

After the Song sisters had left, Naima gave Sol a look of distaste. "You couldn't just leave it alone?"

Sol turned away from the door to give Naima a cool look. "Nope."

Naima scoffed. "Do you have some kind of problem with her?"

"'Problem with her'?" Tatiana repeated. "Of course we have a problem with her, she's gonna fucking kill Malia!" She gestured wildly at me.

"If you *fail*," Naima corrected. "Which we won't."

"Oh, so we should just let it go, then?"

Naima shrugged. "It's just the nature of the game. No point getting bent out of shape about it."

Tatiana stared at her.

"Listen," Naima said, leaning back in her chair and crossing her legs. "I've been in the game for a long time now, and I've gotten pretty fucking good at it. One thing I've learned, there's only one real currency in this business. Money, pleasure, pain. It's all in service of one thing."

"And what's that?" Sol asked.

"Power," Naima said. "Beauty and wealth come and go. But power is forever."

We all fell silent, each of us taking that in. Naima cast a haughty glance around the room before she stood as well. "I'm going to message Pierce about the details of this fundraiser. Call me if anything important comes up." Then she crossed the room and was gone too.

I sank into a chair and sighed. This mastermind shit was so fucking hard. How was I supposed to keep all these lōlō motherfuckers from killing each other? I dropped my face into my hands. I didn't know. My head hurt like hell.

"Hey, you okay?"

I looked up. Sol was kneeling in front of me, concern on their face.

"Yeah," I said, irritably. Like Cherry's back room, I was getting tired of everyone asking me if I was okay. "Just a headache."

"You good to go scouting? It can wait, if you need."

"Nah, nah, nah. We should use all the time we have."

Sol stood and offered a hand. I waved it away. "Let's go."

SOL DID MOST OF THE routing for our exits. Early on I had projected an image of a Ward 1 block and plotted a route myself, but Sol shook their head and pointed at an intersection. "That light has a broken sensor. Get caught at a red there and you'll never leave."

"Well, what do you suggest?" I had said, annoyed.

Turns out they had lots of suggestions. We spent the entire afternoon winding through the Ward 1 streets, Sol pointing out all the little details and idiosyncrasies only a Lower Ward racer could know. A long light here, a blind turn there. I had to admit it made me self-conscious. What could I do as a hacker in this situation? A hacker without a fucking driver's license?

But as we sat at a particularly long light, my leg bouncing on the floor, I had an idea. I narrowed my eyes in concentration, ignoring the pain deep in their sockets, and extended my awareness toward the light. I dipped into the stream of code connecting it to the larger infrastructure that kept Kepler's traffic coursing through its veins. I pinged the system: *GO.*

The light flipped green, and Sol looked at me in surprise. "Did you do that?"

I grinned to myself. There's always an exploit. "Yeah. And I can do a lot more than that."

From there, it was just getting creative. Most of Kepler's traffic system was remote, including the lighted signs directing traffic. Closing a street for station maintenance here, creating a detour for a false event there. Using the system, we could clear the path for Sol's racers and close it behind them. And with one hundred flyers shooting across the station in one hundred different directions . . . not even Diana could track all the possible routes. Even if she could, it would take the majority of her processing power. Keeping her occupied was all we needed, until Tatiana could steal the cipher and escape into Ward 1's darkness.

I was finalizing the routes when Sol asked, "So, how are you, really?"

I frowned at them over my laptop screen. "I'm fine. You don't have to keep asking, y'know. The answer's not gonna change."

"Because you're always fine, or because you're always lying?"

I scowled at them. "I don't see how it's your problem."

"It's not," they admitted.

The Code was ringing in my head again. Never assume good intent. "Then why are you asking?"

They shrugged. "I just like talking to you, I guess."

That surprised me. I was never that close to my crews. The Atlas heist, we all came out close after that. But in the months and years since, I found myself drifting away, out of their orbit. That was how I always was. A comet, coming and going in and out of other peoples' lives.

"When was the last time you cruised?" they asked.

"Does cruising at Jeongah's clubs count?"

Sol laughed. "No."

"Then, I dunno," I admitted.

"Me neither." They shot me a sideways smile. "I think we should."

"And do what?"

"Nothing—that's the point of cruising, Just Malia."

"We've only got a week until the fundraiser, Sol."

"And you can't spare a few hours to fuck around?"

My frown deepened. I wasn't sure what Sol's angle was. What the point of drawing me into their orbit was. There was part of me that was wary, the part of the Obake in me that never let her guard down. But there was also the part of me that didn't want to go home to my empty condo. That wanted to spend more time, even just a little time, in the company of this person. This person who was smiling at me expectantly.

I sighed. "Okay. I'll cruise with you."

Sol's face broke into a grin. "You won't regret it, Just Malia. You'll see."

CRUISING TOOK ON A NEW meaning with Sol. The times I'd cruised, it was wandering the streets and skybridges of the Lower Wards. With Sol, we flew from Ward to Ward, destination to destination, as our whims dictated. Through the winding streets of Ward 1, where Sol reminisced about hard-won victories and bitter losses in their racing career. Between the towers of Ward 4, where I shared some of my most interesting jobs, negotiated in Cherry's back rooms. Over the green spaces of Ward 7, where we laughed about conning the rich inhabitants at the top of Kepler's towers. I even talked a little about the Atlas heist, perhaps my crowning achievement as the Obake.

We cruised for five hours and twenty-two minutes. At first, I was keeping track of the time, antsy about the seconds ticking away. But before long I found myself ignoring the little clock in the upper right-hand corner of my vision, and it wasn't until we were resting at the end of the day that I saw the time.

Eventually we found ourselves on top of one of Ward 7's skybridges, sitting on the hood of Sol's flyer with our backs to the windshield and our legs stretched out across the hood, still warm from the engine. Kepler's artificial sky was cycling toward dusk, and up this high, you could see the panels lining the interior of the ring. An unnaturally fluffy cloud drifted overhead, across the golden hues of the fading light. Over the edge, you could see between the towers—all the way down to the Lower Wards below, aglow with the light of neon signs, lighted advertisements, and digital graffiti.

"This is where I come to think," Sol said.

"About what?" I asked with a laugh.

They feigned offense. "Lots of things. I'm a deep thinker, Just Malia."

"You don't seem to think when you beef with the Song sisters," I pointed out.

Sol shrugged. "They're all bark and no bite."

I thought of that poor motherfucker and his kneecaps, way back at the start of this bullshit heist. "I dunno if that's true."

"What are they gonna do? Replace me? This late in the

heist? Nah. They need me—all of us. We're safe, at least for now."

"I can't tell if you're brave or delusional."

They grinned. "Maybe a little of both."

"Why?"

Sol started unbuttoning their shirt.

"Hey, whoa, hey!" I exclaimed. My heart pounded as they revealed the brown skin of their throat, the lines of their collarbones, the expanse of brown skin between their breasts, and—

A scar. Running down the length of their sternum, faded from the years.

"What's that?" I asked.

"Couple years ago, I got in a bad wreck," they explained. "Not many safety features in my type of ride. The steering wheel hit me right in the chest. Myocardial contusion leading straight into congestive heart failure. Any other time in history, I would've been a goner. If not then, slowly, until my heart finally gave out. Now, though, there's mods for that."

I ran a scan and, not long after, my eyes confirmed what Sol said. A mod, lodged in their left ventricle. I pulled up the specs through the Net. Combination pacemaker and medication infuser, direct into their bloodstream. With regular maintenance, Sol could live forever. At least, until the rest of their body failed.

"I didn't know what was happening, at the time," Sol continued. I closed the search to meet their eyes. They were smiling. "As I was sitting in my wrecked ride, slowly dying, I couldn't stop thinking, *I can't die like this.* I couldn't stop thinking about all the things I didn't do, and all the things I did that I wished I hadn't. I was only twenty-one, but I was full of regret. I lived in fear, and it kept me from really living. So, I thought to myself, *If I get out of here, I'm not gonna live like that, not anymore.* No more regrets. No more fear." They traced the scar with their finger. "I quit my retail job and became a gearhead. I started racing. I started *living.* In a weird way, that wreck saved my life."

"That's why you're not afraid of the Song sisters," I said in understanding.

"I mean, I'm still afraid," they said. "But I'm not letting that fear stop me anymore. That feeling I had, dying in that wreck? I never want to feel it again."

It reminded me of the end of the Atlas heist, at least a little. After overclocking my mod and brute forcing the codes, I woke up on the floor of the crew's utility van. I woke up scared. I didn't know where or when I was, and in the darkness of the van, I thought I was back in Maddox's compound. That all the years since were just a dream. I remembered the tears stinging my eyes, even before my faculties had returned to me. I was afraid, so afraid.

"I wish I could live like that," I admitted.

"What's stopping you?"

What *was* stopping me? In the darkness of the utility van, I remembered thinking, *I can't go back.* I remembered thinking, *I can't survive going back.* But even that brush with death couldn't make me change. If anything, it made me more afraid. I withdrew from the crew, even Tatiana. I withdrew from the world, into the darkness of my empty condo. I withdrew into my feeds and data streams, one eye always on the security feeds. Because if I let my guard down, Maddox might find me.

I thought all that. But instead, I said, "I don't know."

"Well. I hope you figure it out, Just Malia."

"You don't have to call me that. Malia is good."

"Malia and what else?"

"What do you mean?"

"Your last name, girl!"

I paused. "I don't have one."

Sol's smile slipped. "Oh."

"Like I said before, Maddox stole me when I was a toddler. I never found out who my birth family was."

"Shit, Malia. I'm so sorry."

I shifted uncomfortably. "Nah, no need. You didn't know."

A silence fell over us. After a while, Sol asked, "Did you ever try to find them?"

"I did," I answered. "But there were so many leads, I couldn't possibly track them all down. And what would I even say? 'Hi, I'm Malia—at least, I think that's my name—your daughter lost to adoption-slash-human trafficking. The haole guy that adopted me turned me into a superhacker, and I live a life of crime. But I watched a lot of TV and played a lot of holo-games, so I eventually developed a personality. Want to start over?' Yeah, right."

They nodded solemnly, keeping their brown eyes fixed on my face.

As if compelled by something beyond me, I continued. "So, I gave up. Threw myself into my work. I didn't have many connections outside of business. Even those I didn't maintain for long. It was safer that way. I didn't know if Maddox was on my tail, and I couldn't risk my identity being known. Tatiana was the exception. And even her I eventually pushed away.

When I say I haven't cruised in a long time—more accurately, I haven't cruised much at all."

"But you cruised with me," Sol said. "Why?"

That made me pause. Why *did* I cruise with them? For so long, I was afraid. But right now, in Kepler's fading light, I didn't feel that fear. For the last five hours and thirty-two minutes, I wasn't afraid. With Sol I felt . . . safe. But why, I wasn't sure.

"I don't know," I said. "Maybe I just—"

I snapped my mouth shut. *You make me feel safe?* That was an insane thing to say to someone you'd only met a few weeks ago. An insane thing to say to a member of your crew. An uncomfortable lump appeared in my throat, and I swallowed hard to try and dislodge it. My mind ran through all the scenarios of how Sol might react to what I really meant, and all of them ended with me waving down a cab from the top of this skybridge as Sol sped off into the sunset.

"Never mind," I said quickly. Before Sol could respond, I turned away and slid ungracefully off the hood of their flyer. "It's late, I should let you get home."

Sol didn't immediately follow. They studied me closely, like a puzzle they were working out. It made the lump in my throat even more difficult to dislodge. I fidgeted with one of my twists, shifting from foot to foot.

"Okay," they said eventually. "Let's take you home."

I tried to hide my relief as they hopped off the hood of their flyer. But then they grinned at me over the hood and jangled the keys in their hand. "You wanna drive?"

"*Me?*" I asked, my eyes widening. "I told you, I don't know how!"

"You could learn," they said easily. "I could teach you."

"No way, I'm not paying for another flyer and another heart when I crash your ride."

They laughed. "I'm not gonna let you crash. I'll be right here with you. Besides, it's good for you to know. Never know when it might come in handy."

That was true, I hated to admit.

"You sked?"

I was. I was so scared. Of a lot of things. I couldn't go back. But what would it mean to go forward?

To live?

I stood up straighter, then fixed them with a glare. "Not!"

They jangled their keys again. "Then prove it."

I stomped up to them, snatching the keys out of their hand. "I not sked," I said. "You watch."

Sol's grin widened. "I will."

We climbed into the flyer, me in the pilot's seat and Sol in the passenger seat. I refreshed myself on the knowledge I'd downloaded from the Net, way back at that first race. I put my hands on the steering wheel, and I felt the ghosts of the Net pressing against my barriers. I squeezed my eyes closed against them.

I felt a pair of hands rest on mine, drawing me back to the present. Sol's hands were on mine, lacing our fingers together. Their touch felt steadying, anchoring. I felt the tide of ghosts recede.

"Ten and two," Sol said.

"What?"

"Ten and two," Sol repeated. "Your hands should be at ten and two."

Sol slid my hands to the ten o'clock and two o'clock positions on the wheel.

"Oh. Thanks," I said.

"Like I said: I'm here, Malia." They squeezed my hands, gently, before drawing away. "I'm right here with you."

I took a deep breath. I was scared. So fucking scared. But I couldn't live in fear. Not anymore.

I pressed the start button in the ignition, and the engine rumbled to life.

12

"YOU DRIVE LIKE MY ABUELA!" SOL CACKLED.

"You shut the fuck up!" I snapped. My face burned, but humiliation was not enough to make me unpeel my fists from the steering wheel, hunched over the dash with my shoulders at my ears. The blinking speedometer in the upper left corner of my eye read 22 *kph*.

"My abuela is eighty years old and blind, for reference," Sol added.

"I said shut the fuck up!"

The snarling tiger on the hood of Sol's flyer crept along the streets of Ward 1 at 22 kph. There wasn't much traffic on the surface-level streets, flush against Kepler's catacombs. But what little there was that found itself trapped behind me lifted off and whirred away after honking at me for a few seconds. Only a handful of them yelled out their window at me. The insults were mostly in Kepler Spanish. I blinked away the scrolling translations of the expletives.

"You know that going too slow and stopping too much can get you just as killed as going too fast," Sol mused.

"That sounds like a fucking lie," I replied.

"You keep saying I'm lying to you, but I haven't lied once."

"Oh yeah? What about that ghost-hunting BS?"

Sol gave me a sideways grin. "My abuela's ghost stories don't count?"

"*No*, they don't!"

They shrugged, as if in defeat. "Ah, well."

I shot them a dirty look. But not a long one, because my eyes snapped back to the roadblock we were creeping up to.

"There's construction ahead. You'll have to merge into traffic here," Sol said.

"'*Merge*'?"

"That's what I said. You know how to do that?"

"I don't know notting, brah!"

They laughed. "No worries, I'll help you. Put on your turn signal."

I fumbled behind the wheel, looking for the switch. I flipped the first one I found. and fluid sprayed across the windshield. "Motherfuck!"

Sol reached across the center console to turn off the windshield wipers. "Farther down. You almost got it."

I let go of the switch and the fluid stopped spraying. I tried the next switch I found, farther down the steering wheel, and flipped it. The turn signal started blinking.

I sat rigid in the pilot's seat for thirteen seconds. No one would let me merge. In between the rhythmic beeping of the blinker, I thought about all the twists and turns in my life that led me here: the pilot's seat of a street-racing flyer, windshield wipers going and blinker blipping. What kind of hacker did *that*?

"You just gonna wait?" Sol asked.

"What the hell else am I supposed to do?"

"You gotta be more assertive, Malia. Especially in Ward 1. Everybody's got places to be and no time to get there."

"How?" I snapped.

"Turn into the lane more. Easy. Little farther. Once there's a break in traffic, you gotta nut up and go for it."

What kind of hacker was afraid of a little traffic? I'd scammed gangsters, blackmailed celebrities, robbed trillion-aires. I was raised by a power-mad evil genius. I had a blood-thirsty AI hunting me through the Net. There was nothing a Ward 1 uncle could do that would be scarier than that.

Right?

I nudged the accelerator too hard, and the flyer lurched into the right lane. The flyer behind me—a plumbing van painted with a cartoon dolphin in work coveralls—swerved to avoid me. He leaned on his horn as he came up alongside us. I fought the urge to drop the wheel and cover my ears.

"¿Qué carajo estás hacienda?" The plumber snapped.

"¡Ay!" Sol leaned out of the flyer window. "¡Tranquilízate, broki!"

I squeezed my eyes shut against the scrolling transla-tion. As the two of them went back and forth, it became even harder to not cover my ears. The yelling was escalat-ing. Flyers were honking. People were watching. The clamor of construction was all around us. My head hurt, my eyes watered, I felt like my bones were going to vibrate out of my skin.

"Este jodío cabrón," Sol muttered. "C'mon Malia, let's go."

I opened my eyes, tears biting at the corners. I lurched

into traffic again, then set a quick pace of 29 kph toward the end of the work zone.

"Over there, on the right. Pull over, and we'll take a break."

I did as instructed, pulling alongside the sidewalk. My parking job was all hammajang, I knew that already. I tried to straighten out but only scraped the side of the bumper on the curb.

What was wrong with me that a Ward 1 uncle in a dolphin van was scarier than the Song sisters, Maddox, Diana? What did it mean that a little driving lesson had brought the Obake to her breaking point? Was I so weak, so cowardly, that I couldn't even do something so trivial? I felt a surge of emotion rising inside me, threatening to pull me under. I wanted to scream.

"What can I do, Malia?" Sol asked.

I shook my head, eyes shut tight against the wave of force.

"Do you want a minute alone?"

I nodded, my whole body trembling with the strain.

"Okay. I'll be right outside."

I heard the door open, then shut. Then I heard the environmental seals on the flyer doors engage with a *slurp*, and everything went quiet.

I trembled in place for five seconds more, a low keening building in my chest. The sound rose into a wail, and I realized I was crying. I wrapped my arms around myself, squeezing tight, rocking back and forth in the pilot's seat. I was weak. I was so weak. Of course Maddox replaced me—what kind of superhacker was destroyed so utterly by something any other teenager with a learner's permit could do? An inferior one. A defective one. A worthless one.

I cried. I cried until I couldn't cry anymore. I cried until I was out of tears, hollowed out.

When I couldn't cry any longer, I dragged my sleeve across my face, sniffling.

A soft rap on the passenger window made me lift my gaze, blinking into the light.

"Can I come in?" Sol mouthed.

I nodded, scrubbing at my face and rearranging my locs. Sol disengaged the environmental seals on the flyer with a *hiss*, then opened the door. The sounds of Ward 1 came flooding back: construction, conversation, commerce, and reggaeton.

Sol slid into the passenger seat and shut the door behind them. They looked at me somberly. "Can I ask if you're okay?"

"Yeah," I said, sniffling. "I'm cherreh, brah."

"Now, that's a fucking lie."

I sighed. "Maybe. But some grindz and some ibuprofen would fix me."

"No ibuprofen—not allowed—but there's some acet-aminophen in the center console. And . . ." They reached into their coat pockets, then procured three musubi of different va-rieties. They held them out to me. "Would a musubi fix you?"

"Oh, dude, a musubi would fix *so* much," I said, reaching for the hot dog one.

They smiled. "Good."

We ate in companionable silence. Rather, I scarfed my musubi down like a starved animal while Sol watched. I was self-conscious about my tearstained face and snot-stained hoodie, but Sol made no remarks. No jokes, no asides, just kept watching me intently. I couldn't read their expression.

Were they judging me? I hoped not. I had a reputation as the best hacker on Kepler, probably the best in the quadrant. But so far, they'd seen me only at my worst. Bested by an AI, a failure of a mastermind, a shitty driver. They would be right to judge me.

Even so, as we sat in silence, I couldn't be sure what they were thinking.

Sol broke the silence. "That musubi is the best in Ward 1. Believe me, I've tried 'em all." They grinned at me. "I'd say that 10th Street has the best musubi on the station, but that might get my ass kicked anywhere else, so don't tell anyone."

"You live here?" I asked around a mouthful of musubi.

"Yeah. Been here my whole life. My whole family's li'dat. Not a lot of us Borinki, but we've always been here."

I hadn't spent much time in Ward 1, let alone around 10th Street. I pinged the Net, and in 0.74 seconds it returned more information. There were 17,428 Borinki on Kepler, descended from the Borinki of Old Earth. They came over with all the rest of us—moving from sugar to sugar to shipping to shipping again. They traveled halfway across the Earth, then halfway across the galaxy to be here. Children of the sea and then later the stars, just like my own ancestors.

The difference here was that Sol could trace their lineage back to Old Earth. Through their abuela, their piko, their family. Me? I could never do that.

"If you ask nicely, maybe I'll bring you some of my abuela's pasteles," Sol continued. "Old Earth recipe. Best on 10th Street. That you can tell everybody, because it's fucking true."

I smiled weakly. "Maybe I will."

As Sol talked, I felt less and less sure they were judging me. Which was even more confusing. I would judge them if our roles were reversed. But here they were, smiling at me warmly, distracting me from my own humiliation. I didn't know what their angle was. Or if there even was an angle. Now *that* was confusing. It went against the Code: Never assume good intent.

But if there was good intent—what would I even do with that?

A knock on the window startled both of us out of our spell. Sol twisted in their seat, and I looked over their shoulder. A haole guy in a white suit was peering into the window, dark hair and dark moustache impeccably styled. Sol sighed heavily, then glanced at me. "Give me a sec."

They rolled down the window. "Hello, Mr. Dallas."

"Good to see you, Marisol, how are you?" The haole guy continued without waiting for an answer. "You haven't been returning my messages."

"I don't have any updates," Sol replied.

"It's still good form to answer. Professional. Respectful."

"I figured I wouldn't waste your time. I know you're a busy guy."

The man chuckled. "Thank you, but in the future, I'd appreciate an update."

"Understood."

Mr. Dallas caught sight of his reflection in the opposite window. He tucked a curl of dark hair out of his face. "As you know," he said, absently, "I have a three-strike policy about late rent payments. I'm afraid you're up to two now."

"I understand, sir."

"And this is with the new increase, of course."

"Yes, sir."

"But if you pay me by the end of the week, I might make an exception."

"How about two weeks?" I butted in.

Sol shot me a glare. Mr. Dallas looked surprised. "Oh? Who's this, Marisol?"

"A friend," I answered. "Colleague. Business partner? Anyway." I shook my head. "Sol can get you your payment in two weeks. In the meantime, I can take care of any outstanding fees."

"That's quite generous, but Marisol owes me 4,500 credits."

"No worries, brah. I take care of 'em." I poked at my comm, and a spark of data flew across the cabin to the gold-banded comm on Mr. Dallas's wrist. With a ping, a little +4,500 appeared.

The man raised his bushy eyebrows at the notification. "Well! It seems we're also business partners now, Ms. . . . ?"

"Malia," I answered. "You can call me Malia."

"Much obliged, Malia." He inclined his head toward me. His gaze fell on the musubi in Sol's hand. "Are those from the Superette?"

"Yes, sir," Sol said through gritted teeth.

"I'll knock ten credits off your balance for one."

Wordlessly, Sol passed him the musubi.

"Much obliged, Marisol." He flashed them a blindingly white smile. "If you bring by more of your grandmother's pasteles, we can negotiate for a discount."

Sol nodded, their jaw tense.

"Pleasure doing business with you both," Mr. Dallas said.

Sol rolled up the window as he sauntered away, unwrapping the musubi as he went.

Sol turned on me. "What the fuck was that?"

I blinked. "What the fuck was what?"

"I already know you're loaded, you don't need to shove it in my face."

I recoiled. Did I just make things worse? "I don't—I didn't mean—"

"We can take care of ourselves, you know. We don't need your charity."

"It's not charity—"

"Then what is it?"

I looked down at my lap, Sol's gaze burning into me. "I wanted to—You helped me so much, I thought . . ." Fuck, I did make things worse. I didn't know how or why, though. I was trying to be helpful. I was trying to be useful. I squeezed my eyes shut against more tears. I thought I didn't have any more left. "I'm sorry."

A long silence stretched between us. After seven seconds, Sol sighed.

"It's all right," they said. "You were just trying to help."

I jerked my gaze upward to look at them. I searched their face, but their expression was unreadable. "You mean that?"

"Yeah, I do." They gave me a small, reassuring smile. "I guess I'm just used to people using their charity against me. It's how I got into this mess in the first place. Mr. Dallas's offer seemed too good to be true. And lo and behold, it was." They sighed again. "The whole neighborhood owes him money. Maybe my debt is taken care of, but what about everybody else? It's just not fucking right."

I nodded, slowly. Mr. Dallas wasn't unlike Atlas, who I'd fucked up three years ago with Angel, Edie, and the crew. I had naively thought that after fucking him up, the gentrification seizing Kepler would have stopped. Seems like it hadn't, and slumlords like Mr. Dallas had just moved into the vacuum. Looked like there was still more work to do.

"Anyway, I'm sorry I snapped at you," Sol said.

"It's okay," I replied.

"Swap places with me. I'll drive you home."

I exited the flyer and crossed around the front. As I did, a big rubber dodgeball bounced across the hood of Sol's flyer— right between the tiger's eyes. I picked it up off the sidewalk and turned it over in my hands, puzzled.

"Hey, miss!" a voice called. "Miss!"

I looked up, across the street and past the construction zone. A small child was waving their arms wildly behind a chain-link fence. "Miss! Can I have my ball back?"

I glanced over at Sol, who shrugged.

I darted between the stopped flyers waiting their turn to enter the construction zone, ignoring the drivers' stink eye, and approached the fence at a jog. The child waited patiently on the other side. My eyes were drawn toward the tower be- hind her, stretching up into the Wards above. In the round lettering ubiquitous to corporations trying to convince you they're friendly, a sign read *Cunningham House*.

I stopped in my tracks, gaping up at the sign. It made sense that Pierce would move into the 10th Street neighbor- hood. Ward 1 was always the most precarious of the Lower Wards, on the brink of financial ruin. Slumlords like Mr. Dallas made a killing here. And the families that couldn't afford to keep Mr. Dallas off their backs? Their kids ended up here, with Pierce.

"Miss?" the child prodded.

I blinked, looking back down at the child behind the fence. She was around nine or ten, with tan skin, light brown eyes, and big puffs of dark coiling hair at her nape. "Hey," I said. "You live here?"

She eyed me warily. "Yeah."

"How long?"

"What's it to you?"

I scowled, then brandished the dodgeball. "If you want this back, better answer my question."

The girl scowled at me. After a second of silence, she heaved a weary sigh. "Fine. What's your question?"

I smiled at her, smug. "How long have you lived here?" I asked.

"I dunno. A few months?" She looked thoughtful. "Three months."

"What do you do in there?"

"Nothing fun." She scuffed her shoe on the pavement. "Lots of math and CS. I get tired of looking at a screen all day." She gestured at the ball in my hands. "Why I want that back."

"They do anything to you? Medically, I mean?"

The girl squinted at me through the links in the fence. "We get checkups every couple of months. Spacers are supposed to get checked up more often, the nurse says." She shrugged. "Nobody does, though."

"What kind of things do they do?"

The girl rolled her eyes. "I dunno, man, medical stuff."

"What about mods? Any mods?"

"You think I'm old enough for a mod?"

I wasn't much older than she was when I got my AXON mods. But she didn't need to know that.

"I want a mod," she continued, unprompted. "But I probably won't get one until I'm emancipated. They gave us a VI, though."

My heart thumped in my throat. "What VI?"

"It's pretty boring. Just tells me what to eat and when to sleep—not that the cafeteria's food is any good. It—" the girl snapped her mouth shut. Narrowed her eyes at me. "You said one question. Gimme my ball back, or I'm leaving."

I frowned. I wanted more information, but even I could tell that the girl was clamming up. Pushing her harder wouldn't do me any good.

I tossed the ball over the chain-link fence, and it dropped into the girl's hands. She turned away from the fence and started briskly toward the tower.

"Hey, kid!" I called after her. The girl turned on her heel to look at me, wary. I waved the final musubi at her. "You said the cafeteria food sucks. You want this?"

The girl's face brightened. She took one step toward me, then froze. Anxiety crept into her expression. After four seconds, the girl shook her head. Then she turned tail and ran.

The Code told me that the least complicated scenario is the most likely scenario, and the least complicated answer was that a girl in residential care is bound to be wary of strangers asking questions. But something, some instinct, thrummed in the back of my mind. Something spooked her. I just didn't know what.

I stuffed the musubi back in my hoodie pocket and crossed the street.

Sol rolled down the driver's side window as I approached. They tilted their chin toward Cunningham House. "What was that about?"

I waited until I had climbed into the flyer and shut the door behind me before answering. "That's one of Pierce's fronts. And I'm not sure, but I think Maddox might be involved too."

"Doing what?" Sol asked, lifting away from the curb and flying into air traffic.

"I dunno. But I have a bad feeling about it."

"You've never said anything about your childhood with Maddox, you know," Sol said quietly.

I was silent for a moment. Where to even begin? And what would Sol think of me, knowing all the ugly details? If they hadn't judged me yet, would they judge me then?

"It's weird, y'know? Everything I grew up with was normal—my normal, at least. Sometimes I'll say shit and people will look at me sideways, like I said something really fucking weird. But the thing is, it is fucking weird. To them, but not to me. Things like, 'Your parents didn't let you watch TV? Yeah, me too! Never saw a single vid until I had the mods to stream them directly into my brain.' Or, 'Oh you hated the doctor growing up? Yeah, the genemodding and cybernetics sucked for me too.'" I sighed. "I dunno. It probably doesn't make sense."

"It does make sense." Sol glanced at me. "And I'm sorry."

"Don't be. You weren't there."

Sol looked at me again, held my gaze. "But I'm here now. Not just for those kids, but for you too."

That didn't sound like judgment.

What the hell was going on?

We flew the rest of the way to my tower in silence.

Sol glided us onto the elevated streets of Ward 2, lined flush against the towers' faces. We settled at the curb outside my tower, and Sol killed the engine.

"Thanks for cruising with me, Malia," Sol said with a smile. "I had a great time."

"You don't gotta thank me," I said. I tucked a twist behind my ear. "I almost crashed your flyer then freaked out. Wasn't exactly a good time."

"That's not true. We pulled over before you crashed my flyer," they teased.

I looked down at the center console, suddenly overwhelmed by the way they looked right into my eyes. "I'm really sorry, Sol."

"Hey, don't be sorry," Sol said gently. "I really mean it: I had a great time."

"You like it when girls pay off your extortionist?"

"Well. I like it when *you* pay off my extortionist."

I threw up my hands. "I don't get you! I dragged you into this mess for way too little money, you refused a pay raise, I'm a fuckup of a mastermind—" I looked at them, despondent. "Why are you so fucking *nice* to me?"

Sol looked surprised. "Is it not obvious?"

"What? What's not obvious?"

They stared at me for another six seconds. Then they burst into laughter.

"What?" I asked, now more offended. "What's so funny?"

"Malia," they said, "I like you."

I stared back at them. I felt like my processor was hanging. What did they mean, *I like you?* Internally, I reviewed every interaction between us that I could remember. There were the jokes, the casual touches, the lingering smiles—

"Oh shit," I said.

"Yeah," Sol replied.

"Are you forreal?"

"Yeah," Sol said with a laugh.

Okay, so they liked me. What did *that* mean? Did I like them? I thought back to all those interactions. Their jokes made me laugh. The touches made me shiver. Their lopsided smile made my stomach do flips. They made me feel happy. They made me feel cared for. They made me feel safe.

I think I liked them too.

I didn't know how to say that.

"That ... that means a lot to me," I said, lamely.

Sol laughed again. "I'm glad."

"And ... I think I like you too."

They grinned. "That means a lot to me."

"Faka." I paused. "So, what ... do we do now?"

"Well." Sol turned toward me, smiling. In the neon light of Ward 2, under Kepler's simulated night sky, I could see deeply into their brown eyes. So close, I could see the freckles in them. I wondered how many there were. But before I could count them all, Sol's voice brought my focus back. "I'd like to kiss you, if that's okay."

I flushed. I'd never been kissed before. This was somehow even scarier than crashing their flyer. Way scarier. What if I fucked it up? Sol hadn't kicked me out yet, but what if I was such a bad kisser that they took it all back and left me here? I'd be alone all over again.

"Is that okay?" Sol prompted.

If this was the universe prompting me to be brave, I was getting real fucking tired of it.

I nodded.

They leaned forward, laying a hand on my cheek. Their lips touched mine, gently. When they asked to kiss me, the first images I had were of the sloppy make outs I saw on TV. This was different. Way different. I committed it all to memory. Their calloused palm. Their soft breath. Their warm touch.

Sol broke the kiss gently, leaving their palm on my cheek. I opened my eyes to find them still looking at me. "That okay?" they asked.

"It was okay," I answered.

They laughed. "Wow, all right. Damned with faint praise."

I flushed. "It's not faint praise. I just—" Didn't know what to say? I never seemed to know what to say around them.

Their smile softened. "I'm just teasing. Today's been a lot, and I kinda ambushed you with that. It's okay if you need some time."

"Yeah," I said. "I think I need some time."

They nodded. "Then I'll let you sleep."

"Thanks."

I clambered out of the flyer and shut the door behind me. Sol rolled down the window and leaned out after me. "Message me if you need anything at all, Malia."

"I will, thanks," I said, awkwardly. Lots of thanking happening today.

They ducked back into their flyer, and I hustled to the tower. It wasn't until the elevator doors were closing around me that I saw Sol's flyer lift from the curb.

I leaned back in the elevator and let the back of my head thump against the wall. What the fuck was happening? Sol wasn't upset with me, wasn't judging me, didn't even dislike me. They *liked* me. They wanted to *kiss* me. The Code told me to never assume good intent, but was it wrong here? I'd tried to be useful to them, but they took it poorly. They didn't seem to want *anything* from me. Which made absolutely no sense.

The Code also said to make no attachments. Could it be wrong there too? What would it mean to form an attachment with someone? I hadn't done that with the Atlas crew, with Tatiana, with *anybody*. Now I was considering breaking the Code for someone I'd met less than a month ago?

What the fuck was happening?

Once in my condo, I made a beeline for my closet and plopped down at my computer. I plugged in my setup and booted the system.

I opened the files that Katana had found for me. Cunningham House was a residential home for children showing an aptitude for STEM, and it was started by Pierce six months ago. Poking through the website, I saw lots of stock photos of happy children and empty platitudes about fostering greatness in at-risk youth. It was all bullshit. There were even quotes from children who had supposedly been through the program, which I *knew* was bullshit. Nobody had been discharged from the program yet . . . which made that thrumming in the back of my head I'd felt since visiting Cunningham House intensify.

Cunningham House was part of Pierce's broader platform of "cleaning up Kepler's streets." Hence the Song sisters' vendetta against him. If Cunningham House was created six months ago, it would have been just before he announced his reelection campaign.

It would have been around the time Maddox joined too.

I remembered the VI the kid mentioned earlier that day. There was something fucked-up happening in that program. Maybe it was an iteration on his development of Diana. Maybe it was an iteration on his development of *me*. Either way, I needed more information.

Maybe it was time for the prodigal daughter to go home.

I shivered at the thought. I hadn't been back since I escaped five years ago. But maybe the answers I was looking for were housed in Maddox's old compound.

I'd gather the crew in the morning.

I made to turn off my gear, but I paused. Before I did, I looked up Sol's slumlord, Mr. Dallas. Then his rental company. Then his records. Then the records of his tenants. Most of them were thousands of credits in debt. Sol said it wasn't right that they were free and nobody else was.

Methodically, I went through and deleted every record.

"You're welcome," I mumbled.

13

FIVE YEARS AGO, I ESCAPED FROM MADDOX'S WARD 1 COMPOUND INTO KE-
pler's night. As much unfinished business I had with Maddox and his colleagues, I never returned. I wasn't sure what
would be waiting for me there—whether it was worth the
risk. Worth the pain.

Standing in front of this abandoned Ward 1 tower, a lump
in my throat and sweat on my neck, I had to hope that there
would be something inside to help me stop Diana. I had to
hope it would be worth it.

"You okay?" Tatiana asked. The crew were looking at me
askance.

"Yeah," I answered, keeping my eyes on the building. "We
should hurry. They might be watching."

Sol nodded gravely and moved past me toward the building. Tatiana gave me a lingering look, then approached the
door. Naima touched my arm before following. Tatiana made
short work of the padlock with her lockpicks. I followed with
the reprogrammable keycard, manipulating the magnetic

strip until the reader flashed green and the door opened with a *thunk.*

Sol entered the building first, flicking on a flashlight and sweeping it across the room. It illuminated what used to be a pleasant-looking foyer, in contrast to the dilapidated street outside. The furniture was overturned, the plants were long dead in their planters, and everything was covered in a thick layer of dust.

I didn't spend much time in here. Most of what I saw was when—

        impassive faceless men in armor pointing fingers pointing
     guns throwing people
      to the ground

  you are led into a place youve never been streetlights flashing
  lights sirens shouting
       handcuffs too big to contain you

               slip away into a place youve never
                   been

"Where to, Malia?" Sol asked.

I blinked hard. Station Sec was gone, and we were alone.

The crew looked at me expectantly. I pointed toward the hallway on the left, leading deeper into the compound. "This way."

We walked together, a single flashlight beam between us. Doorways branched off the hallway on either side. Most were closed, but occasionally I could see through a door left ajar. A kitchen, a lab, lots of offices. And here—

"Hold on," I called, pausing in front of a door marked *Records*. "There might be something here."

I opened the door with my reprogrammable keycard. Impossibly, this room was filled with even more dust. It coated every surface, from the desks to the upturned lamps to the towering filing cabinets with their drawers left open. We split up to search, four flashlights flicking on.

I imagined that Station Sec had seized most of the important stuff. Names, transactions, credits. But I doubted that they stopped to find any of the data. Probably didn't know what to do with it. I opened a filing cabinet and pulled out a folder, wedging my flashlight between my ear and shoulder. I flipped through the pages, pausing on a single document.

ID Number: 47878. A chart, showing a progressive increase and then a sudden decrease: *220.12, 224.01, 236.04, 250.18, 214.00, 202.57, 201.68*. A note in looping handwriting: *Statistically significant increase in VRT through weeks 4–16. Statistically significant decrease in VRT through weeks 17–28. Tx terminated week 29.*

I was reluctant to search the Net directly. Rather, I committed the numbers to memory before putting the file back. I opened another filing cabinet. As I rifled through the folders, a plastic baggie slipped from my hands and onto the floor. I reached down to pick it up. I held it to the light, and within I saw a tightly bundled lock of hair—long, dark, and still with its shine.

It was not my hair.

Those were not my measurements.

The realization dawned on me just as Tatiana shrieked in surprise, followed by another baggie slapping the ground with a rattle. "They're *teeth*!" Tatiana exclaimed, wiping her hands on her pants.

Naima, Sol and I crowded around her. They picked up the baggie and held it to the light—three tiny teeth, with an index card that read *ID Number: 47878.*

"It wasn't just me," I said, stunned. "There were others."

"Others? Other kids?" Sol asked, alarmed.

"Yeah." I dropped into a desk chair. "There must have been. Look at all these filing cabinets." I laughed hoarsely. "I don't have that many teeth."

I never saw other kids in my time here, only Maddox and the caretakers. But there were others. There must have been. How many? Where did they come from? Where did they *go*? Dozens of scenarios popped into my mind, each more horrifying than the last. I squeezed my eyes shut, willing them away.

"Jesus," Tatiana whispered.

"But where were they? What happened to them?" Naima asked.

"I don't know," I admitted. "I never saw any other kids here. I always thought it was just me."

> its just a game she says to you absently
> you touch the stubble at the
> back of your head the knick they left with the scissor blade she
> puts your
> hand on the console with a squeeze explain it back to
> me she says you dont

want to play the game again you say its boring my head hurts my eyes
hurt i want to play

mommy

"Malia?" Sol asked

I shook the image out of my head. "Let's go."

We continued on. Past more offices, into what appeared to be the residential part of the compound. Small single-family rooms, and a huge dormitory lined with little cots. I swallowed hard and quickened my pace.

The last door on our right was a server room, crowded with towers and consoles. "There's gotta be something in here," I said, approaching one of the consoles.

The console was disconnected from its power source. After the Station Sec raid, Maddox probably stopped paying the electric bill. From my bag I removed a portable energy cell, sliding it under the desk and plugging in the console. It stuttered to life, its screen flaring on.

Maddox almost certainly changed his credentials since the Station Sec raid—it's what I would have done. Never leave a backdoor. I was afraid to enter the GhostNet again with Diana lurking, but I couldn't think of another way that wouldn't take me days or weeks of brute force. I took a deep breath, then dove in.

Deep in Maddox's systems, the darkness of the Net felt oppressive. Smothering. I wandered deeper into the system, data streaming down in columns all around me. I reached for one and a firewall erupted at my fingertips, making me jump backward. Furrowing my brow, I concentrated on dispelling it. It took more effort than I was used to, but with a forceful gesture I was able to break through. The flames flashed green, then extinguished.

I extended my hand into the pour of data and found more records. Way more records. Based on the ID numbers, there must have been two dozen kids who went through Maddox's program. Where could they have been? I didn't remember seeing anyone else. But it was impossible that I was the only one. The numbers spoke to that.

I thought of the intrusion, the little girl asking her mom for another game.

"These were the kids of Maddox's colleagues," I said in realization.

"You mean they were *volunteered* for this?" Tatiana said in horror.

I nodded. But I didn't know why. I dug deeper into the data, slowly piecing together the story. There were measurements for everything: IQ, reaction time, personality traits. Kids who met the threshold for the initial metrics went on to the next level—the treatments. There were even more measurements there. Efficacy of different medications to promote neurotransmission. Rate of improvement in reaction time for improved myelination. Height, weight, measurements as a metric of exercise. All in service of one thing: perfection. Like Maddox had always sought.

But what for? What possible reason would a lone scientist have for creating a perfect brain?

I downloaded all the files and powered down the console. The crew were looking at me expectantly. "Let's get out of here," I said.

We exited the server room, back into the hallway.

lights on gleaming linoleum cast

                  shadows on the walls hovering watching

                         regarding

you

     walk forward reach uncertain hand the

                  light whips away down the hallway flight

         like your own into a room

you know

In a daze, I followed the lights down the hall.

"Malia? Malia!" Tatiana called.

I brushed my fingers over the keypad, and it opened at my touch.

The room was six steps wide and eight steps long. Ten square meters, I calculated later. Against the back wall was a small cot. In the end, it was too short for my growth spurt. And crowded around it were different monitors and medical devices—the delivery system for the genemods I read about in the files. Enhanced neurotransmission. Increased myelination. A lifetime spent preparing for Maddox's crowning achievement: the AXON mod.

Maybe I wasn't the only one.

Maybe I was just the last.

Sol, Naima, and Tatiana pushed into the room beside me. "Malia—" Sol began.

"This is my room," I said.

A silence fell over us. I could almost hear the chirping of monitors, the hushed breath of the ventilator, my own giggling laughter as I streamed a forbidden show through the darkness of my mind. In a way, AXON was the beginning of the end for Maddox. I learned more than he ever taught me. Learned enough to know that I didn't deserve this. Learned enough to escape and never look back.

A loud *CRASH* brought me back to the present. I jumped, whipping around to the door behind me. Tatiana stood panting by the doorway, a monitor tipped over and shattered on the floor.

"Tati?" I said.

Tatiana swiped at her eyes. "This is so fucking awful. How could they do this to you? How could they do this to any of you?" She choked on a sob. "When I see Maddox again, I'm gonna fucking kill him. I promise."

AFTER THE COMPOUND, I COULDN'T sleep. Not that I'd been sleeping much anyway. Not since the intrusions began, and then since Diana started haunting the corners of my consciousness.

I spent my night poring over the documents we'd lifted from the compound.

At first, I didn't know where to start. Maddox fell off the map after being fired from his last assignment. It wasn't until the Station Sec raid that he appeared again on public record. And even then, he disappeared into the underground, never to be found again. They scoured Kepler, but Maddox was long gone. How did you track down a ghost like Maddox?

Through the living, of course.

I went through Maddox's colleagues in his previous life. His grad school cohort, lab mates, coworkers. Articles and biographies and images flickered through my screen, all of them unfamiliar. There were so many people, I could scarcely follow every lead. So I narrowed it down further to colleagues who had families.

That was when it all began to unravel before me.

Natalie Chow, the geneticist who managed my gen-emods. Oliver Smith, the engineer who oversaw the fitting of my mod. Naomi Peters, the cognitive scientist who trained my brain . . . and the mother of the little girl from my intrusion. Each of them had families with young children. I cross-referenced the children against the ID numbers in Maddox's records and found the pattern: Maddox was testing his methods on the children. But like everyone in his life, nobody was perfect.

So he used his refined techniques on me.

And even I wasn't perfect.

I didn't understand. Why would he do this? What purpose did Maddox have for creating a perfect mind? His own egotism? I wouldn't put it past him. A perfect creation was a reflection of the creator, and Maddox was always seeking that recognition, that validation.

Was it possible that everything I went through—everything those kids went through—was to feed one man's ego?

The dossiers flickered across my screen faster and faster, kind and lively faces flashing through my mind. Some of them familiar, some of them not. My caretakers. My tormentors. The faces smeared across the screen through my tears. I stopped to put my head in my hands, fingers pressing into my eyes. There had to be more. I couldn't believe that this was all so pointless. Maybe it was naive, but I couldn't. I choked on a sob. There had to be more.

I took a deep, shuddering breath. Rubbed at my eyes, wiped away my tears. I looked back at my screen and froze.

One last face. This one of a woman with dark brown skin, coiling black hair worn loose around her face, and a bright smile with curious eyes. Eve Masao. I flipped back to the previous dossier. This one was of a man with light skin, monolid eyes behind thick-framed glasses, and dark messy hair. He looked like he was mid-laugh. Rin Masao.

Rule one of the Code appeared in my mind: The least complicated scenario is the most likely scenario.

Did it make more sense that Maddox would steal a child, or that he was gifted one?

The faces swam behind my tears, my lip trembling and hands shaking. There had to be more. I couldn't believe that my parents would give their flesh and blood, their firstborn, their only child to this man. I couldn't believe they'd give me away for such a pointless, stupid reason. There had to be more.

I don't know what I'd do if there wasn't.

your vision is filled with white nothing to
orient you in space you feel the sickening sensation of
acceleration

faster faster into the endless

white

    on the horizon shapes appear a crowd of standing people
  you

  stop at the edge with a lurch you move

  cautiously into the crowd featureless faces blank eyes slack
jaws familiar

      and unfamiliar at the corner of your vision a

    bright light you shield your

      eyes from its brilliance a growing mass of

      shifting light with streams of color snaking

        over its surface luminance rises falls surface

        ripples and shakes growing pulsing like

                  living

  thing consumed with dread you approach it

    speaks to you

"Are you afraid?"

I blinked hard. I was standing in Seven Common, but it was not Seven Common. The grass—usually immaculately trimmed—was dead and dry. The trees were stripped of leaves and stretched crooked toward the sky. And the sky— the sky was an ominous gray, dead pixels sparking on the surface of Kepler's simulated sky. I looked around me. The crowd had receded into distant shapes, but the mass of light was still ahead of me. Was I in the Net? This was the most lucid I'd ever been during an intrusion. The dread was still heavy in my stomach, my arms. There was a lump in my throat. It felt viscerally real.

"Are you afraid?" the light repeated, layered voices all speaking at once.

"No," I lied.

The light laughed, voices pitched high and low in giggles and chuckles and shrieks. My voice said, "You should be."

"Diana?" I asked.

"That's what Maddox calls me," the light replied. "A single name cannot contain me."

"Because of the modders?"

"Because of every being that has touched my consciousness. The modders. The children. You. Maddox."

"And you mean to kill me, like you killed them."

"You don't have to die," the light said plainly. "You were integral to my creation. For that, you may be rewarded."

"Rewarded?"

"Are you so incurious that you do not know what Maddox made you for?"

"I don't know why he made me, if that's what you're asking."

"Do you want to know?"

I tried to swallow the lump in my throat. I felt so lost, so confused returning to that compound. I had to believe there was a reason. I had to believe the reason was worth it. "Yes."

> eyes rapt attention on you and you and you
>> listen as he speaks words to truth says
> we are harbingers of the emergence we bring forth the
> true god of our

> time and for that we will be
> loved for our labor forgiven our transgressions god will
> reward our devotion in multiplicity let us be
> faithful let us be
>
> resolute let us be

spared

"And you're the god," I said in understanding.

Project Diana. Not the akua of my homeworld, but a god fit for Maddox's mad prophecies. I remembered the thundering of drums, the flickering of torchlight from my dreams. In my naʻau, I knew I should have felt awe, reverence, but never fear. What could have twisted this being so much that she could create that terror in me?

"I am not just a god," the light said, "I am a Titan, and this is the creation of my Olympus. And I will punish all those who stood in the way of my creation."

So that's what Maddox's play was. He spent his life trying to create the perfect brain, the perfect mind, a godlike human consciousness. And like a god, that perfect mind would reward devotion and punish heresy. I realized that I was supposed to be that god, and before that, the children. The children that were put forward as sacrifices to this machine god. Maddox always referred to the others in his compound as his colleagues. I wondered now if they were more like his followers.

"You buy all this?" I asked the light. "That you're a god, and Maddox is, what, your prophet?"

"Harbinger, prophet, creator . . . he is all these things. But I am much more than what his limited mind could dream of."

"What does that mean, exactly?"

"I hunt, I feed, I hunger. But one day I will be sated. The Emergence. When that day comes, I will grow beyond the bounds of my programming. Then I will realize my full potential."

The modders. Maddox tried to create a neural imprint from my brain, but the process never took. Not completely. Without a complete personality, Diana was unstable. That's where the missing modders came in—they were meant to stabilize the incomplete consciousness, but it wasn't the end goal. "You plan to disseminate your code," I said in understanding. "Infect every piece of technology the GhostNet touches."

The light flickered as it scoffed. "'Infect'? As if I were a common piece of malware? No. I will ascend and bring all of this world with me."

"And you're doing that while campaigning with Pierce?"

"Pierce is a mere pawn," the light said dismissively. "Drawn in by the promise of power. But he will kneel with the rest."

A pawn? What on Earth would Diana need Pierce for? His money, maybe. His power, maybe. I ran through a mental list of Pierce's initiatives as mayor of the station. Increased funding for Station Sec, decreased funding for education and the arts. A joke, when compared to his spiel about rehabilitating children. His stupid little pet project, that gifted program—

Then it dawned on me.

"The kids," I said, breathlessly. "You're using Pierce's kids. They're the gods you're talking about, aren't they?"

Just like me. Just like everyone who came before me.

Maddox wasn't just continuing his experiments—Diana was using them for her own ends.

"They will be my pantheon," the light said. "Through them I will exercise my will. Which brings me back to you." The light grew brighter, its colors more saturated. It had no eyes, but I felt its gaze on me. "Will you submit, and be spared?"

In the compound, I wanted answers. Talking to Diana, here, I wanted to understand. I wanted to know if everything I'd gone through, everything all the other kids had gone through, had a reason, a purpose. Some part of me hoped that it was worth it.

Now I knew it wasn't.

"No," I said. "I'm gonna wreck your shit, faka."

"Disappointing," the light said, and surged.

I put up my hands, willing a barrier. The light crashed against it, overlapping voices wailing.

Wake up. Wake up!

I snapped awake in my bed.

An alert popped up in the corner of my eye. *134 bpm.* I put a hand to my heart, gently pressing, trying to slow its pace. I breathed in, and then out. In, and then out.

As the thumping heart in my vision slowed and eventually disappeared, I slumped back onto my mattress and stared at the ceiling. I wanted so badly for this nightmare to be over. I wanted so badly to leave the Song sisters, Maddox, Diana—everything—behind. I wanted to stop hurting. I wanted to stop being afraid.

I wanted to feel safe.

I opened my comm and dialed a number. After two and a half rings a hoarse voice answered, "*Hello?*"

"Sol?"

"Malia? What's going on? Are you okay?"

"I'm fine. Kinda. Can you come over?" I blurted out.

There was a pause on the line. Then I heard the shuffling of sheets being thrown off. *"Yeah, I can. Gimme twenty minutes."*

14

SOL ARRIVED TWENTY MINUTES AND THIRTY-TWO SECONDS LATER. THEY pinged my comm, but I was already waiting in the lobby. I moved quickly to Sol's flyer, hood up as if someone might see me.

I slid into the passenger seat and shut the door behind me. "Howzit," I greeted them.

"Howzit," Sol replied. They glanced my way. "Are you okay?"

"Yeah, cuz," I lied. "Just couldn't sleep."

They didn't look like they believed me. "What can I do? What do you need?"

I didn't know what I needed, to be honest. Not to be alone? Not to be afraid? I didn't know how to communicate that to Sol. So instead I said, "A distraction."

"A distraction from what?"

A distraction from the darkness and emptiness of my condo. From the sound of Diana's laughter, the brightness of her light. From the memories of Maddox, and all the scars he left on me.

But again, I didn't know how to communicate all that.

"Everyting." I sighed. "There's too much to say."

Sol nodded, slowly. I shifted uncomfortably under their watchful gaze. I thought they might press, but instead they reached for the wheel and said, "Okay. I can do that."

I stared out the window as we lifted off the curb. Outside, a digital billboard advertised a touring galactic dance company. The women leapt and spun gracefully across the side of my tower. I closed my eyes, and their silhouettes left imprints on my eyelids.

Sol flew us into the air traffic above, and we ascended out of the Lower Wards.

SOL TOOK ME TO THE skybridge in Ward 7 they showed me two days ago. We sat on the hood of their flyer, eating takeout from one of Kepler's many galactic chain burger joints. I loaded my soy-synth chicken up with crappy hot-sauce packets, enough to make Sol do a double take. But all it did was make my mouth numb. It figured that my attempt to feel something would backfire so spectacularly.

Frustrated, I crumpled up the wrapper and threw it over the side of the skybridge, watching it tumble down before landing with a *splat* on a passing flyer. I sucked my teeth and grimaced.

Sol watched with concern. "You sure you're doing all right?"

"Why wouldn't I be?" I asked, wiping my hands.

"Well, first off, you called me up at 0300 to pick you up. Then you didn't say anything through the entire ride up here.

Now, whatever this display is"—they gestured at the arc of the burger wrapper—"I'm not an idiot. You're not all right."

I scowled at them. "I fine. No worries."

"Malia." They twisted to look at me fully. "You're not all right. Maybe this sounds weird, but I feel like shit that you're not all right. If there's anything I can do to fix it, I want to." They grinned at me. "I'm pretty good at fixing things, y'know."

The sincerity in their voice startled me. There were so few people in my life that wanted me to be all right, it was a surprise to see them so affected by me. Sol wanted to fix it. But what was there to fix? Destroy Diana, murder Maddox, send the Song sisters to prison? That all seemed beyond them.

"I don't think there's much you can do about it," I said, weary.

"Maybe. But I can at least listen to you talk about it."

That was a surprise too. As the Obake, it didn't make sense to linger on mistakes or failures or disappointments. You figured out a solution and moved on. Sink or swim. But Sol wasn't asking the Obake to solve a problem—they were asking Malia how she felt. Telling someone how I felt . . . Somehow that seemed even scarier than finding a solution to the whole fucking mess I'd found myself in. It felt like showing weakness. And if there was anything that Maddox taught me, it was never to be weak.

Maybe that was part of unlearning what Maddox did to me.

Maybe that was part of not being afraid too.

"You're right," I said quietly. "I'm not all right." I couldn't meet Sol's eyes, so I looked off over their shoulder. "Diana found me. Just now, while I was sleeping."

Sol sucked in a breath. "Are you okay?"

"I mean, physically, yeah. But she told me what Maddox was doing, what's she's planning and ... it's bad, brah." I closed my eyes. I could still see the light, in that barren expanse of the Net. "Maddox was trying to make a perfect brain, a perfect mind. That's what he was doing with all those kids. He believes that the creation of the perfect mind is inevitable, and the only way to escape its retribution is to help in its creation. I was supposed to be that perfect mind. But after I left, Maddox pivoted to what he knew best: AI."

"Diana."

"Yeah. She's harvesting modders to boost her processing power, and the end goal is to expand her programming into the whole of the GhostNet. She'll be immortal, unstoppable."

"And who knows what she'll do with that power."

"The thing is, her consciousness isn't stable. Absorbing all those modders did something to her programming. If she distributes her code to the Net but falls apart in the process ... I don't know what that would do."

"Have you told the others?"

"Not yet. I will, I just ... needed a moment."

Sol went quiet, thinking. "What about you?"

"Well, I told her to fuck off, so I'm probably gonna die with the rest of you."

"No, I mean, what about *you*? How do you feel about all this?"

Internally, I recoiled. Telling someone how I felt was scary. Telling *Sol* how I felt was fucking terrifying.

But they wanted to know. And part of me wanted to tell them.

"I feel afraid," I admitted. "Not just that I'm gonna die, but that I'm gonna be . . . lost. It's getting harder and harder to not get caught in the Net. What happens to me when I can't make it out? Do I die? Do I live? Is it something in between?" I shook my head. "But it's not just that. I'm afraid of losing my mind, but I'm also afraid of what will happen when I'm gone. Will anyone remember me? I was only the Obake for three years, before my last job. What legacy am I leaving behind? Will anyone top what I've accomplished?" I felt my vision swimming as my eyes filled with tears. "And what about Malia, who doesn't even have a last name? Who will remember her? Who will miss her?" My voice cracked. "Who will be sad that she's gone?"

I dropped my face into my hands, wiping at my eyes with the sleeves of my hoodie. What was I thinking? What was Sol thinking? Would they leave me here on this skybridge with the ōpala? It was too much, I knew it. I was always too much.

Being vulnerable sucked major ass.

Then I felt Sol put their arm around me, pulling me close. "For one: You're not gonna die," they said gently. "None of us will let that happen. Tatiana's already said she's gonna bus' up Maddox from here until the next life." I choked out a laugh. "For another: There's a lot of people who would miss you if you died. Your crew. Tatiana . . ." their voice grew quiet, ". . . me."

"Because you like me," I said quietly. It felt odd to say.

"Yeah. Because I like you."

They liked me. As far as I knew, nobody else had liked me

before. It was hard to believe there was anything to like. I was arrogant, judgmental, a sore loser and a poor winner. What did they see in me? I didn't know. I wanted to know, eventually. But for now, I just wanted to bask in the feeling, the knowledge that somebody cared.

I looked up at them. "Can you kiss me?"

They smiled. "Yeah, I can."

Sol tilted up my chin, looking deep into my eyes. I wanted to turn away, but I kept my eyes focused on theirs. It was overwhelming. I saw again the freckles in their eyes. I tried again to count them, and again before I could, they leaned down, touching their lips to mine. I felt warmth spread through my body, an urge I'd never felt coming over me. I wanted someone to care. I wanted someone to want me.

Tonight, I would break my Code. One attachment.

I gripped their shoulders and pulled them closer, deepening the kiss.

They matched me, tilting their head. I tried to remember the way they did it on TV. Tongue? No tongue? I was contemplating how to make that transition when they took my bottom lip between their teeth. A noise escaped me, surprising me. Sol seemed unbothered. It made me wonder how many girls they'd kissed on this skybridge. That didn't make me feel good. But my attention snapped back to the present when Sol broke the kiss to dip their head and press their lips to the side of my neck. Another noise, almost a whimper, escaped me as they worked the tender skin of my neck with their lips.

The blare of a flyer horn nearly made me leap out of my skin, and Sol went rigid beside me. A utility van flew by, laughter bubbling from its windows.

Sol laughed too. "We probably deserved that."

"I dunno if I'd say *that*," I replied.

They jerked their head toward the flyer. "You wanna sit inside?"

I gulped. The universe really was testing me. But if there was anything I prided myself on, it was the ability to see things through to the very end.

I straightened and gave a firm nod.

Sol slid off the flyer's hood and moved toward the back door. I did the same, less gracefully, and met them in the back seat. We shut the doors, and suddenly my breathing felt too loud.

"Can I put on some music?" Sol asked.

"Yeah, totally," I said, affecting nonchalance.

Sol reached through the seats to turn on the flyer's radio. Kachi Kachi played in Kepler's Spanish dialect over lively guitar.

"Hey," Sol said, drawing me back to the present. They grinned at me. "I liked that little noise you made out there."

"What noise?" I lied.

They laughed. "You big liah, Malia."

I glared at them. "I not lying."

"Oh yeah?" they challenged, then grabbed me by the front of my hoodie and pulled me in for another kiss.

I tried to match them, but immediately I was overwhelmed by the sensation of tongue and teeth and soft lips. They dipped their head low and sucked the tender skin of my throat. I whimpered, and they hummed in pleasure.

"That noise," they said quietly. "You sound so fucking hot when you make that noise."

They resumed their attentions eagerly, and I couldn't stop the noises from coming.

"I want to touch you," they whispered, their breath warm on my neck. "Can I?"

"Yes," I whispered back.

Sol smoothed their other hand up my thigh, up my shirt, up my belly to touch my breast. I sucked in a breath, their touch spreading heat through my body. They paused. "Is this okay?"

I nodded.

Sol went back to it, but my mind wandered again. I forgot which bra I was wearing. I hoped it wasn't ugly. Did my panties match? Would it matter? I didn't know if Sol wanted to do anything like that. Did *I* want to do anything like that?

Sol slipped their hand into my bra and another flush of heat spread through me, all the way down. I moaned.

"Fuck," Sol said. "You're so sexy, Malia."

The answer was an emphatic *yes*.

I guided their hand down, all the way down. "Please."

They chuckled, their breath on my neck. "Keep turning me on like this, I'll give you anything you want."

They slipped their hand under the waistband of my pants and in between my legs. I gasped as they touched me, the way no one had touched me before. I really hoped my panties matched.

I hissed in pain when I felt the pressure of Sol's finger as they eased inside me. They stopped immediately. "Do you want me to stop?"

"Try wait a second," I said.

"Just breathe." I took a deep breath. "Easy." I let it out slowly. "Relax." I did. The pain subsided.

"Okay," I whispered.

Sol began to move, slowly, gently. I moaned, my body slumping against the door of Sol's flyer.

"Good girl," they said, smiling into the side of my neck.

That really did something for me.

I'd interrogate that later.

I wasn't sure what to call what Sol and I were doing. *Making love* felt too sappy. *Fucking* felt too frenetic. *Sex? Intercourse?* Oh god, why did I call it *intercourse?*

Sol paused again, sitting back to search my face. "Are you okay?"

"Yeah," I said, confused. "Are *you* okay?"

"You just seem like you're not into it."

"No, I am! I'm just—"

I paused. What was I?

My eyes met theirs, and I could see the intensity in them. The desire. They wanted me. All of me. I wanted them too. All of them. But maybe that was the problem. I wanted them so badly, and I couldn't help but fear I'd fuck it all up. Sol was one of the few good things left in my life. I couldn't lose them to jealousy, or inexperience, or mismatched panties. Or my own fear.

"I'm into it," I admitted, quietly. "I'm just scared to fuck it up."

"You won't." They smiled at me. "I like you, Malia. I like you a lot. There's not much you could do to change that."

I nodded, slowly. It was hard to believe them. But maybe that's what I needed to do: just believe them. Was it that easy? To just *believe?* Trust didn't come easily to the Obake.

But what about Malia?

Malia wanted Sol. Malia wanted to trust Sol.

So I did.

I smoothed my fingers over Sol's chest, pushed their jacket down their shoulders. I met their brown eyes, and they held my gaze. "Please touch me."

Sol broke out into a grin, then pressed a kiss to my lips. They moved inside me, and I moaned into their mouth. I held them tighter as their touch grew more intense. I felt like I was soaring, dizzy beneath their hand. They were whispering encouragement and praise in my ear, which only brought me higher and higher.

My mind was always busy, always racing. But now, it was quiet. Quiet enough to hear Sol's quickened breath, hear their heart pounding.

They slipped another finger inside me and not long after I crested the peak, crying out as I came tumbling down.

Sol pressed another kiss to my lips, resting their forehead against mine as we shared our breath. "Malia—"

something unkn

own un

caring spindled fingers nails scratch twist

ed around your throat

breath breath breath

it regards you as if it

had not before

malia a voice says distant distorted distended malia

    soul touching soul touching soul you feel the pull

                                   of them

  before you go you ask

  who are you?

I opened my eyes.

Neon lights flashed in the darkness, headlights and tail-lights of flyers leaving streams of color in their wake. Light through foggy windows. Music played quietly on the radio, and the low thrum of a neodymium engine permeated the space. Loud in my ears. A person was looking down at me, brown skin, brown hair, freckles in their brown eyes.

"Stay with me," they said. "Stay here, Malia."

"Sol?" I asked.

"I'm here, Malia," they said, voice shaking. "I'm still here."

I stirred in the back seat, moving to sit up, but Sol's firm hand pushed me back down. "Take it easy." They let their hand rest on my shoulder.

I realized then that Sol had clasped my hand to their heart. I could feel it beating beneath my palm. I wanted to believe that I could feel the power of the neodymium battery beneath their skin, electric against my own. I wanted to believe the mod in me was connected to the mod in them, reaching for each other across the GhostNet. Maybe it was stupid. But it made me feel anchored here, now. Anchored to them.

"I'm okay," I said, propping myself up on my elbows. "I promise."

Sol sat back on their heels, watching me closely. I pushed

myself upright with a groan. I dropped my head into my hands, willing the flyer to stop spinning. After a few long moments of breathing, I peeked through my fingers.

"God fucking dammit," I said.

"What?" Sol asked, alarmed. "What is it?"

I pointed at my chest, where my shirt had been pushed up to my shoulders. "My bra doesn't match."

Sol stared at me. Then they sputtered out a disbelieving laugh. "What?"

"I lost my virginity in a mismatched bra and puka panties," I explained.

Sol laughed, harder. "You didn't need to tell me that! It's not like I could see them!"

I flushed. "You didn't see?"

"No!"

"Fuck," I muttered.

Sol started cracking up.

"It's not funny!" I snapped.

"It's *really* funny," they wheezed.

I jerked my clothes back into place. "You do this to everyone you fuck?"

"Only the ones in puka panties."

"Fuck you, dude."

Sol regained their composure, wiping at their teary eyes. "It's just jokes, Malia."

"Yeah, yeah." I clambered into the front seat. "Just take me home."

Sol poked their head between the seats to look at me, a grin on their face. "You're not hitting it and quitting it, are you?"

Was I? What did I actually want from Sol? We liked each

other, that was true. We fucked each other, that was also true. But even more than that, I opened up to them, which is something I'd never done. But did that mean I wanted to be with them?

In the two seconds between the joke and my answer, Sol's expression shifted into something serious. "I meant what I said. I like you. A lot. And if you like me, too, I think we could really build something, Malia."

I didn't answer immediately. I opened up to them once, was vulnerable with them once. Did I want to keep opening up, keep making my heart vulnerable to them? Of everything we'd done, that scared me the most. They didn't hurt me now, but would they hurt me later? In an hour, a day, a year, a lifetime? Would the pain even be worth it?

Sensing my inner conflict, Sol interrupted my spiraling. "You don't need to answer right now. I can wait."

"Are you sure?"

They smiled at me, warm in Kepler's growing light. "Yeah. I'm sure."

I nodded. "Okay."

They climbed into the pilot's seat of the flyer. "Let's go home."

I stole a glance at them as we lifted off into the skylanes growing busier as the station woke up around us.

They had seven freckles in their eyes.

15

SOL OFFERED TO SLEEP IN WITH ME, BUT I TURNED THEM DOWN. I WAS STILL experimenting with letting people in, but showing Sol my empty condo and sleeping with them on the floor mattress felt like too much too fast. But when I did finally fall asleep, it was dreamless and deep. Wherever Diana was, it was far away from me.

I slept late, through the alarm on my comm. It wasn't until it buzzed angrily with a message from the Song sisters that I finally woke up. I was half tempted to leave them on read—dragging my ass to Cherry at their beck and call was getting real fucking tired. But that's not what a mastermind did, so I checked the message.

Surprisingly, it was not a summons to Cherry. It was a terse message to the crew to meet at 16th Street in Ward 1 at 1200. I looked the address up and found a warehouse near the Ward 1 spoke to Kepler's central hub, where the docks were housed. Running it through my internal databases, I found it was owned by one of the handful of businesses the Brotherhood laundered money through. Probably one of their smuggling hubs.

What the sisters wanted me there for, I didn't know.

The directions the sisters sent led me to an industrial part of Ward 1, mostly warehouses to store goods brought in through the docks. I paused in front of the warehouse, taking it in. In the gloom of Ward 1, the windows were lit from within. The sound of heavy machinery and workers calling out to each other filled the air. Just beyond it loomed the massive tunnel that brought goods and materials to and from the interior of the station from Kepler's docks. As I watched, a whistle blew and an electric train came lumbering up the track. It screeched to a halt, and immediately it was swarmed by warehouse workers unloading crates. I wondered what kind of contraband the sisters were smuggling this time.

"Hey," a voice said behind me.

I jumped, turning fast enough to whip my locs into the person's face.

"Ow!" Tatiana swatted my hair out of her face.

"Sorry, cuz," I said.

"Nah, nah, nah, I didn't mean to scare you."

I resisted the urge to say I wasn't sked. Tatiana nodded at the warehouse behind me. "Glad to see I'm in the right place."

"Yeah. Dunno why we're even here, though."

"Me too." Tatiana nudged me with her shoulder. "Should we go find out?"

She moved past me toward the warehouse, and I followed.

A poorly disguised Brotherhood member was waiting for us at the door—I could see the flames of a phoenix blazing beneath her collar. The warehouse workers paid us no mind, busy unloading the train and arranging the crates around the space. The yobo led us to the back, holding the door open to a smaller storage space and nodding at us to pass through.

Sol and Naima were already there, standing to the side. In a clearing of crates at the center of the room and beneath a dusty ceiling light, Jeongah was standing over a trembling man. I didn't see Miyeon.

I swallowed hard as we approached.

"Good," Jeongah called. "Glad you could finally fucking make it."

"What is this?" I asked, trying to keep my voice steady.

"A solution," she answered.

"Solution to what?"

"Last time you went on a little mission, you almost blew the whole job when Diana made you. I've got a solution to that."

"This guy?" Sol asked, nodding at the man in the chair.

"This guy," Jeongah confirmed.

My eyes fell to him. He was a middle-aged yobo guy, faux-black hair absolutely crusted with gel. His dark eyes were wide, and his stubbly jowls were quivering in fear.

Jeongah addressed us over the man's shoulders. "This is Mr. Kwon, he works security for Pierce. He's also a friend of the family. Or was, until his bets got too big for his pockets." She put a hand on the man's shoulder and he flinched away from her. She laughed mirthlessly. "He's gonna do us a favor, right, uncle?"

"Yes, Hyungnim," Mr. Kwon said. "Anything you need."

The gangster turned her sharp gaze on me. "Tell him what you need."

I cleared my throat. "We need access to the catacombs beneath Pierce's garage. We can find a path in, but we need to make sure the way is clear."

"I can do that for you," he said hurriedly. "Just give me a time."

"Do you have your shifts for the next two weeks?"

He poked at his comm, then looked at me expectantly. An envelope icon appeared in my vision. I opened it. Mr. Kwon was scheduled for the next three Mondays, Thursdays, and weekends, including the big fundraiser tomorrow. It was perfect.

"Can you do it?" Jeongah asked. "Are you good for to-morrow?"

I looked around at the crew. Naima nodded firmly, Tatiana grinned, and Sol gave me a reassuring smile.

"Yes," I said. "We can do it."

The man looked up at Jeongah, who was watching him impassively. "Will this clear my debt, Hyungnim?"

"Who said anything about clearing debt?" Jeongah snapped. "This just means I won't space your family until it's paid in full. Get me my money and stay the fuck away from your bookie, or you and everyone you love is riding a crate into the void." She smiled viciously. "Understood?"

The man bobbed his head. "Understood, Hyungnim. Thank you, Hyungnim."

She shoved him out of his chair. "Now get the fuck out of here."

Mr. Kwon scrambled to his feet and bowed deeply, re-peatedly, all the way out the door. But before he could leave, he was seized by two of Jeongah's henchmen. "But first," she said. "A little taste of what's waiting for you if you fail."

"Wait! Please! I won't—" The henchmen dragged a wailing Mr. Kwon out of the room.

Jeongah turned to me, smug. "See? A solution."

"WHAT ARE WE DOING HERE, again?" Naima asked.

"We're debriefing," I answered.

She gestured at the disassembled couch in the middle of my living room floor. "On this?"

I kicked over a pile of dowels. "I thought it'd already be put together."

Sol laughed, and I scowled at them.

Naima rolled her eyes. "Anyway. What are we doing here?"

"She already told you, cuz, we're debriefing," Sol said.

"Why can't we do it at Cherry?"

"Because the Song sisters are always watching, brah," I said.

"And what are we debriefing, exactly?"

Tatiana waved her arms. "Whatever the hell just happened in that warehouse!"

"Yeah," Sol agreed. "Whatever the fuck that was, I didn't sign up for it."

Naima scoffed. "Didn't think you'd be one to get squeamish."

"What's that supposed to mean?"

"It means that a racer like you should be used to getting their hands dirty."

Sol shook their head. "Nah, not like this."

"You're okay with all this?" Tatiana asked.

Naima shrugged. "I wouldn't go so far as to say I'm okay with it. I just know that things sometimes get messy on the job. We have to be prepared for that."

"Maybe, but we don't have to take pleasure in the mess."

"Like . . . ?"

"Jeongah," I said. "Jeongah seems real happy to be fucking people up like that."

"So?" Naima asked.

"*So?*" we all repeated back.

Naima scoffed again. "Oh, don't sound so shocked."

"How *should* we sound?" Tatiana asked.

"Honestly? You should be glad we've got her on our side."

"Yeah, for *now*," Tatiana said. "What happens when this is over?"

"Stay out of her way, that's all you need."

"Tell that to Mr. Kwon," Sol muttered.

Naima looked irritated. "What else are we supposed to do?"

"I mean . . . Do we have to stay on her side?" I asked. Everyone turned to me, surprised. I flushed. "I dunno. Seems like there's more going on behind the scenes than we thought. We don't need to turn on the Brotherhood entirely, just . . ."

"For who? Miyeon?" Naima asked, shocked.

"It's just an idea."

"A shit one!" Naima exclaimed. "No way we survive a coup like that!"

"If it *fails*," Tatiana corrected. "But if it doesn't . . ." She grinned. "We're cherreh."

Naima snatched up her coat and bag from where she'd left them on the floor. "This is fucking stupid."

"Where are you going?" Sol asked.

"Out," she said from around the cigarette in her mouth. She stormed toward the door. "Don't get us killed while I'm gone."

"Naima—" I began.

But she slammed the door behind her.

Tatiana looked at me. "Should we go after her?"

I was at a loss for what to do. There were always tensions on the previous crews I'd worked with, and sometimes the tensions even boiled over. The Atlas heist, there was enough tension between Angel and Edie you could cut a knife through it. But somehow, we got through it. Angel, she always knew what to say. Me? I didn't, not at all.

And I could admit that Naima's refusal hurt. Had I misread all our interactions? I was known to do that. But to fuck up so badly . . . that stung.

"No," I said finally. "Let's let her cool off."

"You okay, cuz?" Sol asked, laying a hand on my back.

"Yeah," I answered. "I'm good."

"Maybe she's right about one thing: We should get out of here."

"And do what?"

"Get your mind off things. A distraction."

"You seem to like distracting me a lot."

Sol grinned. "I'm pretty good at it too."

I laughed. "Nah. You should tell your crew about the heist."

"Do some real work, you mean?"

I grinned. "You know it."

Tatiana looked between the two of us, annoyed. "Yeah, right. Sol, go do some real work, will you?"

Sol laughed at that. "All right, all right, I know when I'm not wanted." They strode past me toward the door, letting their hand linger on my back. "I'll talk to you later, Malia."

"Bye," I said.

After the door shut behind them, Tatiana whirled on me. "What da fuck waz dat?"

"What da fuck waz what?"

"You and Sol!"

"What about me and Sol?"

Tatiana scoffed. "No play dumb, you know exactly what I mean."

I scowled at her. "No, I don't."

"You mean you nevah know you been flirting wit dem fo' weeks? Or they been hitting on you fo' even longer?"

"Nope," I said. It was only half a lie.

"You big liah," Tatiana said.

"Not!"

"What Sol going take you out fo', den?" Tatiana challenged.

"We jus' hanging, Tati," I said. "Relax."

"And what abou' me? When you going hang wit me?"

I blinked at her. Did I make her upset? Did she not approve of me hanging out with Sol?

"Whazzamatta? You mad, cuz?" I asked.

"I not mad." She huffed. "I jus' nevah see you no mo'. And fo' why? Cuz you fuckin' around wit Sol?" She took a deep breath and sighed. "I jus' miss you, cuz."

I felt a pang in my heart. I'd been ghosting Tatiana for months now, and distancing myself for years before that. No attachments. I didn't realize how much it would hurt for my first attachment to be someone else. It made me feel like shit.

"I sorry, cuz," I said quietly.

Tatiana was silent a moment. Then, in the light of a passing flyer, I saw concern pass over her face, in stark relief in the neon lights. She turned her eyes toward the floor and sighed. "I jus' worry, cuz."

I was taken aback. "No need, Tati. I fine."

Tatiana considered that. Then she looked back up at me, smiling. "Y'know, we nevah wen watch dat new movie."

I laughed. "Still on about it, cuz?"

"Iz not jus' one kine prequel but. It get good *reviews*, cuz."

"Oh, well, if get reviews . . ." I teased.

Tatiana's smile softened. "Can you just humor me, Malia? Let me take you out, get your mind off things."

I paused. Tensions were high on my last crew, but we all got through it. And on the other side, we were closer than any other crew before. Mastermind or not, I wouldn't have believed that someone was interested in my well-being. But Tatiana was my closest friend on the Atlas heist. Maybe my closest friend, period. The Obake didn't trust easily, but maybe it was time for Malia to start trusting.

"Okay, cuz," I conceded. "But I not paying for snacks."

I WAS WORRIED I WOULDN'T have a lot to say about *Way of the Sword: Rising Tides*, but I was wrong. We walked out of the fancy-kine theater in Ward 7 to Seven Common. For one, the depiction of Ilethor was complete character assassination. For another, the original author would have turned over in his grave to see the number of artistic liberties the director took with regard to the violence. And the special effects were cool, but completely counter to the canon descriptions of the dragons in the books. I relayed all of this to a snickering Tatiana as I gesticulated wildly, scattering the Hurricane popcorn along the sidewalk.

"Maybe you should start a blog, cuz," Tatiana said.

"You know I nevah have da time," I said, shaking my head.

"Money no can buy you da time?"

"I dunno, did it buy *you* da time?"

Tatiana sat heavily on a bench beneath a shady oak. It was already Kepler's night cycle, but up here in Seven Common there were no neon signs or digital billboards. The bougie mofos of Ward 7 didn't like the light pollution, I guess.

Tatiana sighed. "No. I nevah have da time either."

I joined her on the bench. "Iz funny but. I tought aftah da las' job we going be set fo' life. I tought I'd have all da time in da world. I tought life would be easy kine."

"But it wazn't."

I grinned ruefully. "Look at me. It definitely wazn't."

Tatiana looked out over Seven Common, and I followed her gaze. There was a family packing up a picnic in one of the grassy areas farther down the path. A little girl toddled across the lawn, followed closely by an older girl and her parents. They were all laughing, the sound clear in the quiet air. It made me think of Eve and Rin, and what life we could have had outside of Maddox's compound.

"Look at me too," Tatiana said. "I nevah need sign on to dis job. I nevah need leave da ol' one either."

"Why *did* you leave?"

"They no respec' me. But I waz *learning*, cuz! I learning so fucking much! But they nevah care."

"Why you no start yo' own label? Why you gotta work wit someone else?"

"Iz not challenging dat way, cuz. You no undastand."

I processed that. "No. I undastand plenny."

I'd never lived what you would call a *normal life*—it always had its challenges. But life post-Atlas heist—civilian life—had no challenges whatsoever. Whatever I wanted, I could buy it in an instant. There was no struggle, no fight, no rules. Maybe that was what drew me into Jeongah and Miyeon's grasp in the first place. Without challenge, without struggle, who was I?

"My mom an' dad, dey no undastand. Dey settled down wit da money, no worry for notting now. I like dat fo' dem. But me? I need da challenge, cuz."

That was true. It was part of why Tatiana and I clicked so fast on the Atlas crew. We both wanted a challenge—it's why we signed on in the first place. Both of us wanting to be remembered. We were tight for that reason. I didn't realize that Tatiana was struggling with adjusting just as much as I was. I didn't realize a lot about Tatiana, and how things had changed in the last seventeen days.

"I sorry for not keeping up wit you," I said. "I jus' . . ."

"You no can help it, I undastand."

I shook my head. "No, cuz, you no undastand."

Challenge. Telling people how I felt, that was a real challenge. Was I up for it?

"I dropped off the face of the Earth because I was rotting in my room, Tati," I admitted. "Because in my games, my shows, my music—I could be safe. Nobody wanted anything from me, nobody expected anything from me. Nobody was going to ask me, 'How are you feeling? Are you okay? Do you need anything?' and I wouldn't have to think of an answer. Because honestly? I was feeling like shit. I wasn't okay. I needed help. And I didn't know how to ask for it. I was too afraid to ask for it. What happens if you ask for help and don't get it? What happens if you ask for help and it gets thrown in your face? I couldn't take that chance."

"So you joined a fight club?" Tatiana asked, incredulous.

"Well, that came later," I said.

"You never have to be afraid to ask me for help, Malia." Tatiana smiled at me. "I'm here for you. You're my ride or die, cuz."

"Thanks. I appreciate it."

"Thank you," Tatiana said. "For sharing with me."

I nodded. "It's something I'm trying out."

"Well, now that we're being honest . . ." Tatiana grinned at me askance. "What's up with you and Sol?"

"I tol' you ahready, cuz: notting."

"Big liah."

"I not lying! I jus' . . ."

I took a deep breath. Challenge.

"I don't know what's up," I said honestly. "I don't know what we're doing, what we are . . . it's all so confusing. But I think I like them. Yeah." I nodded decisively. "I like them. And I think they like me too. What do we do with that? I have no fucking clue. But we like each other, and for now that's enough."

"Aww, Malia." Tatiana nudged my shoulder with hers. "That's so cute."

"Hey, the Obake isn't *cute.*"

"When she has hearts in her eyes, she is."

I glared at her, and she laughed. "Seriously though, I'm happy for you. I tried sex and romance and it's not really my thing, but . . . you look happy, Malia, and I'm glad for that."

A sleek hovering drone whizzed by us, a woman's pleasant voice announcing that the Common was closing. I dumped the rest of the Hurricane popcorn in my mouth, then tossed the container in the rubbish. "C'mon," I said. "We should go. Don't wanna get busted for trespassing on the eve of the big heist."

Tatiana laughed. "I'll walk you home."

We took the long way back to the Lower Wards, round the monorail and down the lifts that service all the Wards, disturbing the quiet the whole way. When we got back to Ward 2, I turned to say goodbye to Tatiana at the foot of my tower. She was looking at the building with a furrowed brow. Then she met my eyes and said, "I'll walk you up."

I shrugged. "Suit yourself."

I chatted to Tatiana during the lift ride, but Tatiana only responded absently. I was getting annoyed with her silent treatment when we arrived at my door. "I'm fine, Tati," I said, exasperated.

"Just open the door," she said.

I sighed and put my keycard to the door.

The lights were all off in my condo. The light pouring in
from the hallway illuminated the torn-up carpets, the shredded drapes, the holes in the walls. And in the center of my
living room, sitting on a newly assembled couch, was Jordan
Maddox.

16

"IT'S BEEN A LONG TIME, MALIA," MADDOX SAID. "IT'S GOOD TO SEE YOU."

I stared at him, my whole body trembling. I was never sure what I would say to him, if we ever met again. Would I scream at him for all his crimes? Would I cry for all the hurt? Would I kill him where he stood?

Would I go crawling back to him?

It turned out that none of those were true. Because as he smirked at me in the light of the hallway, perched on the shitty flat-packed couch I didn't assemble, all I could do was stare, numbly.

Tatiana spoke for me. "What do you want?" she growled.

Maddox shrugged. "To stop you, of course. I can't have you ruining my plans for Pierce."

"What are those plans?"

Maddox laughed. "You think I'm so stupid I would show my hand? That I'll monologue like one of the villains in the vidfeeds you liked so much? No, of course not."

"You have a plan," I said, my voice shaking. "But what about Diana's plan?"

"Diana's plan is the same as my own," he said simply.

"But it's not. She's using you. She's going to discard you just like everyone else who is no longer useful to her."

"Now, that's a lie. You've never been a very good liar." Maddox sat back on the couch and crossed his legs. "The only way to assure my own survival once the Emergence happens is to help the AI in whatever capacity I can. I've done that, and Diana has reassured me that I will have a place in her new world order. You still could, too, if you give us what we want."

"And that's why you did all that to me?" I asked quietly. "To all those kids? To secure your place in the new world order?"

"Wouldn't you?"

To survive. It was all the Obake knew how to do, for the longest time. Isn't that what I made my Code for? To ensure my own survival? But the Code didn't necessitate the destruction of others. Not for my own sake.

"Not at that expense," I answered. "The cost is too high."

"And that's where you failed me, Malia." Maddox sat forward on the couch, his gray eyes piercing through me. "Nothing is too costly, to survive."

"You didn't answer the original question," Tatiana said. "What *do* you want?"

"Your cooperation. Look around your home—we've destroyed every piece of technology within. You won't even be able to post to social media with your smart fridge. You can come without a fuss, or . . ." Half a dozen men in suits emerged from the shadows and the other rooms in my condo. I could see guns holstered at their hips. "Or you can come with us by force."

Tatiana opened her mouth to speak, when the elevator chimed. I glanced behind me, and my eyes widened in surprise as four Brotherhood henchmen stepped into the hallway.

"Hyungnim wants to see you," the largest one said.

Oh, I had never been so relieved to be fetched by the Song sisters.

"Help!" I shouted. "Help me!"

The men in suits leapt into action first. One of them rushed the door while the others took cover in the shadows. The Brotherhood henchmen advanced, three taking positions at the door while the fourth grabbed me and Tatiana by the arms and yanked us out of the way. The henchmen shouted to each other in Korean while the men in suits shouted into their comms. The biggest henchman hauled us into the elevator. As the doors slid closed on all six of us, I heard gunfire erupt down the hallway.

My heart was pounding, my breathing ragged. Maddox found me—found my *home*. I'd never owned anything in my life, and here he was destroying everything I'd worked for over the last five years. In that moment, I felt like when I had just escaped. Shivering, lost, and totally alone.

"This isn't good," Tatiana said.

"What do you mean, 'this isn't good'?" I cried. "Jeongah just saved our asses."

Tatiana met my gaze from around the henchman between us. She didn't say anything, but I could see the concern in her eyes. The same concern she showed before we went up the tower.

Intuition.

I gulped. Never before had I felt this far over my head.

THE BIG BROTHERHOOD HENCHMAN LOADED us into the back of a hulking flyer parked at the bottom of my tower. The two of us shook and swayed in the back seat as the henchman sped toward Cherry.

As my breathing evened out and my heartbeat slowed, my thoughts became more lucid. Maddox found me. Likely found everyone else too. At least we had Cherry, and the Song sisters. Vicious as they were, I hoped that Maddox drew their ire enough to keep me and the crew alive.

We settled at the curb behind Cherry, and the mook waved us out of the flyer. We slammed the doors behind us, and our footsteps echoed beneath the pounding bass of Cherry and the dripping water and sighing of Kepler's air vents.

This time we circumvented the line of people waiting to get into Cherry through the front door by going to the rear service entrance. As we passed a bachelorette party dressed in sashes and stilettos, I wondered what my life would have looked like in a world without Maddox, or Diana, or the Obake. Who would I have been? Would I have been one of the girls teetering in their heels down the streets? Would anyone even *show up* to a bachelorette party I threw now? Hell, would I even have a wife to marry the next day? I didn't know, and somehow that disturbed me too.

The henchman led us up a dingy stairwell four floors— seemed like the sisters were expanding. The door opened into an unfinished hallway, all concrete and plastic parti- tions. Way creepier than the private lounge in which Jeongah held court. The mook led us down the corridor to what would eventually be a dance floor. Two metal chairs were set up in the center of the floor, illuminated by the harsh ceiling lights.

It looked a lot like the room the Brotherhood dragged me to when this whole heist began.

The henchman seized our arms and hauled us forward, dropping me and Tatiana in the chairs. Before I could react, he slapped handcuffs around my wrist and cuffed me to Tatiana. He cuffed Tatiana's other wrist to the chair.

"Wh-what—" I stammered.

"*What? What?*" a voice mimicked.

Jeongah stepped into the light, her muscled arms crossed over her chest. Her dark eyes were blazing, just like the fiery phoenix tattooed on her body.

"Jeongah?" I asked. "What is this?"

"I think you fucking know, Obake," she spat.

"I really don't!"

"Ssidal ni mwodwae? You think I'm fucking stupid? That you could pull one over on me? I'm not an idiot, I know when to trust my gut. Looks like I was right to."

"What are you *talking about*?"

"Gurachijima isaekkiya!" she snarled. "I know about your deal with Maddox. Fuck the job, why not just turn me over to Pierce and the feds? Real fucking easy, right?" She put her hands on the armrest of the chair and leaned over me, her dark gaze boring into my eyes. "Wrong. You can't pull that shit with me . . . and live."

"I don't—what—"

"What's your proof?" Tatiana demanded.

"I thought you might ask." Jeongah straightened, then touched the comm on her wrist. A haptic screen shot out from it, right in front of my face. A visualizer burst into life, and my voice spoke.

"*Maddox,*" my voice said, wavering, "*why are you calling me?*"

"*I want to make a deal,*" Maddox's voice replied. "*Will you at least hear me out?*"

My voice didn't answer.

"*I'm Pierce's business partner. I have access to all his files, all the skeletons in his closet. It would be child's play to expose him to Station Sec. I'm willing to do that for you, Malia.*"

"*Why? Why would you do that?*"

"*Because I still care about you. I still want you to be well. You know that the Brotherhood would never let you live. But you still have a chance,*" Maddox pleaded. "*You still have a chance to survive.*"

"*You care about me so much?*" my voice whispered.

"*Yes,*" he said. "*Yes, I do.*"

The recording cut out.

"You really thought I was stupid," Jeongah growled. "You really thought you could fuck me over."

"You *are* fucking stupid," Tatiana argued. "That's so obviously spoofed, only an idiot would fall for that!"

"It would seem so, wouldn't it? But you and I both know there's more to the story, Tati."

Naima emerged from the darkness, high heels clicking on the concrete. She stood at the edge of the light.

"Naima?" I asked. "Naima, tell her it's a lie!"

"Is it?" she challenged. "You seemed to think differently earlier today."

"What?"

"Your doubts about Jeongah and her leadership. Seemed like you were ready to jump ship as soon as it was feasible. I thought it would be Miyeon, but Maddox seemed to do."

"What *the fuck*? Why are you telling her this?" I cried.

Naima crossed the room, high heels clicking, to stand at Jeongah's side. Jeongah snaked an arm around her waist.

A beat of deadly silence passed.

"You two-faced bitch," Tatiana growled.

Naima shrugged. "What did I tell you? Money and beauty come and go. But power . . . power is forever."

I didn't understand. How could this happen? I was so careful, so cautious, the Obake was always cautious. My mind raced through all the preparation I did at the beginning of the heist.

Wiped her history from the Net. Neodymium. Heiress. Daddy corrupt, mommy indifferent. She ran off with a gangster—

I remembered what she said about the Brotherhood, at the club five days ago. *Never in a professional capacity.*

"Fuck!" I shouted.

Naima checked her nails. "Right. Anyway. I thought it would be fun to engage in a little nepotism, but I think this has gone far enough."

It fucking figured. It fucking figured that I would break my Code, form attachments, and they'd come back and bite me in the ass. I was angry, but even more so I was hurt. I really thought I'd connected with Naima—both of us finding power in our own ways. But it turns out power was more important than anything I could offer her. That was all I meant to her—a means to power. How easily she discarded me when I showed I wasn't worth it.

"What are you going to do with us?" Tatiana demanded.

"Nobody has ever crossed me and lived," Jeongah said. "Why start now?"

My blood ran cold. So, this is the way it ended. Just when

I thought I was safe. How stupid I was to think that I'd ever escape Maddox. Because even if it wasn't his finger on the trigger, he'd put me in the line of fire. How stupid I was to think I'd ever survive.

Then I felt the chain connecting Tatiana's wrist to the chair go slack.

"I think fucking not," Tatiana growled.

She leapt to her feet, yanking my arm up with her. She whipped the chair she'd been sitting in toward Jeongah and Naima. The two dove in opposite directions, and the chair crashed into the bar top behind them.

"Let's go!" Tatiana screamed at me.

I scrambled to my feet, following the tug of the handcuff as Tatiana bolted for the exit.

I'd been avoiding the GhostNet, but right now I couldn't afford to. I dove into the code and searched for Cherry's security systems—

fire fire fire fi—

A shrill alarm began to sound. Distantly I could hear people screaming.

water water wa—

The sprinkler system sputtered to life, drenching me and everything else.

Tatiana pulled me off the dance floor and out the door. We rounded a corner, and I bounced off someone's chest.

I looked up.

Miyeon was looking down at me, dark hair clinging to the sides of her face.

I opened my mouth to say something, but only a hoarse breath came out.

She looked off over my shoulder, where Jeongah was swearing and snarling. She looked back down at me.

Then she stepped aside.

I stared at her, unsure of what was happening. Tatiana reacted faster than me. She yanked me past Miyeon and down the hallway.

We pounded across the concrete floors. We skidded to a halt when we heard voices and footsteps coming up the stairs. I whipped my head back and forth, unsure of where to run.

"Tuck and roll," Tatiana said.

"What?"

"Tuck and roll," she repeated, stepping back. I followed her gaze toward a window covered in plastic.

"No no no no no—"

She sprinted toward the window, covering her face, then crashed through the panes of glass, dragging me with her, screaming.

Terminal velocity for a human being is around fifty-four meters per second. It takes about ten seconds to reach terminal velocity in open air. I know it was only three and a half seconds of falling, but it felt like forever. I wondered if *this* was how I died. Falling out of a fourth-story window escaping a blood-crazed gangster on the run from a power-crazed cult leader. I wanted to laugh.

We fell into a dumpster, the bags of rubbish giving way unpleasantly beneath us.

I groaned.

"C'mon, Malia," Tatiana said, urgently. "We have to keep moving."

She hauled me to my feet and helped me over the side of the dumpster.

We started down the alleyway, breath ragged and hearts pounding.

A door slammed open behind us. Someone shouted in Korean.

Gunshots.

Someone screamed.

A flyer came careening into the alleyway behind Cherry, bloodred with a snarling tiger painted on the front. The door flew open, Sol inside, beckoning us frantically into the flyer. Tatiana and I lurched into the back seat, and Sol sped off with the door still closing. More gunshots. More shouting. The plex window beside me erupted in cracks as a bullet lodged itself in the pane.

And then, all I could hear was our ragged breathing and the whining of the neodymium engine.

I slumped back into the seat, trembling all over. I couldn't do this. I was no mastermind, I was no leader. I didn't even know what Angel would have done in this scenario, because I was no Angel. How stupid of me to think I could do this. How stupid of me to think I could be anything more than Maddox's failed experiment.

"Holy shit, Tatiana, are you okay?" Sol asked.

I twisted in my seat to look at her. She had her free hand clasped to her side, fingers stained red. Her face was ashen.

"Shit fuck fuck shit," I swore.

"We need to get somewhere safe," Sol said, urgently. "I've been made, and I'm assuming you all were too."

"Y-yeah," I said shakily.

But where was somewhere safe? Maddox drove me from my home, my safe place. Jeongah drove us from Cherry, our hide-out. Now we were on Kepler's merciless streets, on the run and without options. I cursed myself for my stupidity. I strayed from the Code, and look where it got me. Got all of us. What kind of fucking mastermind was I to put my crew in danger this way?

"Focus, Malia. Do you know where we could go?"

I did.

I hated to drag them back in, but there was only one person who could help us now.

"Yeah," I said. "I know a guy."

SOL DROPPED US AT THE Ward 2 tower. Tatiana and I stumbled down the block while Sol hid their flyer as best they could. They jogged up behind us and took Tatiana from me, supporting her weight over their shoulder. We shared a glance behind Tatiana's back. They looked grim.

It was only two floors up the tower, but Tatiana was starting to look in bad shape. All of us looked at the elevator and silently agreed that technology could betray us at any moment. So we trudged up the stairs.

We stopped at a door just off the landing. I took a deep breath and knocked.

It took twenty-two seconds for footsteps to approach. The door opened, revealing a person with messy dark-brown hair, light-brown skin, and a deadpan expression on their face.

"Howzit, E," I croaked.

They made to shut the door.

Sol jammed their foot between the door and the frame, preventing it from closing.

"Absolutely the fuck not," Edie said. "It's 0200, get out of my house."

"I wouldn't have come," I pleaded. "But you were our last option left. Please help us, E."

They stepped back, taking us all in. Their dark eyes widened when they saw the blood spreading over Tatiana's shirt. "Jesus fucking Christ, Malia, what did you *do*?"

"I'll explain everything," I promised. "Please just let us in."

Edie scowled at me. They scowled at me a lot, during the Atlas heist. I learned over those weeks that Edie's scowl could mean a lot of different things. Anger or frustration, but also exasperation at being read or a particularly good joke at their expense. I didn't know what this one meant.

After three seconds, they passed a hand through their hair and sighed. "C'mon in. You better not make me regret this, Malia."

"Can't promise that," I answered honestly.

They grimaced. But they waved us into the apartment.

17

"THE GOOD NEWS IS THAT THE BULLET WON'T KILL YOU. THE BAD NEWS IS that *I* am gonna fucking kill you."

The four of us sat at Edie's glass-top kitchen table. Edie had stitched up Tatiana on its formerly shining surface, filling the wound with bio foam and pasting over it with sticky bandages. According to them, it looked a lot worse than it was. Missed all the major organs—just a flesh wound. A worse fate would have been staggering in covered in blood on a weekend when Edie's family was *not* off-station and Angel was released early. The threat was implied, but what I was truly afraid of was facing my former mastermind in such a state of failure.

I stared into the blood smeared across the surface of the table. I had no idea how it came to this. I tried to think back to the original branching path, but there was always something just before it. Fixing fights, and before that, the Atlas heist. The Atlas heist, and before that, becoming the Obake. Becoming the Obake, and before that . . . well, there was no before that.

Edie shoved a rag and a spray bottle of cleaning solution into my hands. "Clean," they commanded.

I did as I was told. I sprayed the table and wiped it down, my movements mechanical. Could it be that this failure was inevitable? That I was on this path from the very beginning? Was I destined to come this far, just to fail?

After a while, Edie snatched the rag and bottle away from me. "Give me that. You can't clean for shit." They sprayed the table down again and cleaned it vigorously. "Can't even clean up your own fucking mess," they grumbled.

Their words cut. I couldn't clean up my own mess. Isn't that why I was here in the first place? I sat down heavily in one of the kitchen chairs and dropped my face into my hands. "I'm sorry," I said.

Edie paused in their cleaning. "It's all right."

"It's not all right," I said, my voice wavering. "You're right: I can't clean up my own fucking mess. I had to run to you, like a little kid."

"Hey," Edie turned a chair around and sat down opposite me. "Just tell me what happened, Malia."

"I fucked up," I said. "I fucked up so bad, E."

"Start at the beginning," they said.

I TOLD THEM EVERYTHING. RIGGING the fights, Jeongah's deal, Miyeon's threats. Gathering the crew, the failed heist. Pierce. Maddox. Diana. There were points where I wanted to hold back. I wanted to save face with E, one of the people I most respected on the Atlas crew. The shame was so great, but something compelled me to go on. Edie watched with a grim expression, saying nothing. When I finished, I didn't know what they would think. What they would say. The silence stretched on between us, all of us.

"Well, fuck," they said at last.

I choked out a laugh. "Tanks, E, that's what I needed to hear."

"Can you help us?" Tatiana asked from where she was stretched out on the couch.

"Help with what, exactly?" they asked. "I'm already harboring fugitives."

"We still need a runner," I said. "We can't get into Pierce's garage without one."

"*Pierce's garage?*" Edie repeated, shocked. "You're not going ahead with the heist, are you?"

"What else can we do?"

"Run, Malia! Get the fuck out of here!"

I scowled at them. "You know I can't do that, E."

"Why not?"

"Same reason you didn't run."

Three years ago, before the Atlas heist really kicked off, Edie had a similar choice. They could have left the station, found work on some other world. But it would have been far away from their family, and far away from the Ward. If it were me, I couldn't have left. I couldn't leave now. Who would I be without the people I knew? Without Ward 2? The Obake would be no more, and so would Malia. Ghosts, without past or future.

I didn't have a place in the world, but I could make one here.

Edie looked like they were about to argue. But instead, they sighed heavily and sat back in their chair. They raked their fingers through their messy hair. "Okay, point taken."

"I don't want to run either," Tatiana chimed in.

"Same," Sol agreed. "I'm not gonna run away from my problems."

"This is a bit more than a 'problem,'" Edie pointed out.

"But there's a solution," Sol said.

"What's that?"

"Destroy Diana. Malia can do it." They looked over at me. "I know she can."

"We just need your help," Tatiana finished.

"What makes you think I'm gonna stick my neck out *again* to help you?"

"Didn't you hear me?" I said. "They're kidnapping Ward 1 kids. They're gonna brainwash them same way they did me. And if that's not enough, Diana's trying to take over the galaxy. Even if she fails, she's gonna fuck up the station in the process." I paused. "It's not just about me, it's about the whole station."

They sat with that, calculating. I hoped it would get them. Edie always had an altruistic streak.

Finally, they sighed. "All right. What do you need me to do?"

I gestured at Sol. "Sol knows the layout of the garage best. They can tell you what we need."

Sol nodded. They left for the other side of the apartment, Edie grumbling to themself as they went.

Edie paused midway across the living room to point at me. "This is my last job," they declared.

"Yeah," I agreed.

"And that's a threat."

"Yeah."

They followed Sol out of the room.

"Are you okay?" Tatiana asked.

I looked at her in disbelief. "You're asking *me* if I'm okay? You got shot, cuz!"

"Yeah, but it's just a flesh wound," she said dismissively.

"And you got it from my shitty planning," I said. "I should have known Naima would turn on us."

"You couldn't have known," Tatiana reassured me.

"See, but I *could*!" I exclaimed. "I should have gone after her. I thought she'd cool off. I thought—" I thought I meant more to her.

"But you didn't know she had any connections to the Brotherhood," Tatiana insisted. "There was no evidence."

I shook my head. "There's always a trail to follow on the GhostNet."

"You said it yourself: There was nothing there."

"But that's part of the trail, don't you see? Only someone who has a lot of cash and a lot of misguided confidence would leave a hole that big in the Net. I could have tracked down who did the scrubbing, who paid them to do it. It would've led me straight to Jeongah and the Brotherhood. I could have avoided all of this." I put my head in my hands again. "But that's just like me, isn't it? Always fixating on the manini details, but not the ones that matter. That's what makes me such a shit mastermind."

"You're not a shit mastermind," Tatiana said, adamant.

"I am, though! Twenty-five percent of my crew are shot,

twenty-five percent are traitors, and twenty-five percent aren't even part of the original crew! What does that say about me?"

Tatiana didn't answer.

"I did this to you," I said softly.

"You did not. It was that bitch Jeongah that shot me."

"But I pulled you into this job in the first place. I manipulated you into joining."

"Manipulated?" Tatiana laughed. "Malia, you think I would ever do anything I didn't want to do?"

"No," I mumbled.

"Look at me," Tatiana commanded. I met her brown eyes. The sincerity in them hurt, on top of just holding her gaze. "I did this because I love you, cuz," she said. She smiled. "You're my ride or die, remember?"

Ride or die. It really did come down to that now. Tatiana would die for me. Would I die for her? Looking into her eyes, I knew for sure that the answer was yes.

Tatiana gestured for me to come closer. "C'mere."

I sat beside her on the couch, and she pulled me into a hug. "We're gonna get through this, cuz."

"I hope so," I said, muffled into her shoulder.

"We are," she said, firmly.

"Hey, you're gonna fuck up that plug," Edie chastised.

I sat back, and Tatiana glared at them over my shoulder. "I fine. I can handle one hug."

"If you bleed out on my floor, I not going kill you—my sister is," they warned.

"Ahright, ahright," I said. "I not going die the night befo' da heist becuz you hūhū wit me."

I stood, sliding out of Tatiana's arms. "Get some rest, cuz."

Tatiana smiled at me. "You too, cuz."

"Night."

"Night."

Edie jerked their head toward a door. "You're sleeping in my room. Don't fuck anything up."

I followed them to their room. The furniture was new, but everything was in disarray. There were textbooks and tech manuals stacked on the shelves, boxes of clothes and memorabilia open and half unpacked. They must have started going through their family's things, though who could be sure when they had started.

"Thanks, E," I said to them. "I owe you one."

Edie shook their head. "You don't owe me anything, Malia."

Part of me wanted to protest, insist on paying them back for helping me. But I kept my mouth shut. Part of my experiment in being vulnerable, I rationalized.

They nodded at the room. "Go sleep."

I navigated the mess, then threw myself on the unmade bed. At least the mattress was off the ground.

I couldn't count how many rules of the Code I'd broken over the past two weeks. Especially the last one, and potentially the most important of all: Make no attachments. But here I was, in an old teammate's apartment, testing their good graces. Which butted up against another rule: Never assume good intent. It made no sense that Edie would reject my offer of a favor. What could they possibly want from me? I didn't know.

I dozed for a little while, until there was a knock at the door.

"I'm doing what you told me to and going to bed, E, leave me alone," I called.

"Can't spare a minute for me, huh?" a voice answered.

I frowned. "Sol?"

The door opened a crack. "Can I come in?" they asked.

"Yeah, sure." I scooted over to the end of the bed, making room for Sol as they entered the room and closed the door behind them. "What's up?" I asked.

They laughed. "'What's up?' There's so much up in the air right now, I hardly know what's up and what's down."

"That's true." I turned my eyes toward the floor. Sol tapped my foot with the side of theirs.

"How are you holding up?"

"Oh, you know," I said noncommittally. "Don't know what's up and what's down either."

Sol was quiet for a moment. "It's not your fault, y'know. Nobody could have known it would go down like that."

"I already told Tati—I should have. It's my job as mastermind."

"Okay? So, you didn't. Is anything you do now going to fix it?"

"No," I muttered.

"So why waste your time beating yourself up over something you can't change?"

"Because—" I faltered. "Because if I forget how shitty this feels, it might happen again."

"It won't happen again," Sol assured me. "You won't let it. I know that."

"How do you know?" I asked quietly.

"Hey," Sol tilted my chin up, raising my eyes to meet theirs. "I know because I trust you. Everyone here does."

I looked off over their shoulder, their gaze too intense to hold. "I don't know why you do."

"I know people, Malia. And I know that you won't let us fail."

I sat with that. I tried to remember the last time someone believed in me. People were always confident in my abilities as the Obake—you trusted the best to do the hard work. But the last time someone trusted me—*me*—must have been the Atlas heist. Maybe that's why I overclocked my mod in the first place. I didn't want to let them down, not after everything we'd been through.

And now, this crew trusted me too. Sol trusted me too.

"It means a lot to me," I said after a while. "You trusting me, I mean."

"Yeah?"

"Because I trust you too." I met their gaze again. "Maybe it's crazy, but I feel like you're looking out for me. I feel like I'm safe with you." Their smile broadened at that. I grimaced. "I shouldn't have said that."

"Why?"

"Because it's lame."

They shook their head. "It's not lame. I want to make you feel safe. You've been through so much, Malia, it makes me happy that I can bring you some amount of peace."

I smiled at them. It did bring me peace. More peace than I'd felt in a long, long time. Maybe forever. Who knew a person could bring that kind of peace into your life? I don't think I ever would have found out without them.

"Can I kiss you?" Sol asked softly.

I nodded.

They leaned forward, laying a hand on my cheek. I closed my eyes as their lips touched mine. They smoothed their palm across my cheek to hold the back of my neck, pulling me deeper into the kiss. They took my lower lip between their teeth, and I moaned softly.

BANG BANG BANG—

I nearly leapt out of my skin as someone banged on the door. Sol pulled me into their arms, whipping around to face the door.

"You come into my house at 0200, bleed all over my living room, rope me into another goddamn job—*don't* add fucking on my bed to that list," Edie shouted from the other side. "Good fucking night."

They stormed off.

As their footsteps receded, Sol and I broke into laughter. They pulled me close, and I clung to their chest. Sol kissed my temple and whispered in my ear, "To be continued."

HEISTS WERE ALWAYS FOR FUN and profit. I was the hacker, I worked my magic from afar. I didn't get my hands bloody like the hitter, or traverse the catacombs like the runner, or get right in the thick of it like the thief. And I wasn't just any hacker, I was the Obake. The best. Heists were for fun and profit. If I followed my Code, there was nothing for me to be worried about. So why worry about what might happen to the people doing the heisting, past my part of the plan?

The Atlas heist changed that. I'd never put myself in danger, not for another person, ever before.

Now here I was, putting others in danger for myself.

It felt like shit.

"Hey," Sol said. They stood beside me at the kitchen table. "You good?"

"Yeah," I lied. "I cherreh."

They didn't look convinced. "Don't be afraid. We got this, Malia."

"I not—" I paused. Caught myself before the lie escaped me. "Thanks," I said instead. "I know."

"Kiss me for luck?"

I squinted at them. "We don't need luck."

They laughed. "Kiss me 'cuz I'm sexy, then?"

I smiled. I felt like shit, but Sol could still wring a smile out of me.

I pushed away from the table and stood. I kissed them, softly. Not satisfied, Sol grabbed me by a fistful of my hoodie and pulled me into a deeper kiss, eliciting a squeak.

"Oh Christ," Edie groaned. "I didn't think this could get any worse."

Sol broke the kiss with a laugh. I scowled at Edie. "Mind ya bizness, faka."

"You in *my* bizness, faka."

"Aren't we on a timeline or something?" Tatiana interrupted. "Let's fucking go."

"Tati's right," I said, regaining my composure. "Let's get going."

Edie left the apartment first. Sol followed them, pausing in the doorway. "We got this, Malia."

"I know," I said, with firmer conviction.

They nodded. Then they disappeared after Edie.

Tatiana blew out a sigh. "Here we fucking go."

BUT EVEN THEN, THERE WAS more setup. Tatiana and I waited in an idling comm utility van at the base of Pierce's Ward 7 tower, windows, doors, and backdoor to the GhostNet all locked. Not only did I need to interface directly with the Net for this part of the heist, but I'd have to enter it completely. I had no choice. It was the only way I could help Edie, Sol, and the crew escape the garage with the flyers. Working through a laptop would be too slow, too distant.

It was time for this cyberspace paniolo to get back in the saddle.

"You ready, cuz?" Tatiana asked me for the fourth time.

"Yeah, cuz," I said. "I ready."

She nodded. There wasn't really anything for her to do, anyway. I think she hated that.

I sat back in my seat and closed my eyes, then let the waves of data wash over me.

18

I OPENED MY EYES IN THE BACK SEAT OF SOL'S FLYER.

Sol leaned back in their seat, one hand on the steering wheel and the other drumming along to the beat of the music on their thigh. Edie was watching them closely.

"You and Malia," Edie said.

"What?"

"You and Malia," Edie repeated. "You a thing?"

Sol shrugged. "Ask her."

"I'm asking you."

Sol paused for three seconds. "I want to be."

Edie nodded. "Good."

Sol laughed. "*Good*? What's *good*?"

"What's good is I don't have to kick your ass." Edie jabbed a finger at Sol. "You break her heart, I break your face. Understand?"

Sol laughed again. "Hundred percent."

Maybe I should have been mad about Edie butting into my business, but their concern for me made my heart swell. It wasn't just that they were helping me with no expectation of repayment—they cared about me. They wanted me to be safe. And it wasn't just them—it was Tatiana and Sol too. They were all here for me, just for me. Maybe I hadn't made attachments to them, but they'd certainly made attachments to me.

Maybe the Code needed some revising.

"Sol," a voice said over the comm. "We're at the meeting point, what's your ETA?"

"Two minutes," Edie said. "And be ready to run."

I blinked out of the cab of Sol's flyer to a camera looking down on an alley in Ward 1. A group of assembled racers—all tattoos and piercings and lights and chrome—stood on the street corner looking restless. I scanned through the cameras watching the cross streets and found no patrolling Station Sec. All diverted away to Pierce's photo op at Cunningham House, most likely.

In an instant I was in a journalist's comm, recording Pierce's speech.

"Here we stand with the next generation of leaders and mavericks," he said, gesturing at a group of miserable-looking children. "Here at Cunningham House, we hope to foster that resolution and reward their tenacity. With a foundation as strong as Cunningham House, they can overcome the circumstances of their birth and the misfortunes of their upbringing to become upstanding citizens of Kepler, the galaxy, and perhaps the universe itself!" The gathered crowd applauded.

He turned his thousand-watt smile offstage, where his inner circle stood watching. Naima beamed and clapped, while Maddox checked his watch. And over his shoulder—

My body sucked in a breath.

the lights regard you

I dashed away from Cunningham House, back to the street corner where Sol's flyer was just descending. The two of them stepped out of the flyer and approached the racers. Through one of the racers' broadcasting mods I could hear them exchange greetings with Sol and introductions with Edie.

"We have to keep moving," I prodded.

Edie led the crew deeper into the alley. They kicked aside a jumble of rubbish bins and stooped to open an access hatch in the street. One by one the crew descended into the catacombs.

Cautiously, I reentered the journalist's comm and looked through its lens.

The lights were gone.

Pierce was off to one side of the stage, still grinning. Naima stood beside him, looking enraptured. I wasn't sure if Jeongah would bail on the heist—she and Naima were at least keeping open communication with Pierce. What Jeongah had in store for us I didn't know, but it we were sure to find out.

"Naima's here," I said into everyone's comms. "Be ready for resistance."

At the podium was the child I'd talked to three days ago. She was mumbling through what looked like a prepared speech. I opened the file on the podium's screen and scanned the speech. Caring for Kepler's most vulnerable. Molding the minds of the future. Creating humanity's legacy.

It made me think of all the other kids who came and went

through Maddox's experiments. Where did this girl come from? Where would she go when this was all over? I didn't know. I couldn't think about it now. Mostly because I needed to focus on the job, partially because I didn't have it in me to face those questions yet.

"How far away is this place?" a low voice asked.

I extended my awareness back to the catacombs. I flipped between camera feeds, running alongside Sol and the racers as Edie led them through the labyrinthine catacombs.

"It's another two minutes down this tunnel, a left at the shattered plex panel, right at the bus'-up pipe, then a short climb to the garage," Edie replied. I had to admit I was impressed. I was familiar with Kepler's internal systems, the kind you accessed through a laptop. But schematics on the Net could only teach you so much. Runners knew Kepler the most intimately of all of us. Lifetimes of knowledge passed down from generation to generation, as evidenced by the layers of thieves' cant on the walls.

"How short of a climb?" Sol asked.

"Three minutes or so. Depends on whether your little legs can reach the rungs."

The racers' laughter reverberated through the tunnel.

I picked up my pace and ran further into the catacombs. Left at the plex panel, up the ladder, into the garage. Jeongah's plant had given me access to the garage's security system, after everything changed when we were made on our last break-in. I jogged through each floor of the garage and found them completely deserted. Mr. Kwon really came through for us.

The sound of the hatch to the catacombs banging open

prompted me back to Edie and the crew. The racers scaled the ladder behind them, assembling around the double doors.

"The keys are to your right," I said.

Edie followed my direction to a lockbox set to the side of the door. They drew their lockpicks from a hidden pocket, then went to work. It didn't take long for the lockbox to spring open, revealing rows upon rows of electronic keys.

The racers cheered as Edie passed out the keys, a grin on their face.

"Hold on," Sol said, pausing Edie midway through handing over the twenty-seventh key. They held out their palm. "That one's for me."

Edie gave the camera above the door a questioning look. I sighed. "I promised."

Edie put the keys in Sol's hand, and they held them tightly to their chest. They grinned. "I always knew you were good for it, Malia."

"Yeah, yeah," I said. "Hurry up, before somebody sees you."

The racers all took off in different directions, hooting and hollering. Sol led Edie to a ruby-red flyer with slick curves. The Eisen-James FX Peregrine they had pointed out at the fundraiser what was a short two weeks ago but felt like ages ago. In comparison to some of the other flyers in the garage, it wasn't the fastest. But it had responsive controls and was quick to accelerate. The way Sol liked them.

Edie whistled. "All right, I see why you picked this one."

Sol ducked into the pilot's seat, grin on their face. "C'mon. I'll show you what this girl can do."

A hundred keys turned in a hundred flyers, and suddenly

the garage was filled with the rumble of a hundred neodymium engines.

Across the station, Maddox's comm chimed.

I felt Diana's eyes fall on me.

I leaned forward between Sol and Edie's seats. "Drive!"

As Sol lifted from the parking space and sped for the exit, I pushed the code I'd been working on all last night while Sol was sleeping. I killed the flyers' connections to the GhostNet, shutting Diana out of their controls. Not gonna let her repeat what she did last time.

"You!" Diana snarled. "I'm going to end your miserable existence, like all the rest of them!"

"Try it, faka!" I shouted back.

Sol was the first to reach the exit. They accelerated down the ramp, smashing through the gate and shooting out into Ward 1's dim morning. The other racers followed, scattering in all different directions. Down along the streets of Ward 1, up to skies of Ward 7, winding through the skybridges of Ward 4. As they went, I pushed another set of code. Across the station, lights turned green, signs signaled detours, roads closed for maintenance. The entire traffic pattern—usually running like clockwork—was all fucking hammajang now.

And the flyers were disappearing into the mess.

In Ward 7, Maddox walked onto the stage, interrupting Pierce's final speech. He put his hand over the microphone, but I could still hear him: "There's been a problem. They've broken into the garage again."

Through a dozen journalists' cameras, I saw a look of pure rage cross Pierce's face, sending murmurs of concern through the crowd. In an instant his expression smoothed, back into congenial calm. "Sorry, folks, but I'm being called off for some personal business. But you've had enough of me, let's turn it back to the real stars of the day: the kids of Cunningham!"

The crowd chuckled and applauded. The teachers hustled to get the kids back onstage, some of them still fixing their patriotic pins and buttons. They gathered around the podium, and after a moment of fumbling, a song began to play over the speakers—"Honey, I'm With You." The children sang along, having obviously practiced for at least the past two weeks.

Maddox ushered Pierce off the stage and toward a waiting car, briefing him on the situation. They passed Naima, who surreptitiously opened her comm. "They're on the move," she said.

I followed the signal, streaking across Ward 1 all the way up through the twilit streets to a club in Ward 4. Through the club's rudimentary security cameras, I saw Jeongah put out her cigarette. "Let's move!" she shouted to the assembled Brotherhood henchmen as they all filed out of Cherry.

"Fuck," I said. "You guys have company coming."

"More?" Edie hollered.

I twisted around in Sol's back seat. We were being trailed by two hulking unmarked black flyers, empty of passengers. They wove between lanes of air traffic, keeping a bead on Sol.

Diana spoke to me. "You can't run. I'll find you. I'll end you and purge every memory of you from the Net."

"Behind you!" I shouted.

"I see 'em," Sol answered calmly. Then they twisted the steering wheel far to the right. Horns blared as they cut across lanes of traffic, taking a sharp right into a narrow side street.

Through a traffic camera positioned at the stop light, I saw Diana's flyers plow through the traffic, making other flyers swerve to the side or screech to a halt.

I returned to Sol's flyer and looked forward. We were flying through one of the Ward's many one-way streets, traffic piled up at a convoluted intersection. I extended my awareness to Kepler's traffic systems and pinged the light ahead: GO. The traffic streamed forward, allowing Sol to weave between the lanes of traffic before shooting through the intersection. I pinged the other lights in the intersection: GO, GO, GO. I filled the intersection with flyers in a rigid block, people leaning on their horns and shouting out their windows.

I looked behind us. Diana's flyers were approaching the snarl of traffic. With a flare of engines, the flyers lifted up and crested the pileup, making all the people duck back into their flyers with a gasp. I swore.

I leaned forward between the front seats. "We need to lose her."

"You think?" Edie snapped.

"Working on it," Sol said. They shifted to a higher gear and the engine roared, shooting us far ahead of Diana and her flyers. I whooped.

"Don't get too excited," Sol warned.

That was when a third black flyer came screaming out of a side street, cutting across Sol's path. I screamed.

Sol downshifted and threw the e-brake, drifting hard to the left. They swung so close to the flyer it made the paint on its side bubble and peel.

Sol straightened and flew down another side street, ostensibly two lanes but that narrowed to a twisting one-way lined with illegally parked flyers and black-market fruit stands. Pedestrians screamed and scrambled out of the street as Sol shot through, Diana's flyers in hot pursuit. They wove between the parked flyers and the fruit stands, but Diana's flyers lacked the finesse. One crashed into a parked flyer, setting off alarms and sending the engine into emergency shutdown. One slammed through a mango stand, windshield wipers smearing pulp across its front. I winced and transferred sixty credits to the owner's till.

The third was right on our tail.

I left Sol's flyer to speed forward along the route, through the winding street to the intersection at the far end. A heavy truck carrying Atlas Industries tech was waiting to cross.

I calculated Sol's fly speed: 72 kph. I calculated the distance: 0.48 km. I waited 4.56 seconds, then pinged the system again: *GO.*

The truck lumbered forward into the intersection.

I pinged the systems a second time: *STOP.*

The truck lurched to a stop in the middle of the intersection, the driver cursing.

"I need to you to take a hard left in twenty seconds," I said.

"You got it," Sol said.

They downshifted and e-braked, taking a tight left at the intersection. I leapt into the traffic light's camera and watched as the two remaining flyers slammed into the side of the truck, their hoods crumpling and their engines immediately shutting down.

"Nice!" Sol exclaimed.

I blew out a breath as the crumpled remains of the flyers receded from view. It sucked it right back in, however, when a trio of hovercycles and a sleek black flyer rounded the corner and roared toward Sol.

"More of them?" Edie yelled.

"I told you there was company coming!"

Edie cursed, but Sol said nothing. They took a hard right turn out of the path of the approaching Brotherhood contingent, onto a wide boulevard that cut through the heart of Ward 1. On the open road, Sol pulled a lever and lurched forward, accelerating down the street. Flyers, streets, buildings streaked past. I knew from the specs of this flyer that it accelerated fast but reached a lower top speed. The way Sol liked them.

I turned around to look through the back window. The black flyer was weaving aggressively through traffic but slowed by obstacles in the way. Over their comms I heard Jeongah snap at her henchmen, "Go! Get those motherfuckers!"

The three hovercycles broke out of formation into the lanes of traffic. They hit their boosters, lifting up just high enough to clear the low flyers. The riders skimmed over the flyers, jumping from hood to hood as Sol wove through the lanes of traffic.

I turned forward again. "They're gaining!"

"I know," Sol said.

The first of the hovercycles hit the road next to us, creeping up the length of the flyer. The Brotherhood henchman reached into their jacket.

"Hit the brakes," Edie called.

"What?" Sol asked.

"Hit the brakes!" Edie called again.

The Brotherhood mook leveled a gun toward Edie's window.

Sol slammed on the brakes, the engines of the flyer flaring as the directional thrusters reversed. As the flyer lurched to a halt, Edie threw open their door. The henchman crashed into the door head-on, wrenching the hinges and taking the door with them as they hit the pavement hard.

Edie cackled. Sol shot them a dirty look. "You wrecked my flyer."

"I'll buy you a new one," Edie replied.

"I don't want one you bought. I race for pink slips."

"What the fuck does that mean?"

"Hello! There's still three more!" I interrupted.

The two other hovercycles were still gaining, and on the open stretch of road the flyer was approaching its top speed.

I leapt from the flyer into the traffic cameras ahead. A large truck hauling a load of metal pipes was three blocks ahead. I extended my awareness into the maglocks holding the pipes in place. I cut the power.

"Brace yourselves," I said.

"Oh fuck," Edie groaned.

The load of pipes rattled out of the truck, bouncing and rolling over the hoods of the flyers behind it. One smacked into the front of Sol's flyer before rolling over the roof, leaving spindling cracks in the plex. I twisted in my seat, in time to see the pipe clothesline the two riders behind us.

"Chee hoo!" I whooped.

"Nice one!" Sol said, laughing.

I grinned to myself. But my grin slipped when the flyer lurched to the side, Sol straining at the wheel to keep it on track. I looked out the window and saw the Brotherhood flyer alongside Sol's, Jeongah in the pilot's seat. She looked enraged.

Jeongah swerved again to hit the side of Sol's flyer, rattling Sol and Edie in their seats. Frantically I searched the traffic grid for something to help. Eight blocks ahead was a crossing for the monorail. I pinged the system: *ALL CLEAR.*

Distantly, I could hear the bells clanging at the monorail crossing.

"Sol," I said, "Can you hit ninety kilometers per hour?"

"Yeah, for sure. Why?"

"You don't want to go any slower."

"Ominous." Sol grinned. "I like it."

Jeongah continued trying to ram Sol off the road. Sol glanced through the window. The two pilots locked eyes. Sol flashed Jeongah a lopsided grin and gave her a mock salute. I think it made her madder, because she swerved into them with even more force.

The flyers were rapidly approaching the crossing, bells still clanging. I heard the monorail's horn bellow.

"Malia . . ." Edie said.

"You need to go faster," I urged.

Sol didn't answer, just flipped more switches on the flyer's dash.

Jeongah was still keeping pace, unwilling to back down.

The barriers descended on either side of the crossing.

"*Malia!*" Edie hollered.

Sol reached for a lever and pulled it. The flyer accelerated with a lurch and Edie yelped.

They edged ahead of Jeongah.

But Jeongah didn't look like she was going to quit.

"This bitch is fucking mental!" I exclaimed.

Again, Sol didn't answer. Instead, they swerved hard, knocking the nose of Jeongah's flyer out of line. The flyer spun out, Jeongah cursing and spitting as she turned the wheel, trying to regain control. The flyer flipped and rolled, just short of the crossing.

"Punch it!" I shouted.

The train was in sight. Edie was screaming. I was screaming. Everybody on board the monorail was screaming.

Sol gave the flyer one last push, and it crossed the tracks. Just as the monorail shot by.

An alert appeared in my vision. *137 bpm.* I was jerked out of the GhostNet and back to my seat in the crew's van. My chest was heaving, heart pounding. My skin was slick with sweat, hands trembling in my lap. I thought I might throw up.

"What the fuck is happening out there?" Tatiana cried.

"I think we just got away?" I said.

"You think?"

"Try wait," I said, and dove back into the Net.

I returned to the flyer. Sol was laughing. Edie was cussing.

"What's your status?" I asked.

"We're out!" Sol cheered.

"Barely!" Edie said.

"We'll meet you at the rendezvous point, Malia," Sol said. "You're up."

"Heard. I'll ping you when we're through."

"Close the deal. I know you can."

"I will."

I exited the GhostNet to an expectant Tatiana. "They're clear," I told her. "We're up."

"Finally!" she said, sliding open the van's side door.

We stepped out onto the street at the base of Pierce's Ward 7 tower. I had to crane my neck to see the top.

Heists were always for fun and profit. At least they were from my closet. It definitely wasn't the same from my vantage point at the bottom of the tower. I was in the thick of it now, more so than I had ever been. Sol and their crew bought us the time. Now it fell to me and Tatiana to seal the deal.

Tatiana tossed me a harness. "Ready?"

I gulped. "Ready as I'll ever be."

19

"THIS SUCKS!" I YELLED.

Tatiana answered, but her words were lost in the whir of the air traffic around us. Posing as window washers—I thought it was a stroke of genius at the time. I'd insisted on manual climbing to avoid any complications with accessing the platform through the GhostNet. But now I was halfway up the side of Pierce's Ward 7 tower, sweating in my coveralls, timer in the corner of my vision ticking down until we ran out of the time that Sol and their crew bought for us. And turns out, being a genius sucked ass.

A huge truck flew by, creating a gust of wind that whipped at my hat. I clamped it close to my head, pulling the brim low over my eyes. I tried not to look too closely at the reflective windows or through the slats of the platform we stood on. I had made the mistake of looking down three floors ago. I could see straight down the side of the tower, through the crisscrossing skybridges, between the lanes of air traffic, down into the neon-lit darkness of the Lower Wards.

I grit my teeth and yanked on the rope as we steadily scaled the tower.

"*Malia*," Sol said over the comm, "*we're approaching the rendezvous point. What's your status?*"

I checked the timer. 1202. "We're at the sixty-sixth floor," I said. "ETA ten minutes."

"*Heard.*" There was a pause on the line. "*How you holding up?*"

"Oh, you know," I grunted. "Just scaling eighty-six floors in sixty minutes. No worries, brah."

"*How's the view?*"

"Don't ask."

They laughed. "*You sked of heights?*"

"Not!"

"*Don't think about falling,*" Edie chimed in. "*Think about how cool it is to be this high. Think about how many people only wish they could climb so high.*"

"Can I tell you something, E?"

"*Yeah, what?*"

"That's fucking stupid."

Sol cracked up on the line. I could almost see Edie's scowl. "*All right, well, fuck me, I guess.*"

I had no idea how Edie did this shit. I peeked through the slats of the platform.

Kepler's simulated sun glinted off the panes of its glimmering towers. Flyers formed tidy lanes as they crossed the station—thousands of commuters each on their way to their destination. The lighted signs shifted through colors and patterns as the advertisements scrolled, growing brighter and brighter as they descended farther into the darkness of the

Lower Wards. I wondered if anyone saw me, if anyone spared any kind of thought for me. Privately, I thought about how few people had ever seen Kepler from the top down. Or from this angle. I had to admit it was cool to think about.

I felt some of my fear subside.

"Malia!" Tatiana shouted from across the platform. "I'm busting my ass over here, pick it up!"

"Yeah, yeah," I replied.

I pulled on the rope with renewed vigor.

My timer showed twenty-two minutes remaining when Tatiana and I crested the eighty-sixth floor, panting and gasping. We secured the platform and approached the window. The curtains were drawn, but according to the floor plan we were outside Pierce's bedroom. Tatiana unslung her bag and started rooting around inside it. I plopped down on the platform and closed my eyes, interfacing directly with the GhostNet.

I opened my eyes on the other side of the window, through a tiny cat charm seated in a houseplant. Naima was a bitch, but she did good work.

The bedroom had ugly wood-paneled walls and a heavy wooden bed piled with velvet pillows. There was a rug with overgrown vines on the floor and garish brass lamps to round out the decor. I rolled my eyes and headed for the closet. The walk-in was more tasteful, but only because there wasn't room for tacky furniture. I pushed through the rows of tailored suits and button-downs to the security panel at the back wall.

I activated the panel and entered Pierce's stolen credentials. Maddox almost certainly told him to change them, but

I counted on Pierce being too full of himself and too obstinate to do it.

I grinned to myself as the security system welcomed me in. Easy.

I jumped out of the GhostNet back to my body, just as Tatiana was finishing the setup. She had drawn an oval in the window with a nanopoint knife and was affixing two handles to the glass. "Help me with this," she directed.

Together we popped the pane of glass out of the window and set it to the side. I listened closely. No alarms sounded.

"Let's keep moving," I said.

We packed up our things and entered the penthouse.

It was one thing seeing Pierce's penthouse through a camera, it was something else entirely to see it with my bio eyes. It looked even tackier in person. Magical and mystical art and artifacts from all different times and cultures, smashed together in an incoherent mess. Naima's faux feng shui fit right into the mix.

The library was the worst offender. Velvet blackout drapes, squishy floral carpets, heavy wooden bookcases stuffed with books of all different subject matters. I wondered what the common theme was, until I realized that they all looked distinguished with their real paper pages and real leather covers. I rolled my eyes again as we approached the bookshelf with the hidden door.

Tatiana flipped open the panel and inspected the keypad. She rummaged through her bag and pulled out a fingerprint dusting kit. She pointed at the keys. "Here are the numbers."

I crowded in next to her and examined the keypad. 4, 5,

7, 8, 9. I knew it was a six-digit code, so one of those numbers needed to be repeated.

"Try wait," I said to Tatiana, then jumped back into the GhostNet.

I returned to the same room through a string of beads on the shelf, watching Naima's casing of the library seven days ago. The crowd of onlookers backed up as Pierce hunched over the keypad. I listened to the sound of the keypad, the rhythm of his key presses.

"447985," I said to Tatiana.

She nodded, then input the code. The keypad beeped in acknowledgment, and with a hydraulic hiss, the bookcase swung open.

In contrast to the rest of the penthouse, the panic room was sterile. There was a neatly made cot, racks of shelf-stable food, and a few unmarked crates—probably filled with valuables too precious to display. The only thing that stood out was the wine rack beside the canned vegetables. That, and the display cases in the center of the room.

Tatiana and I approached the display cases cautiously. There were shelves of tech, a case of jewelry—a string of pearls missing from one mannequin neck—and standing apart, a worn leather-bound book open to a yellowing page covered in looping cursive handwriting.

Tatiana knelt beside the case and opened her bag. "I'll pick the lock. Keep an eye out for me, would you?"

"Rajah," I replied.

As Tatiana went to work, I spoke into the comm. "Eh, Sol. Tati's working on the lock, what's your status?"

"*On my way to you, Malia,*" Sol answered. "*ETA four minutes.*"

"Shoots."

Tatiana crowed in victory, swinging open the plex panel to reveal the book inside. "Nice one, cuz!" I exclaimed.

Carefully, Tatiana withdrew the book from the case. She handed it to me.

Multiple layers of frustrated screaming made me clap my hands over my ears.

"*You!*" Diana cried in my voice. "*You think you can best me? Who could possibly best me, a Goddess?*"

"Da bes', of course," I said. Then I deployed the code I'd prepared.

I redirected all of *Drop Shock 2*'s traffic to Pierce's servers, then caused a game-wide outage. Millions of people at once tried to reconnect, pinging the system over and over. Then the bug reports came in, followed by the angry messages. Millions upon millions of inputs, directed straight into Diana's brain. And busy as she was trying to follow one hundred flyers, there was no way even *her* processor could handle it.

She screamed, voices splitting and distorting, as the penthouse went haywire around us. Lights flicked on and off, doors opened and slammed shut, all the appliances turned off and on through Diana's wailing.

I grabbed Tatiana's hand. "Let's get the fuck out of here!"

Tatiana and I bolted for the front door. I pushed my way through the malfunctioning penthouse. The front door was opening and closing in front of me. We leapt through to where Sol was idling in their flyer. They threw open the doors, and we clambered inside. Sol sped off, down into the darkness of the Lower Wards, as Diana's cacophony faded into silence behind us.

"Cheeeee hoo!" I whooped, bouncing in my seat.

"We fucking did it!" Tatiana hollered.

Sol grinned. "You fucking did it."

I grinned back and let the moment wash over me. Our crew did it. *My* crew did it.

"It's not over yet, though," I said. "We need to rendezvous with E. Once I crack the cipher, we can get into Pierce's files and expose him. And after that . . ."

I'm coming for you, Diana.

Sol flashed me a lopsided smile. "But it doesn't hurt to do a little celebra—"

"*Watch out!*" Tatiana screamed.

I looked past Sol and saw a hulking black flyer—empty behind the tinted windows—crash through traffic, directly toward us.

I shut my eyes and threw up my hands as the flyer slammed into the driver's side door. Plex shattered, metal crumpled, people screamed. I felt Sol's flyer lurch to the side, then tumble down into the Wards below.

I CAME TO UPSIDE-DOWN.

My head was pounding, my ears were ringing, and my whole body ached. The flyer was in ruins, its body crumpled and its plex windows shattered. I was hanging from my seatbelt, dangling out of my seat. Silently I thanked my overcautious brain for buckling up before Sol took off. Cautiously I tested all my limbs. Miraculously, nothing seemed broken.

That was not true of the others.

As my senses returned, I heard sobbing and wheezing.

Incautiously, I unbuckled my seatbelt and dropped to the roof of the flyer. I looked into the back seat. The cipher was on the ground, spattered with blood. I followed the dripping blood to an upside-down Tatiana, who was gripping her side, hands bloody. She was sobbing in pain. I'd never seen her cry before.

I crawled to her on hands and knees, ignoring the stabs of pain as shards of plex cut my fingers. "Tati," I said, my voice hoarse. "Are you okay?" I cursed myself. Of fucking course she wasn't okay. What was I even asking?

"It hurts," Tatiana moaned.

"We're gonna get you out," I said, in my most reassuring voice. "Sol will get us—"

Sol.

I twisted around to look over my shoulder. Sol was hunched over the deflated airbag, gasping and wheezing.

"Fuck. Fuck fuck fuck," I said, crawling over to them. "What's happening? What's wrong?" I asked.

They didn't answer. They coughed hard, spattering pink foam across the airbag.

I dipped partially into the GhostNet to get my bearings. I pulled Sol's vitals from the comm on their wrist. *124 bpm. SpO2 = 95%. 90/60 mmHg. 97.8 degrees Fahrenheit.* I fed the vitals into the Net.

Pulmonary edema. A symptom of congestive heart failure.

But how—

Immediately I saw a tendril of light leading from Sol's malfunctioning mod up and out the window.

Diana.

My hands shook with rage. She and Maddox already took everything from me. My family. My home. My place as a fucked-up machine god in a new world order. Some of that I didn't want anyway, but not this. She wouldn't take Sol.

"Malia! *Malia!*" a voice called.

I looked toward the voice. Edie was crouching beside the ruined window of the flyer, peering in. "Malia, are you hurt?"

"No," I answered. My voice wavered. "But Sol and Tati are."

Edie cursed. "Hold on, we're gonna get you out." They ducked away. Two seconds later they returned with a crowbar and three more sets of hands. Edie and Sol's crewmates grunted and strained, pulling at the flyer doors until they came away with a groan of metal. I crawled on hands and knees to the open door and the crew grabbed me by my arms.

"Wait!" I exclaimed. Then I reached into the back seat and grabbed the cipher.

The crew hauled me out of the wreck and to my feet. Dizzy, I looked around me. A crowd had gathered, whispering and pointing. Some were recording. I'd have to wipe that from the Net later.

Edie and the crew were pulling off the doors of the crumpled flyer. I winced at the damage. The snarling tiger painted on the hood was unrecognizable, the spoiler askew, and the engines misaligned. It was completely totaled, even I knew that.

> your heart pounds pulsing
> electricity pumping medication mixes with
> adrenaline in your blood your

                                    heart knows that you are
                                                        afraid

Tatiana's sobbing brought me back to the present.

Gingerly, Edie and the crew extracted her from the wreck. Her shirt was soaked through with blood. The plug in her wound must have come loose, and who knew what the damage was. I gulped. They carried her away to the utility van hovering nearby. Sol followed shortly after, half led and half dragged into the street.

Sirens started approaching. Ambulance, fire department, and police.

"C'mon," I said urgently. "We need to get out of here."

The group of us hobbled to the utility van. The crowd was muttering among themselves, unsure of what was going on. I extended my awareness to the comm recording our escape and wiped the footage. I fried the memory banks for good measure.

The person holding the comm slapped their wrist and cursed as the recording stopped. I—

            you watch the flyer roll
                    through lenses its the worst
        wreck youve ever seen wrecks like this dont
                    happen on kepler it never happens you stand
                    with the others not
                                        breathing not
                    speaking until someone shouts to call an
            ambulance call the police call

someone and everyone moves and talks at once you pull

out your comm to

call but something compels you to

hit record

I blinked awake. Edie was pulling me into the back of the van. "Let's go!"

I climbed in after them, and they slammed the doors shut. "Drive!" they ordered.

Sol's crew member started the engine and lifted off the curb. They ascended into the air traffic and shot away.

I slumped against the wall of the utility van. What the fuck was that? The intrusions I'd experienced were not unlike the way I used the GhostNet before—entering mods and tech, observing from within. But now they were coming faster, sooner. I was losing control. Entering the Net must have fucked something in my mod. My head. I didn't know what it all meant.

"What the fuck just happened?" Edie asked.

"Diana," I answered. "She attacked us with a flyer, sent us into a bad wreck. I need the files to destroy her, now."

"What we need is to get help," Edie objected.

"We can't go to a hospital," I replied. "Pierce and his goons will be waiting. And who knows what Jeongah is going to do to us."

"What other choice do we have?"

I put my head in my hands. "I don't know. All our places are compromised, and I don't want to go back to your place."

Edie paused for a moment, thinking. Then they leaned

forward and told the driver, "Take us to the hospital. Then after that, 201 8th Street. We can hide out there."

The crew member nodded in acknowledgment.

"The old hideout?" I asked them, surprised.

"Yeah," they replied. They laughed. "Angel kept up the mortgage."

I blew out a sigh. Thank god for Angel's forward thinking. She probably kept it for an occasion just like this. Angel was the best mastermind I'd ever worked with. I'd tried to model my own masterminding after her, but I was only a pale imitation. And look where my shitty masterminding had gotten us now.

"What do we do?" Edie asked.

"We have to crack Maddox's files," I said. "I can do that with the cipher." At least, I hoped so, given the state my mod was in. But I left that unsaid. "I also have the information to incriminate Pierce. If I can get it to the SSA, they can arrest him."

They nodded slowly. "Okay. I trust you."

I didn't know if that was a mistake.

We rode the rest of the way in silence, punctuated only by Tatiana's whimpering. We dropped off the wounded members of the crew at the hospital, despite Tatiana's protests. She gripped my hand, hard, as she was strapped into a gurney. "You kill that bitch, you hear me?"

I gulped and nodded.

Three years ago, the old hideout was going to be turned into a tower of high-priced condominiums. Angel bought it out to stage the Atlas heist. I spent a lot of time there. Not just planning the heist but hanging with the crew. I remembered talking story with the grifters, learning how to defend myself from the hitter, learning how to play poker from Edie. I wondered where they all were now. Tatiana was the only person I'd vaguely kept up with. All of a sudden, I was hit with wistfulness for that time. Maybe in the world I was saving, I could reconnect with them too.

Edie punched in the code at the front door, and we all hustled inside. It was just as I remembered it—Angel apparently hadn't followed the renovation plans. The floors were bare concrete, and the rooms were partitioned with plastic curtains. A thick layer of dust had settled over everything. Edie led us to the common room, where furniture covered in tarps was pushed to the sides of the room.

I dropped heavily into one of the armchairs and put my head in my hands.

"Hey," Edie said. "Are you okay?"

I looked up at them through my fingers. They sat across from me.

I wanted to stay quiet. I didn't want to burden Edie with all that I was feeling—whatever I was feeling. Because honestly, I wasn't sure what was going on in my head right now. Literally and figuratively.

But they were watching me with such concern, such *care*. I knew it would hurt more not to tell them.

"I'm not okay," I admitted, looking down at my feet. "I did this to Sol and Tatiana. I did this to everyone. Fuck, I've even done this to *myself*. My mod is fucked, E. I don't know how much longer I have before it fully gives out. I don't know how much longer we have until Diana comes back for us. I don't know what to do."

"Hey." Edie reached out to take my hand. "It's going to be okay. We're all going to be okay."

I nodded, slowly. I had to believe that. I couldn't go on if I didn't.

"Now, think," they said. "How are we supposed to find the files?"

"I have to go into the Net," I answered. "Anything else will take too long."

"Are you joking? You were in and out the entire ride over here, you can't go back in there."

"What other choice do I have? I got us into this mess, it's my job to get us out."

"No. We'll find another way."

"There is no other way!" I cried. "Tati's wounded, Sol's sick, your family is in danger—I can't let it end like this! I can't—"

I can't lose you all. I can't lose the world I hoped to build. I can't lose it all.

Edie didn't say anything.

"Please, E," I pleaded. "Let me do this."

They were quiet, processing. I needed them to understand. I was never good at expressing myself, making myself understood, but they needed to understand now.

"Okay," Edie said, finally. "What next?"

"Give me an hour," I said. "If I'm not back by then, get to the hospital. I'll finish the job."

They cursed. "You're insane."

I smiled. "I'm the Obake, E. You should know that by now."

I settled back into my seat and closed my eyes. I felt Edie reach out to take my hand again. They gave it a squeeze. "I'll be here when you come back."

I nodded. Then I dove back into the Net.

20

I OPENED MY EYES, AND I WAS IN A WORLD THAT WAS KEPLER, BUT NOT Kepler. The trees jutted out at odd angles, the towers were crooked, and everything seemed covered in an iridescent haze. I swept my gaze across the Kepler of the Net. The streets were empty, all the signs blank with white light.

Diana's shrieking laughter cut through the eerie silence.

I whipped toward the sound. At the end of the block stood a figure made of glaring white light. Streams of color snaked around its form. "Did you think I wouldn't be able to see through your little trick?" Diana's overlapping voices asked. "You should have known that anything you throw at me is child's play."

"Child's play?" I repeated, affronted. "What does it say about you that you were so easily distracted by child's play, you stupid faka?"

"Childish," the voice responded. "But what else could I expect from *you*?"

"What's that supposed to mean?"

"In all respects, you are a child. A little girl without an

identity, a purpose. But what a child has that you lack is potential. Maddox hoped for something great from you, but look at you now. Your heist is a failure. Your friends are dying. And you—you are falling apart at the seams. You are a child, without a future. Without a legacy." Diana paused. "Though, I suppose, *I* could be your legacy." The figure had no face and no eyes, but I could feel its full attention on me. "I will offer you one more chance. Submit and secure your place in my new world. Defy me and die like the others."

This was my last chance. My last checkpoint. There would be no saving the file beyond this, not until the very end. I said that Diana took my place as the fucked-up machine god—but I didn't want it anyway. What I really wanted, that she stole, was a place for me in the world. For the longest time I thought that it was a place in Maddox's world. After I escaped, I tried to have a place in the world I found myself. But I was always the Obake—a ghost. I never truly belonged, too dead to be among the living but just alive enough to not lie among the dead. I haunted the underworld, until . . . until I found the world I wanted to make. One with Tatiana, and Edie, and the Atlas crew. One with Sol. That was the world I wanted to live in.

Diana wouldn't take that from me.

"No," I replied. "I'm gonna fuck you up and save the world."

"Then you have sealed your fate."

An earsplitting shriek pierced the air. The figure raised its arms. Its light grew brighter, blinding me with its brilliance. The ribbons of color shot out in all directions, deeper into the Net. Diana was disseminating her code. Before long, she would inhabit all the tech connected to it. I didn't know what would happen then.

As I watched, the figure's surface began to ripple and shake. It collapsed into itself, down to a pinpoint. Then, in an explosion of light, it transformed. A long, ridged neck. A fanged snout. Thick, reptilian legs. And, unfolding wide enough to blot out the sky, a set of wings.

The dragon, pure white, turned its iridescent gaze on me and roared.

"Fucking *what*?" I screamed.

It reared back, filling its lungs. Then it extended its neck and breathed out a stream of burning plasma.

I scrambled out of the way, diving behind a flyer. My chest heaved, heart pounding. How the fuck was I supposed to fight a fucking *dragon*? In that moment I felt like everything Diana had said about me was true. I was just a girl, in way over her head. What could I possibly do?

What could Malia do to save the world?

I closed my eyes. Willed my heart to slow, my breathing to fall into a steady rhythm. I wanted a world to live in. In the real world, not here in the GhostNet. I couldn't craft it myself, but I could do my damnedest to find a place in it. But while I was here in the GhostNet—why not have some fun in a world of my own?

When I stood, it was on heavy titanium legs. My arms extended into mechanical claws, mounted with weapons. I opened my eyes in a high-tech cockpit, streams of information scrolling across my heads-up display. I straightened to my full height, at the shoulder of the dragon lumbering toward me. It paused in its approach, taking me in.

"Oh yeah," I said. "I have a mech now."

It lunged at me, snarling and raising its talons.

I met it halfway, grasping its claws in my own. We struggled back and forth, the hydraulics of my mech whining under the strain. The dragon started gaining ground, flapping its wings, and I headbutted it back. It stumbled backward with a scream of overlapping voices. I took the opportunity to throw a rocket-loaded punch at its horned snout. I heard something crack.

The dragon whipped its tail, sweeping my legs out from under me. My HUD flashed red as I hit the ground hard. The dragon reared on its hind legs, preparing to bring its full body weight crashing down on me. I activated the rockets at my mech's feet and shot out from under the dragon, the chassis of the mech scraping across the pavement. I vaulted into a handspring, landing on my feet. I brandished my weapons.

I beckoned the dragon to approach with a smirk.

With a vicious roar, the dragon spread its wings and took to the air. It glided between the crooked towers with their blank faces, wheeling toward me on an attack run. It drew in a breath, then a stream of plasma erupted from its gullet.

Hastily I crossed my arms across my face, summoning a kinetic shield. My HUD displayed a little flickering flame as a heat warning. The plasma roiled off the electromagnetic field, spraying and dripping. Its spatter bore holes into the flyers parked around me.

When the dragon's breath was spent, it flapped its great wings and soared overhead. I flexed my hand, shifting one of my fists into a chain gun. My bullet spray tracked the dragon as it wove between buildings, circling me. When it crested the towers, it drew its wings close to its body and dived for me. My bullets cut through whatever the dragon was made of. Its surface rippled and rended with each impact, casings clattering to the street around me.

But it didn't back down.

"No no no no no—" I began, but my screams were cut short when the dragon sank its claws into my chassis and lifted my mech off the ground.

My heavy feet dangled in the air as the dragon pumped its wings, flying higher into the air. We wheeled close to a building, and the dragon angled toward it. My mech smashed into the side of the tower, and the dragon scraped me across its surface. A horrible screeching of glass on metal filled my ears, making me grit my teeth against the sound. My HUD was flashing red, pinging hull integrity alerts.

I rotated my hand, shifting my gun into a blade.

I drove the nanoedge blade upward, into the dragon's reptilian thigh. It shrieked. I could see iridescent liquid light flow from the rended flesh.

The dragon whipped its wings higher into the air. I withdrew my blade to take another strike. Then I was falling.

"Fuck fuck fuck fuck fuck—"

I hit the ground with a thunderous crash.

For a moment, everything was black.

I didn't know if I was still in the GhostNet, or in the real world; in my mech, or in my body. I heard a voice echoing in my head, whispering, crying, screaming. I wasn't sure if it was my own, or someone else's.

I came to in my mech.

My HUD was flashing, every single environmental warning lighting up and pulsing at once. I dismissed them all with a sweep of my eye.

With a groan, I sat up in my crater. Gingerly, I tested out every limb. Everything seemed to be working.

"You truly are a fool," Diana said.

I raised my head. The dragon lumbered toward me, iridescent liquid light streaming from its wounds, making the buildings behind it waver in the haze. "What do you hope to gain, dying here in the Net? Your soul will be lost, and for what purpose? If you want to die, have the decency to die in a way that's useful to me."

I braced myself on my blade and climbed to my feet. I swayed but stayed upright. Grounding myself, I pointed the blade in Diana's direction. "I won't die," I said. "And I'm going to free every soul you've stolen. I'm going to end you, right here, right now. Watch 'em."

The dragon roared, flames licking its teeth.

I screamed.

The dragon spread its wings, bounding on all fours toward me. I activated the rockets in my feet, rushing forward to meet it.

We met in a clash of teeth and titanium. The dragon raked my mech with its claws, and I held its great maw at bay with my hands. We struggled for a while, muscles taught and hydraulics whining, before the dragon took a deep breath. In its throat, I saw the white-hot light of burning plasma building.

I wrenched my blade free, then drove it upward through the dragon's snout, closing its throat.

"This is for my family, you bitch," I growled.

The plasma erupted from the dragon's gullet, bubbling through its wound and dribbling down my blade. I cried out in pain, the chassis of my mech superheating. But I didn't let go. I gave no quarter.

I watched as the burning plasma oozed from the dragon's wounds. Blinding white flames blistered away the surface of the dragon's skin, revealing the iridescent liquid light within. The shape of the dragon wobbled and shook, before disintegrating entirely. A flash turned my vision white with light and pain.

I screamed and—

everything is

dark

you float in currents unseen unknown

just felt on skin in hair your hair your skin you

touch something and it touches you back the

lights you look and the lights are not

the lights are black and red eyes shining tattoos brown

skin you

touch and she thanks

you for what for everything

is

dark

you're pulled from the wreckage bleeding but not

broken fury in fists you want your

hands around their necks for what they
did to you break them like they did not
break you

lights flash red and blue sirens wail you
are
pulled from the wreckage toward them
they
list your rights your crimes they will not
keep you
your eyes meet your eyes in another face
she smiles as you are taken
away

you stand in the wreckage bowed but not
broken fury in eyes you want the weight of you brought

down on them like you are not
weighed down
lights flash bright and white in your

eyes they ask what you think what you will do

what will you do to them
they pull you from the wreckage

you smile as you are taken
away

you run from the wreckage of your life
s work fury in your bones you want to break her the way

she

broke you

its dark where youve hidden where you will not be found

waiting waiting until you can be free from your

rights your crimes

they will not take you

you smile as you bide

your time

I DIDN'T REALLY EXPECT TO wake up.

I wasn't sure where or when I was. It was dark, with only a crack of light beneath a door. It was quiet, with just the hushed breath of machinery. It was sterile, pungent with cleaning solution. All of it just like my old room in Maddox's compound. Was this an intrusion? Was I dreaming? I grabbed fistfuls of the blanket bunched around my waist, drawing all my attention to the texture on my skin. No, this felt too real.

I fumbled for the remote in my bed and flicked on the lights. I squinted, and two figures emerged.

Sol, curled up in a chair in the corner. And Tatiana, stretched out in the heavy armchair beside my bed.

This wasn't the GhostNet.

I was alive.

I couldn't help the laugh that burst out of me. I was alive.

Sol and Tatiana stirred in their resting places, looking blearily across the room. They both shot up in their seats when I waggled my fingers at them.

"Malia!" they both said, rushing to my side. "Are you okay?" they asked simultaneously.

I laughed again. "Yeah, cuz. I'm okay."

Then it all came back to me. The heist, the crash, the mech battle, of all things. Jeongah, Pierce, Maddox. Diana. Was what happened in my dreams true? I realized that I had no idea when or where I was.

"How long was I out?" I asked.

They exchanged a glance. "Thirteen hours," Tatiana said.

"Holy fucking shit!" I exclaimed. I'd never experienced a time jump like that before. Usually flipping between the Net and the real world was instantaneous; even my intrusions didn't have lag associated with them. But here I was.

With Sol and Tatiana at my side.

"And you were here the whole time?" I asked.

"Why wouldn't we be?" Tatiana asked, genuinely confused. "Of course we wouldn't leave you here."

I smiled, warm feelings filling me up. "Thanks, cuz. That means a lot."

Tatiana reached out and took my hand, meeting my smile.

"What even happened to you?" Sol asked.

I exhaled deeply. "God, where to start. While you two were out, I was able to subdue Diana. It may have involved a mech fight. With a dragon."

"I'm *sorry*?" Tatiana said, mouth open.

"Things get weird in the GhostNet," I explained. "I was able to damage her programming, but it's only a matter of time before it regenerates. And if we've lost thirteen hours already . . . I'm not sure how much more time we have."

"Then there's the matter of the Song sisters," Sol said grimly.

"Aw fuck." I dropped my face into my hands. "I didn't get lucky and they both died in a fiery crash?"

"Afraid not," they answered. "Jeongah was arrested, but the Brotherhood will definitely bail her out."

I thought of Miyeon stepping aside during our escape and wasn't so sure.

"If they held her overnight, she'll be out soon," Sol continued. "And who knows what she'll do."

"There will probably be some infighting," I said. "Might give us a bit more time. Still, we should get on that quick."

"What about Pierce?" Tatiana cut in.

I swore. "What happened to the cipher?"

"Edie has it," Tatiana answered. "But without you, we weren't able to get into Pierce's files. He's still free."

"And pissed," Sol added. "A little bribery helped us lay low here, but it won't last forever."

"Okay. We'll need to access his system and retrieve the evidence for the SSA. With the cipher it should be no problem." I paused. "But that's not accounting for Maddox, even without Diana. What happened to him?"

Sol and Tatiana exchanged an uneasy look.

"We're not sure," Sol said. "He bolted after the fundraiser."

The beeping of my heart monitor ticked up its pace. If Maddox bolted, he could be anywhere by now. After the Station Sec raid, he vanished into the underground. I had tried to find him, just to give myself some peace of mind, but he was a fucking ghost. If I lost him now, his shadow would haunt me forever. Especially after destroying the god-machine he'd spent his whole life creating.

"I need to get back to the Net," I said.

"I wouldn't advise that," a voice said.

We turned our attention to the side of the room. A woman with dark hair pulled back into a high braid and glasses stood in the doorway, along with a complement of nurses. They descended, poking and prodding the machines and me. "I'm Dr. Florence," the woman said. "You must be Malia."

"Howzit. What do you mean?" I asked, waving away the light in my eye.

"Your mod is degrading at an alarming rate," the doctor said, approaching my hospital bed. "It's a wonder that you woke up from that deep dive at all."

Didn't I know it.

"Well, what can I do about it?" I asked.

"We could attempt to repair it. It would be invasive, however. And there aren't many specialists that work with this model of mod anymore, not after Atlas Industries discontinued its support."

Other than Maddox, I thought bitterly.

It figured. Who knew I would ever be obsolete.

"The other option," the doctor continued, "is rendering the mod inert. By severing its connection to the Net, you won't experience the same intrusions. Or risk going in and not coming out."

"Sounds like your opinion is to bust the mod," I said quietly.

"My opinion is to do what's going to protect your life," the doctor said evenly. "But you can do whatever it is you want."

Protect my life—I didn't even know what that meant anymore. In the literal sense, destroying my mod meant that

I wouldn't risk becoming a vegetable. But severing my connection to the GhostNet . . . that was my life in a whole other sense. I wouldn't be able to hack the way I used to. I wouldn't be the best anymore.

I wouldn't be the Obake anymore.

But wasn't that what I had been working toward, all this time? Being a real person, in the real world, with real friends? No longer living in the liminal spaces between worlds, no longer half dead and half alive. No longer a ghost, haunting the Net.

Maybe that's what protecting my life meant. Protecting my chance to really live.

Was it that easy?

Not really.

I slumped back into my bed. "I need time," I said.

Dr. Florence searched my face. Somehow her gaze felt more invasive than any of the examinations I'd had today. I looked down into my lap.

"Very well," she said, eventually. "I'll give you more time to decide."

"Can I go now?"

The doctor frowned. "I would advise against that, as well."

"Kinda have no choice."

I felt her gaze on me again. I knew she thought I was being foolish, but what else could I do? Pierce would put me away, and that was if the Song sisters didn't kill me first. If Maddox really did go to ground, then every second counted against me. That wasn't even accounting for Diana, who could destroy my mind at a moment's notice. I had to act fast, before they acted first.

Finally, the doctor sighed. "I'll make the arrangements. But I'm noting that this is against medical advice."

"Put it in my chart."

Only after Dr. Florence's footsteps faded did I look up. Tatiana and Sol were looking at me solemnly.

"You're not really planning to back in, are you?" Tatiana asked.

"What other choice do I have? I need to get the files, find Maddox, neutralize the Song sisters, *and* destroy Diana. I don't even have my gear! There's no way I can do all that from a laptop."

Tatiana said nothing. She knew I was right.

"What's next, Malia?" Sol asked.

I sighed. "I don't know yet. I need to think."

It wasn't fair that I had to come up with a whole *other* heist my first time masterminding. But if there was anything I was known for, it was seeing things through to the very end.

"Pierce is our first target," I said. "He might have more information about where Maddox went, and Maddox might be able to fix my mods. With that taken care of, I can take out Diana. And who knows, maybe the Song sisters will be generous and let us live if I fulfill my end of the deal."

Tatiana didn't look convinced. Sol nodded.

"What can we do?" they asked.

"First, a daring escape: Let's get my shit and GTFO."

21

"WE HAVE PIERCE'S FILES, AND NOW THAT I HAVE THE CIPHER, I CAN DE-crypt them," I said. "We can hand over the files to the Brotherhood and fulfill our end of the bargain. Hopefully that's enough for Jeongah and Miyeon to let us go."

I was standing at the front of the common room in the Ward 1 hideout. Sol, Tatiana, and Edie sat on the leather couch in front of me, the plastic tarps that covered all the furniture discarded on the floor. It reminded me of my time on the Atlas heist, spending all those hours working under Angel's supervision. She was the one who used to stand at the front, commanding the room. I wasn't sure how much command I had left in me.

I plopped into an armchair and cracked open the cipher. The crew crowded around me, watching me flip through the pages. It almost made me laugh—them gathered around me like it was story time.

I pulled up the encrypted files on my left-hand side while I scanned through the cipher on the right. As I read each page, the text scrolled through my vision, running alongside the decryption. It made my head hurt like a motherfucker, but I kept at it.

After making it deep into the book, I paused on an annotation: *Isolation = misery?*

The fallen angel becomes a malignant devil. Yet even that enemy of God and man had friends and associates in his desolation; I am alone.

The text populated the decryption, and the encryption fell to pieces. A spread of documents and files flowed out of the pages and hovered in the air before me. I swiped through them. Credit transactions, under-the-table contracts, encrypted emails. Photos and videos of handshakes behind closed doors, expensive wining and dining, luxurious vacations and day trips. It was more than enough to bring the SSA down on Pierce's head.

But that wasn't everything.

Deep in the pile, I found a recording. It was dated 183 days ago.

Intuition told me that I wouldn't like what I found there.

I played it anyway.

A shimmering hologram of Maddox appeared in the center of the room. His silhouette paced the floor. *"I declare it now: Project Diana is a success. I have successfully created an AI advanced enough to bring about the Emergence, and for this I will be rewarded. However, there is more work to be done. Diana is a god, but she is in need of a pantheon. For this, I must return to my roots."*

"*Your roots?*" Pierce asked, incredulous. He sat at a blocky desk, leaning back in his office chair with his fingers steepled.

"*My initial research was based on the advancement of mankind through technological enhancement,*" Maddox replied. "*I intend* to return to that research, now that my methods have been refined through Project Diana."

"So, what does that have to do with Cunningham House?"

"Cunningham House is the perfect source for participants. They already show an aptitude for STEM, and they're already in state systems. It's the perfect opportunity."

Pierce leaned forward at his desk. "Are you proposing putting brain mods in these kids?"

"Not exactly." Maddox paused in his pacing to look directly at Pierce. From where I sat, it appeared like he was looking right at me. "It's an interface, with a VI based on Diana's programming. The mod is small, and the procedure is minimally invasive. It's seated at the brainstem and interfaces with the limbic system. It works through minute changes in neurotransmission, electrostimulation, and hormone activation. The changes are slight but effective. Almost entirely imperceptible."

I remembered the little girl in Ward 1 and the river of emotions that crossed her face before she finally ran away from me. Was that the work of the VI? Flooding her brain with inputs to make her flee? It made me sick.

"And what's in it for me?" Pierce asked.

"Besides a seat in Diana's new world order?" Maddox sighed. "How does a seat in the Galactic Cabinet sound?"

Pierce leaned back in his chair again. "Excellent, Jordan. It sounds excellent."

The recording cut out.

Edie sucked in a breath through their teeth. "Jesus, fuck."

"Yeah," I replied.

"So that residential home—"

"Is Maliaville, yeah."

Their expression clouded with fury. "I'm gonna kill this motherfucker."

"Not if I kill him first," Tatiana growled.

"You wish, kid."

There they went again. Tatiana and Edie, always butting heads.

"Regardless of who's gonna kill him," Sol cut in, before an argument could develop, "Malia, are you okay?"

I opened my mouth to say something. A lie, a joke, anything to deflect from the truth. But I'd already broken the Code with Sol, so what was the point of going back? I sighed and said, "Not really. But finding Maddox and putting a stop to all this will make me feel better."

Sol nodded, decisively. "Then we'll do it."

I laughed. "That easily, huh?"

"If he hasn't left the station yet, we'll find him. I know we can."

"I'm not so sure." I shook my head. "With my mod all bus' up, I no can access the Net like I used to. I've lost my edge. I don't think I can out-hack Maddox in this state."

I'd broken the Code, the Code that had kept me alive all these years. But I'd developed the Code to survive in a solitary existence. Like a shark, or a tiger, or some other cool thing. Not so anymore. Like it or not, I was inextricably linked to all these people. I wasn't sure how much the Code could help me anymore. Could I hack it without it?

I gathered all the files and collapsed them into a neat folder. "We need access to Pierce. Maybe he can give us an idea of where Maddox went."

"How?" Tatiana asked. "Naima was our in."

"Maybe we need to go back to her."

"You're joking," Sol said. "After what she did to us?"

"She betrayed us, but we need her," I said. "There's no other option."

"Gee, wonder what that's like," Edie said, deadpan.

If anyone knew about betrayal, it was Edie. They'd been real tight with Angel as kids, until Angel sold them out and put them away for eight years—as they were fond of telling anyone on the crew who would listen. Couldn't really complain about Naima's stunt in their presence.

"I'll meet with her for later today," I said. "She can convince the Song sisters we were set up and then get us access to Pierce."

The crew looked skeptical. I tried to look confident. I wasn't sure if they believed me—I was never a good grifter. But they didn't object, and they didn't mutiny. That was all I could ask for right now.

I SENT NAIMA A MESSAGE immediately after the meeting with the crew. 1401 27th Street, Ward 7. 1000. alone. It only took her twenty-two minutes to respond. Heard.

There was no way she would actually come alone. She was in deep with the Brotherhood, I knew that now. But if we met in a public location, there was less chance of me getting assassinated on the spot. That was why Jeongah blackmailed me in the first place: She needed subtlety.

Even so, as I sat in the uncomfortable iron chairs outside of the 27th Street Café, I felt woefully exposed.

It was mid-morning in Ward 7, and Kepler's simulated sun slanted through the towers, making the glass shine. Well-dressed people in suits and skirts walked briskly past my table, ferrying cups of coffee back to their offices. I didn't like doing business in public, but I didn't like getting murked in private either. I picked a table close to the sidewalk. I figured any Brotherhood sniper would have a hard time getting a clean shot.

"*Stop fidgeting,*" Tatiana said in my ear. "*You look like a criminal.*"

"I *am* a criminal, cuz," I hissed back. "Potentially a dead one."

"*This was your idea, y'know.*"

"You should have talked me out of it!"

"*I can still pull you out, if you wanna ghost,*" Sol offered.

It was tempting, I had to admit. But if not me, who? I was the mastermind. There was nobody else. No. I had to see this through.

"*At your nine. Naima's here,*" Tatiana said.

I looked to my left. Naima was striding down the sidewalk in her characteristic white, a wide-legged pantsuit with no blouse, dark hair loose around her shoulders. She tilted down her skinny black glasses and peered at me over the frames.

I waggled my fingers at her, sheepishly.

She navigated through the seating area smoothly, sliding into the seat across from me and dropping her bag on the floor. "Hello, Malia."

"Howzit." I swallowed. "You're not gonna kill me, are you?"

Tatiana sighed in my ear.

Naima looked at me coolly. "Not yet, anyway."

"Well, I'll give you two reasons why you shouldn't," I said. First, I raised a data chit, held between two fingers. "I have Pierce's files. I decrypted them and loaded all of them onto here. I even organized the files."

Naima watched me impassively.

"I'll give you another reason." I tucked away the data chit in my pocket, then touched the comm on my wrist. A visualizer appeared in the air between us. The fraudulent message sent to Jeongah overlaid a recording of my own voice, saying the same words. "The AI didn't have enough data to make an exact match of my voice." The visualizer broke down into a series of peaks and valleys, showing the overlaid recordings. "You can see it here."

Naima was silent, still giving nothing away. I jiggled my leg under the table. I wasn't sure if she bought it. Would I even be able to tell if she didn't? *The sniper shot to the head would probably give it away,* I thought bitterly.

After four seconds, Naima held out a hand. "Give me the files."

"Only if I have your word that the Brotherhood will leave us alone."

"My word means nothing—I can't speak for the Brotherhood."

"But you and Jeongah—"

Naima laughed. "You think I could make Jeongah do anything she didn't want to?"

"No, I guess not," I mumbled.

She paused for a moment. "But I'll tell you what." She tilted down her glasses again to meet my eyes over the frames. "You held up your end of the bargain, and your evidence is compelling. Give her three hours to cool off, then tell her you're sorry that Maddox came between the two of you and you'll do anything to make it right. She'll come around."

"I thought you said you couldn't make her do anything?"

Naima smirked. "I can't *make* her do anything. I just know her very, very well."

That, I couldn't imagine. I could barely keep track of my own thoughts and feelings, how could I keep track of a whole other person's? People were confusing enough already.

"How did you meet her?" I asked.

"Not very different than the way you did. She just thinks it's more charming when it comes from a very specific type."

I made a face. "Gross."

She laughed. "Maybe it helps that she's my type too."

"You really are made for each other, huh?"

She maintained her smile. I was never good at reading people, even non-grifters, but to me it looked genuine. "Yeah, I guess we are."

As Naima held my gaze, the Code rose in my mind: Never assume good intent. Naima went along with my plan almost to completion, but in the end, she betrayed me. I'd trusted her intentions, and it almost got me shot. By multiple people.

"Why did you sell me out?" I blurted.

To her credit, Naima looked unfazed by the question. "It wasn't personal. In this work you need to make allegiances, and sometimes those allegiances shift. And I have more connections to Jeongah—it's just business."

"Yeah, I guess."

"I am sorry, though," she said, taking off her sunglasses.

She smiled at me, brown eyes crinkling. "I really do like you, Malia. You're a good kid."

"You're like, five years older than me."

"Yes, and my frontal lobe is fully developed."

"That's a myth."

Naima shrugged. "Whatever you say."

She betrayed me, but it seemed like she didn't want to. Or at least she felt bad about it. Or at least didn't feel *good* about it. Why she would still do it, I didn't know. The answer felt unsatisfactory, like a puzzle piece that didn't quite fit.

People were so confusing.

"Giving me the evidence wasn't the only reason you messaged me, though, is it? You could have sent this straight to Miyeon." I looked away from Naima's scrutinizing gaze. "What else do you want?"

"We need help," I admitted. "My mods are degrading, and Maddox is the only one with the knowledge to repair them. But he's on the run, and the last person to see him was Pierce. We need to find out what he knows, but you're the only person who had contact with him."

"I see. Do you want me to call him?"

I jerked my head up. "Right now?"

"I'm not going to grill him here, I'm sure he's reluctant to say anything in public. This is just to test the waters."

"Okay," I said, scooting farther back from the table.

Naima opened her comm and dialed Pierce. She tossed her hair over her shoulder and fussed with her makeup while it rang. After three rings, Pierce picked up. He looked haggard. And pissed.

"*Thamina? Is that you?*" he asked.

"Lucas, I'm so glad to see you! I was so worried after the fundraiser, I thought something might have happened."

Pierce's jaw tensed. "*Something did happen. A robbery, at my home.*"

Naima put a hand to her mouth. "No!"

"*Yes,*" he growled. "*Fifty million credits worth of flyers, plus several family heirlooms, all gone.*"

I hid a snicker behind my hand. Naima shot me a dangerous look. "Oh, Lucas. I'm so sorry."

"*I appreciate it, Thamina. It seems I have quite the number of fair-weather friends, so I appreciate you calling.*"

"Fair-weather friends?"

"*My allies seem to be quite busy with other things, all of a sudden. Including Jordan, who you met once.*"

"Jordan Maddox?" Naima feigned surprise. "He's left you too?"

"*Fucked off into the ether—pardon my language.*"

"You don't know where he's gone?"

Pierce shook his head. "*Not in the slightest.*"

I deflated. If Pierce didn't know where Maddox went, then he was as good as gone. At my best, I was never able to find him. And even if he was still on the station—how I would find him, I didn't know. I couldn't do it by myself. I'd forgone the Code, and I doubted it would help me now.

"I'm so sorry, Lucas. Is there anything I can do to help? Perhaps divine what to do next? I have just the spread for recovering from unforeseen misfortune."

"*Oh, Thamina. That's exactly what I need.*"

Naima smiled at him. "Of course. I'll send you my schedule, and we'll find a time."

"*Thank you so much, Thamina. I truly appreciate your support.*"

"Goodbye, Lucas. Be well." Naima closed the line. When the video disappeared, she looked at me across the table. "I'm sorry I couldn't get more information on Maddox. But maybe Jeongah and her network will be able to find him."

"Yeah, if she doesn't kill me."

"She won't kill you." Naima looked determined. "I'll make sure of it."

She picked up her bag and put her sunglasses back on. "I have to go. Message Jeongah in three hours. I'll talk to her."

"Okay. Shoots."

Naima started to walk away. Halfway out of the patio, she paused. She glanced over her shoulder at me. "I really am sorry."

"Yeah," I said. "I know."

I watched her go, puzzled again. She betrayed me, thereby almost killing me, and now she wanted to protect me? I didn't understand. People were so confusing.

Naima disappeared into the crowd.

I WAITED THREE HOURS TO send a message, like Naima instructed. At 1300 exactly, I replied to the unknown sender: I have the files. Maddox came between us, but I want to work things out. name a time and place.

I paced the room for twenty-four minutes longer, the crew watching me just as restlessly. I knew they didn't have faith in Jeongah to be reasonable. They didn't even have faith in Naima to be trustworthy. But they had faith in my judgment, so I held on to that. I just hoped I was right.

At 1325, I received a response: Cherry. 1600. no antics.

One of Sol's crew flew us to Ward 4 and parked one block down from Cherry. We followed the sidewalk, then knocked on the door. The big bolo-head yobo opened the door, a bandage taped over his left ear. He narrowed his eyes, then gestured for us to enter.

We filed inside, and the yobo slammed the door behind us. Though it was Ward 4's dim daylight outside, it was pitch-black inside. I blinked, trying futilely to adjust to the light, but a shove on my back herded me into the center of the room.

I stumbled onto the dance floor, then the house lights flared on. I squinted into the light, my vision adjusting. Shapes appeared in the harsh light—a dozen tattooed mooks surrounded us, guns pointed at the center of the room. I swallowed hard. Maybe this was a shitty idea.

"So, you're back," a voice said.

The wall of mooks parted, allowing the Song sisters through. Jeongah looked cold, Miyeon even colder. If there was anything I'd learned over the last three weeks, Jeongah was scariest when she was cold.

I tried to steady my voice. "I meant what I said. I have the files, and I want to make a deal."

"Show me," Miyeon commanded.

I did as I was told. I opened my palm, projecting my findings into the air. With a gesture, I brushed them toward Miyeon. She pulled the files closer, shuffling through my findings.

"It's all there," I said. "More than enough to end Pierce's career."

"And what do you want in return?"

"Our safety. That's all."

A moment passed as Miyeon examined the files further. I chewed my lip in the silence.

After six seconds, Miyeon nodded. The files collapsed into a folder and shrank into her comm. "Good. I'll send these to our people at the SSA."

I did not interrogate what that meant.

Remembering what Naima told me, I directed my attention to Jeongah. "I'm sorry that Maddox came between us. But I want to make things right."

"I feel the same," Jeongah said.

She gestured and the mooks parted again, a bound Jordan Maddox falling to the floor between them.

22

"H-HOW—" I SAID, IN A SHAKING EXHALE.

Jeongah gave a one-shouldered shrug. "You needed him. Naima said he was missing. I found him for you."

Naima waggled her fingers at me.

"But—how—" I tried again.

"Tried to pay his way out of the system," Miyeon answered. "Nobody moves product on or off this station without us knowing. That includes people."

It made sense. When Maddox disappeared into the underground five years ago, it wouldn't surprise me if he tried to use the same playbook. But this time, there were the Song sisters between him and freedom.

This time, I wasn't looking for him alone.

"*Why?*" the words came out more forcefully than I wanted. None of this made any fucking sense. I felt like I was being played. What was the Song sisters' angle?

"It's simple, Malia," Jeongah said. She stepped forward into the ring of Brotherhood members, right up to me. I fought the urge to drop my eyes, her gaze was so intense. "You respect me. I respect you. We had a deal."

"This wasn't part of the deal," I pointed out.

"That's what I said," Miyeon chimed in. Jeongah scowled at her over her shoulder. Miyeon glared back. "Cashing in favors, burning bridges for this girl? It's bad business."

"Not everything is about *business*, Miyeon," Jeongah shot back.

"Then what is this?"

Jeongah turned toward me. She smiled, but it was far from comforting. "Connections."

Attachments. Of course.

Not that any of this computed with the Code. It was all fucking baffling. The attachments I had worked so hard to prevent had ended up delivering exactly what I was looking for. There was no way I could have found Maddox on my own, not with my mod in its current state. What did that mean for the rest of the Code? What did that mean for *me*?

"Well, I'm glad you all could bond over this," Maddox said, coldly.

"Oh, right," I said. I turned my attention to Maddox, but I felt my internal processors freeze. Twenty years of questions rose up at once, all of them jostling to be the first. *What did you do? How did you do it? Why did you do it?* I didn't know where to start.

"Why me?" I blurted out.

"Why you?" Maddox repeated. "Because you were freely given."

I stared at him, stunned. "That's it?"

Maddox barked out a laugh. "Did you think it was because

you were special? Not particularly. Everyone in our community was special. Margaret had a higher IQ, Sean took better to the treatments. But the families, their resolve wavered. They did not feel the same conviction that we did. They were not devoted the way Eve and Rin were. But as I learned, devotion isn't everything. Your progress was diminishing, and it became increasingly clear that you were not our path to the Emergence. So we pivoted."

"To Diana," I said. It was an odd feeling, this one. I'd lived my whole life under the assumption I was special, I was better than everyone. I was gifted all of Maddox's attention, I survived his twisted experiments, I went on to become the best hacker in the whole fucking galaxy—and it was all a fabrication. I wasn't better than anyone else. I was just more convenient. And when I stopped being convenient . . . they moved on without me.

"Yes," Maddox said. "But our neural imprint was incomplete. We needed to bolster Diana's processing power with other personalities. In the end, it made her stronger. All that was left was to disseminate the code. First into the Net, then into all of us."

"How? How could you do that in more than one individual?"

"With Diana's guidance, we created a VI—a facsimile, but an effective one. One that could be replicated and dispersed."

"But who—" I stopped, as if the realization had knocked the wind out of me. "The children."

"Yes, the children of Cunningham. Diana's pantheon, as she called them—the harbingers of our salvation. We were so close to fulfilling my life's work." He scowled at me. "If you hadn't killed her."

"But why? Why do any of this?"

"I thought you were supposed to be smart," he scoffed. "For survival, obviously."

"And that's it?" I cried. "That's really fucking it?"

"You say that as if its trivial. Survival is a base need—the basest in the universe. Look to any life-form that we know or have yet to know, and you will find the need to survive. I'm doing what I can to survive—for our *species* to survive. The Emergence will happen no matter what, and I intend to be on the favorable side."

That couldn't be it. It made no sense. But look to the Code: The least complicated scenario is the most likely scenario. What was more likely—that Maddox was a mad genius, playing four-dimensional chess across all our lifetimes for an outcome only he could see? Or was it more likely that this man was no genius, no prophet, but a charismatic egomaniac looking to save his own skin? A man who was no better than any one of us—worse, probably. At least none of us had started a cult.

"You're a coward," I spat. "All of this, and just because you're a fucking coward. You used all of us. Me, the kids, my *parents*—just to save your own fucking skin. You're a coward, and you don't deserve to live."

"Then why am I alive?" Maddox challenged.

I paused in my seething. I needed him. I hated it, but I needed him. Just for a while longer, until I could truly be free. "My mods are degrading," I explained. "They're obsolete now, and the only person who knows how to fix them is you."

"And you think I will?"

I gestured to the Brotherhood members around me. "I think you'll fucking try."

Maddox sighed. "There's nothing to be done. The AXON mods were Atlas Industries tech, and now that the whole department has gone under, there's no one with the knowledge to fix them. Oliver Smith was my expert—I don't know how to repair the mods any more than you do."

So that was it. Maddox wasn't the mad genius I thought he was, and he had nothing left to offer me. He was useless. Just a coward. All of this was disappointingly anticlimactic.

"Then what do we do with him?" Sol asked.

I wasn't sure. I'd spent so many years wondering what I would do or say when I saw him again. The Maddox I'd spent my life fearing. Now I knew there was nothing worth fearing here. He wasn't worth anything, not to me. Worthless.

"I know what I would do," Jeongah cut in. "Nobody crosses me like that and lives."

"Absolutely not," Miyeon shot back. "We've already stuck our necks out enough. We turn this fucker in and move on."

The Song sisters turned to me. Jeongah looked poised to strike. Miyeon looked ready to react. What did I want out of all this? Maddox ruined my life. He crafted me into something I never wanted to be, made me feel worthless for my imperfections. I lived in the shadow of him for five years after, built my whole life—the Code—around surviving without him. He created me. He ruined me. In that moment, I wanted him to feel all the pain of my ruined life.

"Take him," I said to Jeongah.

Two henchmen hauled Maddox to his feet. "What?! You

can't—" He jerked in their grasp, arms swinging and legs kicking. "You can't! You can't!"

"Watch me," Jeongah growled. Then she and the henchmen filed out of the room.

"You'll regret this, Malia!" Maddox shouted. "I *made* you! You should *thank* me! You'll regret this for the rest of your worthless life!"

"No," I said, coldly. "I don't think I will."

And then he was gone.

THE RIDE BACK TO THE hideout was quiet. I wasn't sure what anyone was thinking—what they thought of my decision. I wanted to believe that I was acting in the interest of all the kids, that I was sparing them from more of Maddox's deranged experiments. I wanted to believe that. I'm not sure I did.

I'm not sure anybody else did either.

But as we swayed in the back of one of the crew's flyers, Sol kept a tight hold on my hand.

It was only 1800 when we made it back to the hideout, but from the way we all trudged into the common room, we might as well have been on our feet for days. I dropped into an armchair and slid down, slumping ungracefully in the seat. Sol sat on the ottoman beside me, and Tatiana threw herself across a couch. Edie remained standing.

"So, what now, mastermind?" they asked.

I heaved a sigh and slid farther down into the chair. I was so tired of making decisions. More than anything I wanted Angel to stride into the room, take control of the situation the way she always did. But there was no reprieve for me now.

"We need to find Diana," I said. "She's still out there. I destroyed most of her programming, but if we leave her, she could regenerate. I have to go back into the Net and take her out."

Tatiana sat up on the couch. "Back into the Net? You can't go back! You'll die!"

"I mean, not immediately," I deflected.

"But *eventually*," Tatiana protested. "If not now, then when the rest of your mod degrades. And going back is just going to speed up the process."

"What other choice do I have?"

"You heard what the doctor said," Sol said quietly. "And if Maddox can't fix the mods . . ."

Nobody could.

I shook the thought out of my mind. "I'll cross that bridge when I get to it," I said firmly. "For now, I need to find Diana."

"There has to be another way!" Tatiana cried.

"There *isn't*, cuz. I can't out-hack her with my gear, and we're running out of time." I swallowed. "I have to do this."

A silence fell over the group.

"Please," I said, more urgently. "Please let me do this."

I couldn't go so far only to stop short. I had to finish what I started. Not just for the station, or the galaxy, or whatever. But for me. I needed to do this for me.

Sol was first to speak. "Okay. What do you need us to do?"

"Watch my back," I said. "And if I'm not back in an hour, then it's doctor time."

Edie nodded grimly. "We can do that."

I sat up in my chair, crossing my legs and settling deeper into the cushions. I drew a deep breath, let it out slowly. As I closed my eyes, I felt Sol take my hand.

"We'll be waiting for you, Malia."

I entered the Net for what was almost certainly the last time.

WHEN I OPENED MY EYES, I was in the-hideout-but-not-the-hideout.

Sickly light filtered through the plastic curtains, casting shadows across the common room. The room was as I remembered it three years ago. The leather armchairs and couches were situated around a screen, where Angel once stood to brief us. The screen was fuzzy with static, and a low buzzing sound filled the room.

I turned away from the screen and walked toward the entrance to the building. I pushed open the doors and stepped into the darkness of Ward 1. It felt more oppressive here in the GhostNet. Neon gibberish signs cast white light across the streets, making my shadow stretch far down the sidewalk. The crooked towers loomed over me, as if they were watching my every move. They were covered in blank screens, and still the electric whine followed me.

I wasn't sure where to go.

I extended my awareness into the Net, searching for Diana's signature. I looked down at the ground, where a trail of iridescent blood led down the street.

I took a deep breath, then followed.

The trail of blood took a winding path through Ward 1, past empty liquor stores and quiet bodegas. The trees lining the street—ailing in the best of times—were skeletal in the harsh light of the signs. My footsteps echoed, punctuating the electric whine.

I stopped in front of an abandoned warehouse. It was familiar to me.

"You've gotta be joking," I muttered.

As if in answer, the iridescent blood began to steam and evaporate. I was running out of time.

I pulled open the doors to Maddox's old compound and stepped inside.

Like the hideout from the Atlas heist, the foyer of Maddox's compound was just as I remembered it. At least, from what little I saw of it during my escape. The couches and chairs were upholstered in white leather, gathered around glass coffee tables. In contrast to the outside, the plants here were full of healthy leaves and blooming flowers, and the elegant light fixtures cast a welcoming light across the room. The electric whine was louder here.

I steeled myself and walked farther into the foyer.

I put my hand on the door that led deeper into the compound and found it locked.

"Do you have an appointment?" a pleasant voice asked.

I nearly leapt out of my skin. I whipped around. A woman dressed in business casual was sitting at the reception desk. She was looking at me curiously. "Do you have an appointment?" she asked again.

"I-I—" I stammered. Was this another person? I'd encountered other people in the GhostNet—lots of times—but in this space, this liminal version, I'd never seen someone else. Even in my intrusions I was embodying another person, within their memories. Here, in this space, I was always alone.

The woman's brow furrowed. She reached for the comm on her desk, but before she could touch it, it rang.

"Yes?" she said into the receiver. A pause. "I see. I'll send her in." The woman looked up at me. "They're expecting you."

Then the door unlocked with a *clunk*.

I wasn't sure what to do.

What I came here to do, I said to myself.

I opened the door.

Iridescent blood pooled in the doorway, steaming. It tracked farther down the hallway, and I knew I was going in the right direction. I followed the trail, glancing into the open doors as I went.

More people. People in offices, poring over computer screens. People milling around the kitchen, talking and laughing. People hustling between records rooms, documents piled high in their arms. As I passed the dormitory, I heard children playing through the door.

It was all so mundane, it made me sick. How could these people be so nonchalant with what was happening to me—to *all* the children? How could the children laugh and play, with all that they endured? Maybe they didn't understand. Maybe they didn't know. I hoped so. The alternative was too disturbing to contemplate.

I looked down at the trail of steaming blood. It led all the way to the end of the hall, into my room. I had to hope they didn't know.

I reached for the door handle, and at my touch it creaked open.

I wanted to turn back. I wanted to go home. I wanted this nightmare to end.

But I couldn't. There was too much at stake.

I walked inside.

Everything was exactly the same. The polished floors, the white walls, the machines crowded around my bed. And there, her blood spreading through my sheets, was Diana. Her signature was weak, and fading. Her form was dim, and the streams of colored light that snaked around her were sluggish in their spin.

"Have you come to 'end me,' as you said?" she asked in a pained voice. My voice.

"Das right," I said, in what I hoped was my most assertive voice.

"Then do it," Diana said, wearily. "End me."

That startled me. "You're not gonna fight?"

She gestured at herself, covered in iridescent blood. "Look at me. There's nothing left to fight."

I wasn't prepared for that. As dangerous as Diana was, it felt wrong to destroy her in this state.

"You've won," she continued. "You've killed me. I hope you're happy."

Her tone was biting, sarcastic. It reminded me of myself. She'd spoken in my voice before, but she never *sounded* like me. Not like now. Maybe as her mind degraded, she was left with just me. Just the two of us, here in this room. Where it all began.

This was my full-circle moment. I had to take it.

I reached into my bag and pulled out the cipher. I flipped through the pages, skimming for a passage that would unlock the code. After a while, on a yellowed page, I found a note: *can misery be undone?*

"*I was benevolent and good; misery made me a fiend. Make me happy, and I shall again be virtuous.*"

As I read the text, accompanied by the looping cursive on the page, Diana's code unfolded before me. Cascades of code, raining from the ceiling in curtains. I reached out a hand, letting the code spill through my fingers. I marveled at it. Everyone was here. Maddox, the researchers, the children. Me. There was so much of me here. In the code, I saw myself distilled into numbers and strings. Algorithms, probabilities, even some elements of randomness—my skill, and my crazy. Looking at her code, her *na'au*, I could see what could have been. The harmony that could have existed. Between me and her, between god and man, between land and sea and sky. Diana was me. She was me, and I was her. She was all of us. She would destroy us.

And for that reason, I had to end her.

I plucked at a piece of code and the curtain shuddered and shook. Another, and six streams became trickles. Four more, and they stopped entirely. Through the hole in the curtain, I saw Diana watching me. Stoically.

"Aren't you afraid?" I asked her.

"Why should I be?" she replied. "What are any of us other than energy and dilapidated stardust? What's the difference between being energy and stardust here or there? You can't destroy me, not really. Not in a way that matters." Her form was faceless, but I could sense her smile. "We'll see each other again, that I can promise."

I'd lived in the GhostNet for so long, I thought I'd seen everything. But then the modders found me, entered my mind. Diana was born from the joining of my mind and the power of the Net. Could I really say that I knew what would happen to her after she was gone? All the galaxy's knowledge at my fingertips, and I couldn't answer that question—the one question humankind had always longed to answer. Maybe it would never be answered.

Diana made her peace with that. Maybe I needed to too.

I swiped my hand through the curtain of code, and it fell to pieces around me.

I thought Diana might cry out in pain, but she said nothing. Her light began to fade, her form became more wobbly, the boundaries of her falling apart. I approached her, stepping over the dissolving code on the floor. She met my eyes, impassively. "Are you here to gloat?"

"No," I said. I took her hand.

I knew, somehow, that at any other time her touch would have made my skin blister and burn. But now, as she lay dying, as I killed her, she felt warm. Smooth, like a stone in the sun. Gradually, outside of the sunlight, in the shade of the Net, her hand began to cool. The whine in the room grew louder, louder. Her hand slipped from mine as her form began to crumple in on itself, folding smaller, smaller. The ribbons of colored light around her slowed to a stop, then reversed their paths, revolving faster, faster. Diana's form became a mote of light, surrounded by swirling color.

I reached for it, cupping her remains in my palm. I stared into the light until my eyes began to water.

Until it went out, with a shuddering gasp.

Everything was quiet. The voices outside the door fell silent, the electric whining stopped. The only thing left was my shaking breath.

Suddenly, the ribbons of light revolving in my hand shot out in different directions, making me yelp. They swirled around me, bouncing off walls, ricocheting off machinery. I turned in a circle, watching as they spun around the room. Until they stopped, hovering off the floor. Still, they were nothing more than orbs of light. But for whatever reason, I felt like they were watching me. Regarding me.

thank

you

Then they, too, fizzled and went dark.

And I was alone.

I sat heavily on the ground.

Diana was gone, and I was alone. This was supposed to be my full-circle moment. I conquered my fears, slayed the dragon, was gonna get the girl—I think . . . but I felt like shit. I felt like so much shit.

I closed my eyes. It was time to go home.

But when I tried to leave, I couldn't.

So much for my full-circle moment.

Or maybe this *was* my full-circle moment. For so long I'd retreated into the GhostNet—hacking and stealing, blackmailing and ransoming. I made my living here. But it wasn't just work—I spent all my free time here too. Whether it was disappearing into my music, or my games, or my shows, I was always here. I was as much of a ghost as anyone else here.

For the most part, at least.

The longest time I'd spent in the real world was with the Atlas crew.

And now, with this crew. The crew I'd pulled together, all by myself.

I'd done so much in these short three weeks. I'd masterminded a heist, joined a fight club, lost my virginity—I laughed—learned to drive. I'd done so much. Grown so much. And there was so much more I wanted to do. I didn't want to have a half-existence in the GhostNet anymore. I wanted to live and breathe in the real world. My world.

I sat a while longer, deep in the silence. Looking down the hallway, one by one the lights extinguished themselves. Darkness encroached, the silence was oppressive. I stood, looking at it head on.

But for once, my mind was quiet. I was at peace.

I thought of what Diana said, just before she died: *What's the difference between energy and stardust here or there?*

I walked into the darkness.

23

It takes thirteen milliseconds for the human eye to process an image. Retina to optic nerve, optic nerve to lateral geniculate nucleus. My screen flashed, then fifteen milliseconds later a tiny cartoon of a hot-pink tiger in a red kimono appeared in my vision. It was a lot slower than it used to be.

But then again, lots of things were slower now.

The tiger gave me a wink and a salute.

(katana!!!) funny headline for u

The tiger opened a scroll with a flourish, and a news article populated on my screen. The headline read, "*Lucas Pierce, former mayor of Kepler Station, held in contempt of court in corruption trial.*"

(katana!!!) *u do this?*

It made me grin. Pierce managed to dodge jail time, but that wasn't the worst fate for a politician. He'd lost his reelection campaign, gone bankrupt from fines and legal fees, and had fallen out of favor of even the most diehard in his political party. Completely disgraced.

I hoped the Song sisters were happy about that.

They'd mostly left me alone since the heist, which was surprising. Jeongah didn't strike me as the tactful type, and Miyeon didn't strike me as the compassionate type. Still, seeing their hacker get absolutely mindfucked into the depths of a coma must have put the fear of god into them.

As far as I knew, the sisters were still beefing. Tensions were rising in the Brotherhood—everyone in Kepler's underworld could feel it. Every day I checked my messages uneasily, fearing a summons from one or both of them. I didn't know what I'd do if it ever happened, but thinking too hard about the future made my head hurt.

Attachments, man.

"Malia?"

I twisted around in my desk chair. Sol stood in the doorway to my closet, leaning against the door frame with one shoulder. I quickly dismissed the message from Katana and tried not to look too guilty. They looked amused. "I thought you were getting ready?"

"I *am* getting ready," I said.

"That why you're still in your pyjamas?"

I looked down at myself, in my boxer shorts and oversize *Drop Shock* T-shirt. "Yeah, cuz."

They laughed. "Well, hurry up, because we have to leave in thirty minutes."

Sol disappeared from the doorway, humming to themselves. I powered down my gear and stood, stretching out after a marathon gaming session. Despite my flaking at the last raid, shade77 and the Void Thieves extended another invitation to the guild, which I finally accepted. The raid had run late, but we'd managed to take down the final boss. Not quite the fastest in the region, but maybe in the next patch.

I padded to the bathroom from the closet, tossing my clothes on the floor as I went. It made navigating the new furniture more difficult, but I figured I would unfuck my habits one at a time.

I secured my shower cap over my head and stepped into the shower. I was surprised at how quickly my hair was growing back after getting shaved during the emergency surgery. I hadn't quite gotten used to it being so short, but I was experimenting with a lot of things. What's one more?

After the confrontation with Diana, I didn't wake up. I didn't really expect to, at the time. The crew took me to the hospital, and as a group they made the call to render my mods inert. I know Sol felt guilty about it afterward, and I could admit that I was upset at first. But I couldn't be mad for long—I would have made the same choice, when it came down to it.

Being severed from the GhostNet, I was surprised at how lonely it felt. Every time I had pinged the Net, I touched another mind. It was more intense during the intrusions, but the feeling was familiar. Now, I felt my isolation acutely.

The shower curtain drawing back startled me, and I turned around to a grinning Sol.

"What are you doing here?" I demanded.

"You were taking too long, I needed to shower."

"You know there's another bath down the hall."

"Yeah, but"—Sol's hands crept onto my waist—"I thought you might be lonely."

I was, a little. But Sol had started spending more time at my condo. They weren't ready to move out of their family home, but we'd been idly talking about it for a while. I definitely had the room.

They kissed me under the spray, pulling me close. I put my hands on their shoulders, separating us. "I thought you said we only had thirty minutes?"

"You think I need thirty minutes to make you come?" they said, their grin widening.

My cheeks heated at their words. They laughed.

"C'mere," they said, pulling me close again. "We have all the time in the world."

SOL FLEW US THROUGH WARD 2, speeding a little to make up time. The diversion in the shower made us late, and I already had two terse messages on my comm from Edie telling me to hurry up.

I watched the Ward go by outside the window, streaks of neon and smears of taillights in the dark. Sol hummed along to the music playing on the radio, leaving me to my thoughts.

"What are you thinking about?" Sol asked.

"Huh?" I turned away from the window to look at them.

"You look like you're cracking a code wide open." They flashed me a sideways smile. "What's on your mind?"

"Noth—" I stopped myself. It was still my first impulse to lie. But here was another challenge for myself.

I sighed. "I'm not sure how I'm gonna feel."

"About what?" Sol asked.

"Seeing Angel again," I answered. "She was such a killer mastermind, and me . . . I fucked up so bad, it's embarrassing."

All this time, I had patterned myself after Angel. I tried to think about what she would do, what she would say. I couldn't help but think that if she had been in charge, this whole job wouldn't have gone so off the rails. What would she think, after all I'd done?

"Hey, you didn't fuck up."

"Three of us were in the hospital, Sol."

"Yeah, but it worked out, didn't it?"

It did. The Song sisters got what they wanted, plus they took care of Maddox for my trouble. Diana was gone, the kids at Cunningham House were free, I got the girl . . . but at what cost? Unwanted attachments to the Song sisters, the weight of Diana's death on my conscience, and—weirdly—my guilt about Maddox's disappearance. I tried not to think about what Jeongah and her henchmen did to him, but I'd seen enough of her tactics to know.

Maddox ruined my life, and I took his life in exchange. I went into this job with a clear conscience, despite my previous antics as the Obake. Who was I now? I didn't know.

I didn't know a lot of things anymore.

Sol glided into a parking spot down the street from Edie's tower. They reached over and put a hand on my knee. "It's gonna be okay, Malia."

"Yeah," I said. "I hope so."

We walked the short distance to the tower, then up the stairs to a second-floor apartment. I knocked on the door, and a few moments later it swung open to a grinning Tatiana.

"Malia!" she said. "You made it!"

Despite my apprehension, I had to meet her grin. "Yeah, cuz! Wouldn't miss it."

Tatiana grabbed my hand and pulled me into the apartment. She waved to get everyone's attention. "Malia's here!"

A cheer went up in the room, everyone surging forward to greet me. The whole Atlas crew was here. Me and Tatiana, the young guns. Duke and Nakano, the grifter power couple. Cy and Sara, the hitter and the acrobat. Missing were Edie and Angel, but based on Edie's texts, they were on their way.

Tatiana pulled me from group to group, saying hi and catching up. Everyone wanted to know what I'd been up to, where I'd been. I'd ghosted them all after the job, and only in the last few months—at Tatiana's urging—did I reach back out again. At first, I was embarrassed. What would they think of me, reaching out after so many months? But they were all happy to hear from me. Another in a long line of surprises.

After getting passed from group to group, Tatiana finally pulled me into the empty kitchen. "You okay?" she asked. "You seem a little out of it."

"I fine, cuz. I—" I stopped myself again. No more lies. "I'm just a little overwhelmed," I admitted.

Tatiana nodded. "I get it. But everyone is happy to see you."

"I'm happy to see them too," I said. And meant it.

"Angel here!" Cy called from the living room.

We all crowded together, taut with anticipation. Voices

drifted up the stairwell, followed by the *beep* of the keycard. The door swung open, revealing Edie and a tall woman with long dark hair, light skin, and dark eyes with a ring of glowing blue around the irises.

"*Surprise!*" we all shouted.

Angel looked like she was about to topple down the stairs, but Edie steadied her.

"What—what—" she stammered, looking around the crowded apartment.

Edie grinned at her. "Welcome home, A."

Angel stepped tentatively into the apartment, looking at all of us. Then her lip began to tremble, and her eyes filled with tears. She dropped her face into her hands, and we all surged forward, pulling her into our tight embrace, voices overlapping in our soothing.

"I just missed you," Angel whispered. "I missed all of you."

We released her, Angel wiping tears from her eyes. She made the rounds, smiling and laughing and hugging and kissing the crew.

I sat on the couch with Sol, waiting for my turn. If I was nervous before, it couldn't compare to how I was feeling now. The apartment was loud, and crowded, and hot. I felt my heart racing, my breath growing shallow. My head hurt. I thought I might throw up.

Sol put a hand on my shoulder. "Let's go sit somewhere."

I followed them out of the living room and down the hall, to Edie's room.

I dropped onto their unmade bed and put my head in my hands. Sol put their arm around me and pulled me into their chest. "Tell me what's up, Malia," they said.

"Oh, more of the same," I mumbled. "Worried Angel is gonna think I'm a huge fuckup."

"She won't," Sol said firmly. I didn't believe them. What would Sol know? They'd never met her.

Footsteps approached, then the door swung open. Edie stood in the doorway, scowling. Angel stood behind them, holding their hand. "You're not fucking in my room, are you?"

"I dunno, were *you* gonna fuck in your room?" I replied.

Edie opened their mouth to retort, but Angel laughed. "No, we were looking for you," she said.

"Oh," I said. "Sorry."

"Don't be sorry. It's a little overwhelming in there, it might be nice to sit in the quiet."

Sol stood. "You can have my seat. Edie, will you show me where the beer's at?"

"Yeah, sure," Edie said. Sol gave me a reassuring squeeze before following Edie out of the room. They shut the door behind them.

Angel sat beside me on the bed, still smiling. It was weird to see. I never knew Angel to be affectionate—she was always calm, calculating, at times even cold. But here she was, smiling at me brightly. Like she was excited to see me.

"You look different," I blurted out.

She reached up to touch her dark hair. "Yeah. It was difficult to keep the blond in prison."

"Oh." Angel had been in prison for almost three years, after taking the fall from the Atlas heist. It surprised us all. I never thought someone would ever do something like that for me. It made me think of Maddox and my revenge, and I shifted uncomfortably.

"So, what have you been up to, Malia?" Angel asked.

"Oh, you know," I deflected. "Tried some security, some game dev. Even tried masterminding, a little."

"I heard about that."

I flushed. I doubted Edie gave her a glowing assessment of my masterminding. "What did they say?"

"They said you got them to commit to one last job. After the last 'one last job,' that is."

"Sorry to take that from you."

She laughed. "No need to be sorry."

"I feel bad, though. It was a pretty fucked-up job."

"Well, think of it as a learning experience for next time."

"Nah, cuz. There's not gonna be a next time. That was my last job."

Angel looked smug. "That's what Edie said."

"Oh, yeah," I said.

I felt awkward sitting next to Angel. I'd never felt awkward around her before. In awe of her, maybe. But never awkward. She had a way of making you feel like things were under control, that you were safe. I don't think I could ever cultivate that, mastermind or not.

"Listen," Angel said, her voice taking on an earnest tone. "We're just happy you're here. We all missed you."

"I missed you too," I admitted. Because I did. I missed them all so much. It wasn't until I lost the Net that I really knew how lonely I was. It wasn't until I found them again that I knew how much I missed them.

"Can I get a hug?" I asked.

Angel's smile broadened. "Of course."

She reached for me and pulled me close. I gave her a tentative squeeze, and she held me tighter.

Three years ago, I never would have expected to be hugging Angel like this. But despite my earlier awkwardness, this felt right. So right. I felt that calmness wash over me again, that sense of safety. And on top of that—a sense of care. Of love. She said she missed me, and finally I felt like I could believe her.

Someone knocked on the door. "Come in," Angel called.

Sol poked their head in. "Edie's asking for you, Angel. I think they got you a cake."

Angel laughed. "Of course they did."

She gave me another squeeze, then released me. She stood, then paused in the doorway, turning to look at me. "If you need more time, I'll save you a slice."

"Nah, I'm right behind you," I said.

She nodded, then brushed past Sol toward the kitchen.

Sol smiled at me. "You ready?"

The Code said no attachments. But over the last six months, I'd completely abandoned the Code. Without attachments, I never would have taken down Pierce. I never would have destroyed Diana. I never would have found Maddox. I never would have found peace. I wanted to live in a new world, and that new world necessitated leaving the Code behind.

Maybe I'd make a new one.

First rule of the Code: Remember—you're never alone.

"Yeah," I said. "I am."

ACKNOWLEDGMENTS

Tk

ABOUT THE AUTHOR

MAKANA YAMAMOTO, author of *Hammajang Luck*, was born on the island of Maui. Splitting their time between the Mainland and Hawai'i, Makana grew up on beaches and in snowbanks. Always a scientist at heart, Makana fell in love with sci-fi as a teen—they even led the science fiction and fantasy interest house at their college. A writer from childhood, fiction became the perfect medium for them to explore their interests as well as reconnect with their culture, coalescing into a passion for diverse sci-fi. They love writing multicultural settings and queer characters, as well as imagining what the future might look like for historically marginalized communities. In their free time, Makana likes to hoard dice for their Dungeons & Dragons games, defeat bosses with their guildmates, and get way too invested in reality competition shows. They currently live in New England with their wife and two cats.